Totally

Owned by the Alphas
Shared by the Alphas

The Omega's Alphas

SHARED BY THE ALPHAS

JAYCE CARTER

Shared by the Alphas
ISBN # 978-1-83943-813-4
©Copyright Jayce Carter 2019
Cover Art by Erin Dameron-Hill ©Copyright November 2019
Interior text design by Claire Siemaszkiewicz
Totally Bound Publishing

Published in 2019 by Totally Bound Publishing, United Kingdom.

Totally Bound Publishing is an imprint of Totally Entwined Group Limited.

SHARED
BY THE ALPHAS

Dedication

To the woman who told me I would never amount to anything if I used vulgar language—I dedicate the first fifteen swear words of this to you. The rest are mine.

Chapter One

Pain twisted Tiffany's small body, so deep she couldn't think. The only thing she knew for sure was that the alpha in the room with her smelled divine.

Her earlier horror paled against her need. The fear, the pain, the panic when the alpha she'd been dating, Randy, had abducted her and drugged her meant nothing now. Her biology had scrubbed that clear, and while she'd have to face it later, only this alpha mattered.

She hadn't known a heat would feel like this. Her mother had talked to her about them, but she'd assumed she could deal with it. She'd figured omegas had oversold the truth looking for sympathy.

If anything, they'd undersold it.

The clawing pain in her stomach made her curl in on herself. Her arm hurt, but she couldn't figure out why. It hung limp and useless against her side while she buried her face in the alpha's lap, although she didn't know him. He'd appeared in the midst of the fog that was her head. She knew nothing about him, but she didn't care about anything beyond what he could do for her.

His cock pressed against her cheek, hard and thick and everything she needed.

"Please," she begged.

He stroked his strong fingers through her hair, letting her nuzzle her cheek against his length. "I can't take you like this."

"It hurts." She twisted, sliding her lips over his jean-clad hardness. "It hurts so much."

"I know." He moved his fingers from her scalp to the back of her neck, digging in as though his touch could ease the rigid muscles. "Breathe through the cramps, nice and slow. It'll pass."

He was wrong, though. She felt like she'd die, like her skin would sear away and leave behind nothing but bone. It consumed her, flames dancing over her skin, her thighs rubbing together. Her underwear and sweats were soaked, and her cunt throbbed around nothing.

She parted her lips and dragged her tongue against the length of his cock. It jerked beneath the touch, and a heavy groan left his lips.

"You can't do that," he growled. "I've got limits, little girl, and you're mid-heat. Don't test them, because you don't want me to knot you."

I do. The thought of his knot stretching her cunt, of him locking inside her, made her soaked pussy clench desperately. It would stop the pain and the mindless need that gnawed inside her.

He inhaled slowly, then that growl started up again. "You're too far gone, aren't you?"

"I need you. Please, help me."

A sigh. "Okay. I can help you, but I won't fuck you."

The filthy word from his lips only drove her need higher. She wanted to argue, to claw open his pants, to mount him herself. She rolled, trying to crawl over him and free his cock.

Large hands set on her waist, keeping her from her goal. "I already told you, not that. I've got something else that will help." He moved her so she knelt before him.

She trailed her hands over his thighs, gripping the firm muscles as he undid the button to his pants.

The moment his cock came into view, her mouth went dry. He was thick, the color shades darker than the rest of his skin, with raised veins running along the length. She wanted to lean forward and wrap her lips around him. She wanted him to fuck her face, to grasp her hair and force himself down her throat, to feed her every thick inch of him. The thought might have shamed her before, when she was clear-headed. Her heat filled her so fully there was no room for shame now.

When she moved forward, his snarl stilled her. It reached inside her to the omega part that submitted to an alpha, that wanted to please one. Hell, she'd do anything if he'd give her what she needed.

"Please."

His lips pulled into a smirk that would have frightened a lesser omega and wrapped his hand around his cock to stroke. "Oh, I'll take care of you, little girl."

Tiffany's scent drove Kieran feral. Each breath drew it deeper into him.

He wanted to fuck her. He wanted to strip off her soaked sweats, spread her thighs and slide deep into her. She'd let him, too. Hell, she'd *beg* him to.

It was her first heat, and she smelled delicious. He wanted to be her first, to claim her in a way no one else would ever be able to. Hell, maybe she was a virgin, too? Damn, she'd feel good stretched tight around the girth of his cock, and she'd make the best sound as he trapped her on his knot.

First-time omegas whined when they stretched, as they got locked in place. Their bodies might know what they needed, but their minds tended to take a while to catch up. Fuck, he wanted to have her pinned on his cock, trapped against him.

He stroked his cock, pre-cum dripping enough to lubricate his hand. It took everything he had not to call her over, not to let her have what she wanted. She'd slide that pretty pink tongue over his length before swallowing him down.

What little decency he had kept him from it.

As much as he wanted her, she was too young, too inexperienced. She was an omega with a dislocated shoulder who'd been abducted by a murderous alpha, whose first heat had started due to a drug. None of that meant he should fuck the poor girl, even if they both wanted it. *Badly.*

Her heat would end, and she'd regret it all. He could picture her sweet, innocent face pinched in unhappy lines at realizing she'd given up her first heat to an older, jaded alpha like Kieran.

That didn't mean anything to his cock, though, as he fucked into his palm. She needed, and even if he couldn't take her, he'd give her something to take the edge off.

A thin whine left her lips, her gaze pinned to his cock.

Stay quiet. Don't say a word. Anything you have to say will only make it worse.

He couldn't stop the words. "Are you drenched, girl? Desperate for me?"

She nodded, her good hand inching forward, leaning closer.

"Have you ever had an alpha? Ever felt a knot stretching you wide?"

"No." The word came out soft, breathless, and had him almost coming at the implication.

"Have you ever had anyone?"

A shake of her head had his cock aching.

Damn.

Even with her dressed, he could see the lines of her alluring figure.

Her shirt hung low, letting him peer down it and see her ample cleavage. Her breasts weren't huge, but they were perky. They pressed together when she leaned forward, her injured arm still tucked against her. Her hips spread out, pulling at the waist of her leggings, hiding nothing.

Especially not the wet spot at the apex of her thighs, proof of what she needed.

To think no one else had satisfied her, that she'd never experienced the stretch as someone slid into her tightness had him groaning. There was only so much a man could be expected to resist. He couldn't think he'd be able to ignore her, her scent, her body, that pleading in her eyes and her voice.

Still, Kieran had done enough things he regretted, enough shit he couldn't take back. Taking a virgin during a forced heat was a nail in his coffin he didn't need.

So instead, he stroked his cock while he let his mind wander, as he let himself pretend her lips wrapped around him instead. When her tongue darted out and slid against her bottom lip in an unconscious stroke, he lost it.

He couldn't hold off his own orgasm any longer. Didn't want to. He came, his thick cum warming his palm, sticky and hot and not at all what he'd wanted.

Tiffany leaned forward on her good arm, eyes begging. Poor little omega, desperate for alpha cum.

Kieran held his hand out to her, but that didn't sit right. The alpha in him snarled at his passiveness, at him ignoring his own needs. Kieran changed tactics. He wrapped his other hand around the nape of her neck and pulled her in. He fed two fingers past her full lips and into the heat of her mouth.

She suckled him, her agile tongue moving against the seam between the two fingers, neck twisting to clean each drop from him. She took it like she'd tasted nothing better, a broken moan leaving her, muffled as she refused to release him.

When she'd removed all the cum Kieran pulled back. He opened his palm, rubbing it against her lips, smearing the remaining cum on her like a mark. He wanted her skin to soak him in, her to carry his scent.

Maybe he hadn't fucked her, hadn't bred her, but instinct demanded he claim her somehow. Her tongue pressed at the creases of his palm, capturing his cum, the taste of his cock, all of it. When he pulled back, white still painted her lips near the corner of her mouth, but her tongue captured it and swallowed it down like the rest.

Kieran ran a thumb along her cheek, her blue eyes clouded and momentarily sated.

Damn, she is something.

Too young. Too naive. Too impulsive, if all he'd heard about her had been true, but still something.

A spark in her gaze and a thin whine said the effect of the cum hadn't lasted long. Swallowing it would take the edge off, but it wouldn't ease her the way fucking her would have. Too bad that wasn't an option.

"Relax," he ordered, a command in his voice he couldn't hide, couldn't stop. "I'll take care of you, omega."

He wrapped his hand around his cock and stroked again, now aided by her saliva coating his palm.

He could hate himself tomorrow for this. For now? For now, he'd feed this omega as much of his cum as she could take.

* * * *

Marshall hated to see injured omegas. It seemed like hurt puppies, something that shouldn't ever happen. Was there even a point to alphas existing if they couldn't manage the one thing they were meant for?

He'd been a doctor long enough, had seen the horrors of what the body could survive, but it never dulled that initial shock. Even at thirty-seven, having worked with injured omegas for a decade, he never lost that anger on their behalf when they came in beaten and hurt.

Though, after hearing the story from Sam, the detective who had brought her in, he knew damned well it had been an alpha who had put the girl in that hospital bed. An alpha was to blame for him having to reset her shoulder, for the cut lip she'd had, the bruises on her knees.

Worse? The alpha had been the reason he'd had to inject her with a sedative to ride out the rest of her heat, and he couldn't quite pretend to be unaffected.

Even unconscious, she threw off an intoxicating scent. At the tail end of her heat, the scent had lessened. He'd opened the window so it didn't fill the small hospital room. The heat, brought on by a drug the alpha had used on her, was stronger than most, and he'd already had to send another alpha to a different floor.

She tossed and turned on the bed despite the sedative. The sounds she made swung between frightened and filthy.

Marshall should have left. He'd set her arm, he'd written her orders. There were beta nurses to deal with the rest who would remain unaffected by the strong pheromones her body was pumping out.

Something kept him there, though. Something had him standing beside her bed, staring at her long blonde hair fanned out on the pillow, the flushed tone of her skin, the quick breaths.

What was it?

Instinct was something he ignored whole-heartedly. Instinct could go to hell for all he cared. He was a man and, while he may have been born an alpha, he refused to let that dictate his behavior. He'd made his own life, carved it out from nothing, and he'd be damned if instinct screwed it up for him.

Yet, that sound in his head, the one that filled his body and scratched against his mind, wouldn't allow him to walk out. The moment he'd seen her, the moment he'd smelled her, he'd known.

What he'd known, he wasn't sure.

It was like a fact written in a language he didn't know, but a fact nonetheless.

So, he'd waited in her room, checking her vitals again and again as an excuse.

She stirred, quick movements that signaled waking. The medication should have kept her under for longer, but omegas never failed to do the unexpected. They reacted poorly to many medications, their hormones wreaking havoc on medical knowledge. It was why specialists like him were so important for omega care.

"You're safe," he offered softly to reassure her.

Her lids lifted and blue eyes met his. She tried to rise, but when she went to set her hand behind her, she gasped.

Marshall placed a hand on her back to help her up. "Your shoulder won't be much use right now. You're in the hospital."

"Hospital?" She peered down at her lap before her gaze shot up. "Where's Claire?"

Marshall pulled his hand back, the fear on her face showing she'd recalled the events. "She's fine. She's in a room down the hall."

"I want to see her."

"You will in a bit. First, I need to check how you're doing, then I'll see if she's up for visitors." He turned to the machines, checking heart rate, oxygen level. "My name is Dr. Brown. I've been taking care of you since you arrived yesterday."

"Yesterday? I've been out for a whole day?"

"Yes. I gave you a sedative to sleep off most of the effects of your heat."

Her cheeks flushed red, the color bright on her pale skin. "Right, *that*."

He nodded, recalling the man who sat in the waiting room, the one who had brought her in. Kieran Elliot. He knew the man only through reputation. He'd offered information without inflection, as though none of it mattered, as if they'd spoken about a toy instead of a living, breathing omega in pain.

He'd claimed they hadn't had sex. The idea had Marshall scoffing, since resisting an omega in heat was something few alphas could manage. Marshall could only because of years of training. Still, the omega

15

carried the other alpha's scent, a low level that supported his story.

They'd had contact, but it seemed he hadn't knotted her. Had he, that scent would have clung to her in far larger amounts.

A petty part of Marshall liked that. It made his alpha side quiet the snarling when Kieran had stood in the room with him.

"How are you feeling?" Marshall lifted the clipboard from the foot of the bed. He didn't need it, but his looking at it relaxed patients. His gaze could unnerve anxious omegas.

Being an alpha working with omegas had challenges, especially when he cared for injured and abused ones. Still, they'd found that nothing calmed an omega quite like the scent or voice of an alpha.

"Tired."

He nodded, gaze down. "You'll be tired for a few days. I'll have food brought in to help. How much do you remember?"

A shudder ran through her. "Everything."

Words perched on his tongue, something reassuring, something to tell her it was okay. Instead, he shook away the impulse. "The alpha who found you, Kieran, stated there was no sex, so no possibility of conception. Is that right?"

She nodded, her fingers running over the sling that kept her arm immobile. "Kieran?"

"You don't know his name?"

"No. We'd never met."

Marshall hung the clipboard on the hook at the foot of her bed. "Yes. His name is Kieran Elliot. He's outside if you'd like me to get him."

"He's still here?"

"He never left. I think he wanted to make sure you were all right."

She huffed a soft laugh that made her chest rise against the hospital gown they'd dressed her in. "I doubt he wants to see me. Let him know I am awake, alive and not his problem anymore."

The hurt in those words caught Marshall. Not venom. Not fear and not anger, but unhappiness. What had happened to cause her to react like that? Marshall rolled his shoulders, telling himself to relax, to breathe in and out, like he told his patients.

He had no reason to believe the alpha had harmed her, but reason had nothing to do with the adrenaline that had started to work its way through his body.

"Doctor?"

Marshall snapped his gaze up. "Yes?"

"Is something wrong?"

"Nothing. Why?"

Her eyebrow lifted, and the vibration in his chest told him.

He'd been growling.

Wonderful.

"Sorry." Marshall cut the sound off before leaning out of the door to order the food, giving himself a moment to collect himself. He didn't go off like that, didn't let his baser instincts free. No, not Dr. Marshall Brown. He'd always been the steady one, the thinker, the one no one would suspect of being an alpha.

After a few breaths, Marshall returned to the room, to the omega, to her scent and her temptations. "Are you in pain?"

She shook her head, but even that had her wincing. Her soft smile said she knew he'd seen. "I'm sore, but I don't want painkillers."

"Why not?"

She curled her fingers into the blanket as she pulled it up tighter around her waist. "I don't want to feel out of control."

Of course. After what she'd been through, she'd want all her faculties in order. "How about anti-inflammatories? They will reduce the swelling and pain, but they won't make you feel drugged or loopy."

A breath full of relief left her. "That would be great."

Marshall added it to her chart, then sat in the chair beside the bed. It lowered him and gave her a position of height. "You can have them after you eat, since taking them on an empty stomach will make you sick. Eat something, take the pills and I'll set up for you to see your friend."

"Thank you, Dr. Brown."

"Marshall." He frowned at how quickly the correction came out, at how much he wanted to hear his first name fall from those pink lips of hers. "Call me Marshall."

"Marshall," she said with a smile.

And, damn, that smile was enough for him to pull in a rough breath and realize he was in over his head.

He liked the omega.

Chapter Two

Kieran wanted to pace. He wanted to move around the waiting room and snarl at anyone who passed too close.

Tiffany sat in a hospital room, and the walls separating them made him want to tear them down. *Fuck. Where did that come from?*

Instead, he sat in one of the chairs far too small for his size, his laptop perched on his thighs. He reviewed the bid for a job in Texas sent by the manager there. It was busy work to keep him occupied and not thinking about Tiffany, about what had happened, about how she'd looked stretched out in that hospital bed unconscious.

The way her lips had wrapped around his fingers, the way she'd swallowed down his cum—he couldn't shake it. Her eyes, full of trust, were the worst.

She was too fucking young. After what had happened with Randy, she shouldn't trust anyone, especially not him. Kieran was at fault for what had happened. He'd failed to see Randy for what he'd been, hadn't recognized the monster in his employee and it had led to the deaths of too many omegas. It had led to what Tiffany had suffered.

After getting her settled, he'd checked on Claire in her hospital room. The other woman had given him some information on the girl, but she'd been tight-lipped. Smitten as she was with Bryce, Joshua and Kaidan, it seemed he wasn't offered that same trust.

Tiffany was only nineteen. A barista at a local coffee shop, from what he understood. That didn't shock him, though. Her sweet nature, and the way she'd pleaded so nicely?

That was the sort of voice he wanted to hear begging. He wanted to see her strip down and drop to her knees, to have her turn those blues eyes up to him and —

"You sure this is the place for that?" Sam's voice cut into his thoughts.

A look down at his groin had Kieran groaning and adjusting the laptop to cover his erection. "What do you want?"

Sam only grinned before lowering into the seat beside him. How the detective managed to deal with all he did and still have that cheerful mood, Kieran would never know. "Wanted to check in on everyone. Besides, I brought Tracy and Karen to see Claire."

A soft snort was Kieran's only answer. Sam was the sort of alpha to settle down, so it didn't shock him to hear he'd put some claim on the broken omega and her daughter. Sam was a family man, the sort who would fit well into the father role.

"How are you?"

"I don't need a heart-to-heart, Sam."

"You sure about that? Because you look even more glum than usual, and you're usually pretty depressing."

Kieran released a low, threatening growl.

Sam only laughed. "That won't scare me off."

He shut the laptop, giving up on the fake distraction. Sam was a hell of a pain in the ass when he wanted to be, and it seemed he wanted to be.

"I'm fine."

"What happened?"

"She was in heat. What the hell do you think happened?"

"You didn't knot her. You wouldn't be this wound up if you had."

Kieran's knuckles popped when he drew them into fists, then released them. "Fine, I didn't. Can you blame me? She was drugged out of her mind, and it was her first heat. Nothing in that says she should have had sex with anyone, let alone me."

"Let alone you?"

Kieran pressed his lips tight at the telling statement. "I mean that I'm not looking for anything long term, and that girl should be. So, no, I didn't knot her. I helped her the best I could until she could be sedated, and now? Now I'm waiting here to make sure she'll be fine. Then she can go on her way, meet a nice young alpha and have a handful of kids. Are we done?"

Sam's chuckle only drove Kieran's temper higher. The draw to knot the female had nearly overwhelmed him, and denying the instinct had left tension. "Oh, this should be fun to watch."

Kieran shook his head, wanting to open the laptop and let the detective fuck off for all he cared. Being rude wasn't something he'd worried much about in his life.

"There's something else," Sam said.

"What?"

"Well, when they brought Tiffany in, they fingerprinted her, ran her history."

"She's nineteen. How much history could she have?"

"More than you'd think." Sam reached into the bag slung over his shoulder to pull out a folder. "She's been in trouble a few times. She was pegged as an omega at fifteen because of a reaction to some medication. At that point, she rebelled a bit. Most of it was small stuff. Went joyriding in a few cars, a bit of graffiti, some breaking and entering."

"Most of this looks harmless enough." Kieran read through the reports.

Hard to think of Tiffany being such a troublemaker. Even the things listed weren't outright destructive. She'd graffitied omega slogans on the wall of a newspaper that tended toward pro-alpha stories. The breaking and entering seemed to be revenge for an alpha who had groped her friend. The joyriding was pure fun.

"Most of it was. Then this happened." Sam leaned across and flipped the page. "She got into it with this alpha. Broke his nose, gave him a concussion."

"That little spit of a girl did all this to an alpha?"

"That little girl had a big bat and a lot of attitude."

Kieran read over the details, his lips tipping down. "Says here she claims the alpha attacked her."

"Yeah, and, judging from what I've found, he probably did. However, the alpha's father is a congressman, and the last thing he wanted was this story in the paper about his son, so he made sure it fell on Tiffany's shoulders. They put out a warrant to have her registered as a delinquent omega."

"Fuck." Kieran slammed the folder closed. "Tell me there's something you can do about this?"

"The alpha's father has a lot of pull, and he's well connected. I'd guess he hasn't let it go, because I ran her prints as soon as she came in, and I got a call within fifteen minutes about her."

"You can't let them register her for that. She'll be given to whatever alpha has been sucking the dick of the council. She'll be nothing but property."

Sam slid the folder back into his bag. "I know, but I don't have unlimited power here. Lucky for you, I have enough strings for one plan, but it's all we've got."

"And what plan is that?"

Sam's smile, wide and full of amusement, didn't bode well. "How do you feel about coming out of retirement to train one last unruly omega?"

* * * *

Kane sighed as the man struggled against his binds. Why did they always struggle? It wasn't like the man thought he'd get out of the rope that bound his wrists, yet there he went, yanking and rolling.

Even calves gave up when hog-tied. Seemed cows were smarter than the fucker Kane had caught.

"Let me go! I'll give you anything."

"Don't want shit from you." Kane opened the desk drawer and rummaged through the items there. Snacks, a magazine, a billion paper clips.

What the fuck? No one used paper clips anymore, yet every desk he looked through had them in spades.

"Besides, you'd lie anyway."

"I won't lie. I'll tell you whatever you want to know, okay?"

"See, that won't fix this. Someone hired me to find you and to get some important files. You being alive or dead at the end of it? Well, that's a fun surprise for us all. I'm partial to dead, but not sold either way."

That had the man struggling again, hard enough he rolled to his side and got stuck. Not the most dignified position.

The ringing of Kane's phone had him sighing. Why did he give out his number? He hated when people called him when they wanted stupid shit. He should hire a secretary, someone to deal with the frustration for him.

He pulled out the phone, and the name forced a smile he tried to hide the moment it appeared. He gave a warning jab in the man's direction then a shush before he answered it. "Hey, Tiff. Been a while."

A soft background beeping came before she answered. "Hey, Kane. Sorry, I've been busy."

He stilled, something on the edges of his awareness raising suspicion. "You okay, doll? You don't sound great."

"I'm fine." The lie, even through the phone, could have been spotted by a blind idiot. "Well, I mean, I will be. There was an accident, and I got hurt, but I'm okay now."

"Accident? You lying to me now?"

The hesitation from her was new. Hell, it almost sounded like she had to psych herself up to answer. "I don't want to talk about it, okay?"

His hand tightened around his phone until a crack warned him to ease off. "Fine. Sure. We'll not talk about the fact I know you're in a fucking hospital. You think that beeping ain't distinctive? But, yeah, whatever you want. Why'd you call? So we could not talk about you being hurt?" The sharpness of his tone would have shut up most people, but Tiffany had never been most people.

A year since they'd started talking, since she'd hired him to do a simple delivery job, and he'd never been able to stop thinking about her. They hadn't met, of course. Too tempting, too dangerous. She sounded like a fucking perfect omega, and him? He was scarred and tatted up and far too dangerous for her. Hell, the girl had no idea he was even an alpha.

Instead, their talks had turned from jobs to actual conversations. They'd laugh, they'd talk and he'd pretend there was something there. Her voice had gotten him through some dark nights, nights when that soft laughter of hers was the only light he knew of.

Her sigh came out soft and tired.

Don't be an asshole.

She'd clearly had a hell of a day, so the last thing she needed was Kane acting like a bastard to her.

"Sorry, doll. What's up?"

At that, the man on the floor shouted, "Help me! He's going to—" A kick to the man's stomach, then a hand over his mouth shut him up.

"What was that?"

"Nothing. TV was on too loud. What's up?"

Suspicion colored the silence, telling him she was too smart to believe his shit. Still, she didn't call him on it. "I wanted to know if you've made any progress. I don't know how long I'll be under this name, and in case I have to go, I wanted to make sure you send anything new you've found."

"You planning on running?"

"Might not have a choice."

The hell she wouldn't. Kane wanted to ask her what the problem was, wanted to tear it apart. He wasn't any good for her, but that didn't mean he couldn't fuck up anything that endangered her. That was what they had—all they could have. Tiffany got the good life, the happy life, and Kane got to watch over her. It had to be enough. "Tell me the truth, Tiff. Tell me what's going on. I can help you."

"You've done a lot for me, Kane, but even you can't fix everything."

"Wanna bet?"

Her laugh eased his chest, the resilience there. Stubborn, feisty little omega that she was, nothing much kept her down for long. "Yeah, well, I don't think I'm going to have much to say about this. Text me that address when you find it, please."

He nodded before remembering she couldn't see him. "Sure thing. You keep my number, though, because if you drop off the face of the Earth and don't bother to let me know you're okay, I'll track your ass down."

"Promise?"

His answering growl came out feral against the teasing she always did.

How many times had she asked to meet? How many times had she'd begged him to stay at their drop-off location? Hell, he still recalled the time he'd scouted it out first, only to see the same car sitting there. A call and her laugh had said, yeah, she'd tried to outwit him.

Fuck, turning her down was hard. Didn't matter, though. Sometimes people did what was right even when it was hard, and he hadn't done much right in his life.

"Don't push me," he said.

Nothing but affection came through her words, as if his growls and threats meant nothing. "I'll do what I can, okay? And, just in case, if things don't work out and I can't talk to you again, I want you to know —"

"None of that. You shut the fuck up with goodbye bullshit, you hear me?"

"There's that charm of yours I love. Okay, fine, no goodbyes. I'll talk to you later."

"You better."

The line went dead, leaving Kane still holding the man beneath him down, his hand over the guy's mouth. Sure, the guy was a two-bit asshole who deserved the shit that was happening, but, even so, it all painted a picture, didn't it?

No matter what Tiffany thought, the girl didn't know shit, and they had no future. The best thing he could do for her was to stay the hell out of her life.

If only he was strong enough to do it.

* * * *

Tiffany shifted her arm, the sparks of pain causing her to grit her teeth but try again. It moved, but pain still spread through the joint.

The pills had taken the edge off the ache. Food had settled her stomach, and she could breathe easily again.

Kane's voice brought a smile, though. That growl he let out and his subtle annoyance with her warmed her. If she had to run—and it seemed she'd need to—she'd miss him.

She couldn't contact him after she cut ties. Claire had taught her enough to know better than to try it. The quickest way to get caught would be contacting anyone from her old life.

She'd miss him. How many people could she count as friends? He'd never been interested in anything, had refused to meet her. Because she'd gotten his number through a forger, she had to assume he knew she was an omega.

Was that the problem? Most betas didn't want omegas. They considered them too much trouble, too prone to running off with an alpha. It meant few settled down together.

Did he not want to risk his heart if she decided she'd rather end up with an alpha? Like omegas were driven by nothing but the need for a knot? She bristled at the idea.

As soon as it happened, the anger melted away. The reason didn't matter. She'd miss him.

There wasn't a choice, though. She'd seen her legal name on the file. If they had that, they'd have seen the warrant and the orders to register her.

And she couldn't let that happen. She wasn't going to be given away like a prize to some alpha she'd never met. The alphas willing to take on delinquent omegas tended to be shitty people. What sort of man was fine with taking an unwilling omega as a mate?

She grasped the needle of the IV. How much time did she have? How long before the police showed up? Before someone came to tell her what happened next?

Before the thoughts could drag her under, before she risked pulling out the IV, a soft knock on the door caught her attention.

"Yeah?" Her voice cracked from the nerves.

The door opened, and a man she didn't recognize came in. One sniff told her. *Alpha.*

Before she could worry, Kieran came in on his heels. He met her gaze, eyes hard, looking so much like he had in that room.

He was tall and impossibly large. Silver hair at his temples showed he was more than a couple of years older than her, but that didn't scare her off. In fact, all the signs of his age, the knowledge in his dark eyes, the lines between his eyebrows that implied he frowned a lot—she liked it all. His hands caught her attention, and they brought back all the ways he'd used them on her the night before.

It forced her gaze down to hide her reaction.

"Hello, Tiffany. My name is Detective Sam Franklin. How are you feeling?" The new man spoke with a kind voice, the sort that made her want to let down her guard.

"Tired of that question."

Snark was always a risk. She never knew how an alpha would react. Would he find her smart-ass comments adorable? Would he see them as a challenge?

Sam responded by letting out a hard bark of laughter. "I'll take that as you feeling pretty well, then. You look better, and the doctor says you'll be fine."

"So why are you here?"

Kieran said nothing as he leaned against the wall beside the door. He stuck his hands into his pockets, his gaze moving between Sam and Tiffany, but remained silent.

Sam, however, seemed more than willing to do the talking. "Well, as I'm sure you guessed, we've run your name. It seems you've had some issues with the law in Ohio."

She swallowed before trying to play dumb. "I have no idea what you're talking about. Must be a paperwork error."

Sam reached into his bag and pulled out a folded piece of paper. Her picture showed on the front, her name above it. "This isn't a mistake. You are Tiffany Hansen, and they are looking for you."

"Please, don't turn me over. Walk out of the room, go get some coffee. I'll take the IV out and be gone before you get back. Say I snuck off again. Say anything you want, but let me go." Her words started to ramble, to spin faster and faster.

Kieran spoke, voice hard and so familiar despite the short time they'd known each other. "Easy there, girl. Listen to your options before you pass out."

She pulled in a shaky breath, not realizing how shallow her breathing had turned. "I have options? That's new."

"To be fair, it's only one." Sam came over and rested his hip against the bed. "I've got an option for you, Tiffany. It's not great, but it's better than being registered."

"What's the option?"

"Go through a training program with a registered alpha. I've gotten a judge to sign off on it. Complete this program, and your history is wiped clean. You'll be free to start over, to live any life you want."

"I've never heard of that before."

"It's not done much anymore. Basically, if there's an omega they feel could do fine on her own after a little training, they'll place her with an approved alpha. He'll teach her, get her set up, and she gets a second chance after completing the program."

"How long?"

"Program takes a year. You'd have to give up that time to it."

Her jaw ached from the way she pressed her teeth together. "So, you're telling me that the cost of my freedom is to give up my freedom to some strange alpha for a full year?"

"It's not perfect, I know, but it's all I've got. And, besides, it's a year versus your whole future, so it's the lesser of two evils."

The idea of agreeing chafed. Still, what had she wanted since she'd run a year ago? She'd wanted her life. She wanted to go home and see her parents. She wanted to be able to use her real name, to buy property, to go to school. An entire year beneath the thumb of some registered, approved alpha wasn't ideal, but it was only a year. She'd been on the run for longer than that.

She could sacrifice a year if it meant her freedom. "Okay."

"Don't you even want to know who the alpha would be?"

"Doesn't matter. I can get my life back this way, so whoever it is? I can handle them."

Sam chuckled, then stood. "Glad that's how you feel right now. Not sure you'll feel that way when you find out who it is."

Her eyebrows inched toward one another. "Why not? Who is it?"

Kieran spoke from his spot against the wall, so still she'd nearly forgotten about him. "You just agreed to be mine for the next year, girl."

Well, shit.

Chapter Three

Kieran didn't crowd Tiffany when she stepped into his home. He stayed a few feet back, giving her the chance to move around and get her bearings. He didn't want her afraid.

"So, you *train* omegas?" She drenched the word in attitude.

So much for being afraid.

"I used to, yes. It's been a long time since I've done such a thing."

"Why am I the lucky one?" She walked by a globe on a bookshelf, spinning it with a single finger.

"You aren't. You were in an unfortunate position, and I was able to help. Sam actually called in the favors to get approval, and I have enough name recognition for the judge to agree." Kieran kicked his shoes off beside the door, then lifted an eyebrow and nodded at her feet.

Tiffany rolled her eyes like a petulant teen and returned, kicking off her dirty sneakers beside his. "What does this whole 'training' thing mean? Are you going to get me a collar?"

"Don't tempt me, girl." Kieran allowed a growl to enter his voice at the thought of how black leather would look against her light skin. He pushed the image aside and cut off the sound. "No. You are not someone who requires the training I've done in the past. Not that a firm hand wouldn't do you some good, but your inclusion on the registry appears a political move. So, while I can't make it so you don't require this year, you will be able to spend it in my care without any real training."

"Why?" She twisted to nail him with a hard look. "Seems like an alpha with an omega who can't say no would enjoy the benefits."

"If you think that, you don't know me well." He fought the desire to make her understand. He wanted her to look at him differently, to understand he wasn't an alpha looking for a forced mate.

But they didn't need to make this any more complicated, and it was already complicated. How could he live with her, share the same space, smell her all day and all night and not take her? His control had limits, and she'd already undermined all his control. Why she affected him so strongly, he didn't care to examine.

"We'll just be roommates?"

"Not exactly. While I can give you a rather large amount of leeway, in the end, you are an omega under my care. You will not risk yourself, and you will keep me apprised of your schedule. I will ensure that you are cared for, that you have all you need, that your finances are in order so that at the end of the year, you have plenty saved up for whatever and wherever you wish to go. However, your day-to-day life will be your own. Make no mistake—I am not looking for a slave or a mate."

"And the rest?" Her words quivered as she asked, as if her nerves had finally gotten the better of her.

"The rest?"

"Will you give me suppressants for my heats? What about sex?" Ah, the way she tripped over the word 'sex' made his cock perk up. *As if the bastard's gone down since I first caught her scent.*

He was taken back again to her soft lips and her agile tongue, to the way she'd lapped his cum from his fingers and the sounds she made. Hell, she'd have to take care of herself during that year. Adults couldn't be expected to forgo basic biological needs. Could he sit in his own bed when her scent drifted through the hallway? When she made those little gasps, quiet as she could, and tried to hide that she was fingering herself in her room?

His lips pulled into a smirk at how the confident omega wilted with the graphic conversation. "I won't be fucking you, but no, no suppressants. They aren't good for you long term, and there is no reason for you to be on them now. Dr. Brown has given me sedatives should a heat strike. Without the drugs Randy used on you, we'll see it coming and be able to prepare the next time. What happened before won't happen again."

Her back went straight. She acted like he'd threatened to beat her instead of telling her he wouldn't treat her like a sex slave.

"Well, I'm sorry you were so *inconvenienced*." Her words came out sharp enough to wound.

"You're twisting my words."

"I'm not doing anything. Do you want to show me where I'll be sleeping, or should I find it myself?"

Kieran's lip lifted at her tone, his alpha side wanting to put her in her place. He wanted to overwhelm her, to cage her in, to offer bites to her throat that would mark for days. He wanted to fuck her until all that attitude drained away.

She breathed in, a long, slow inhalation through her nose. Her cheeks reddened and she took a step forward, as if the scent alone reached out and drew her close.

But he couldn't. It didn't matter what his body wanted, he couldn't fucking do it. Instead, Kieran shook his head and pointed. "Down the hall. Second door on the left, the room with gray walls."

Again, she stopped and pulled back. She wore hurt well, but only for a heartbeat before anger swallowed it up. Her steps came loud, like gunshots, as she stormed down the hallway.

He was too old to have an angry nineteen-year-old in the house again.

* * * *

Kane lounged on the roof of his apartment building, his gaze on the stars. Fuck, he liked the night sky. In the city he couldn't see shit, but that didn't bother him much. He'd pretend he could see each little star, that they shone as bright as they had the few nights he'd gone camping in the middle of nowhere.

No word back from Tiffany. Had she run, already? He'd find her, of course, but he wouldn't stop her from going. Girl was smart, knew if running was her best shot. Still, the silence got to him.

He'd sent the address she'd asked for, a building owned by a corporation name she'd sent him. She'd needed a place they owned that wouldn't get much foot traffic, something without any other payments to it. Seemed the omega was searching for something off the books, and something above both their paygrades, if he had to guess. It had taken him more work than he liked to do to find what she needed.

Found it in an old empty apartment building in the northern area of the city. The company, a no-name corporation where no one knew what they did, had bought it up six weeks prior, then not made another move. No permits to renovate, no construction companies to work on it, nothing at all. Seemed whatever they'd bought it for, they didn't want people knowing shit.

What has that troublemaker gotten herself into?

From what little Kane could dig up, he'd figure drugs. Place would make a nice spot to stash them, and a good base of operations to meet with dealers. Sure, it was higher priced and nicer than most of what he saw, but the security wasn't good enough for it to be guns and too remote to be whores.

In his experience the options were always drugs, guns or whores.

A buzz from his phone had him pulling it from his pocket.

Speaking of.

How do you pick a lock?

He laughed at Tiffany's odd question.

You need lockpicks, doll. Use the pick to set the pins, then the tension rod to twist the lock

And if you don't have a lockpick?

That had him stilling.

This just a hypothetical, right?

Let's say it is. Hypothetically, what would you do if you didn't have those things and needed to get into this:

A moment later, a picture came through of a lock, and he groaned. So, not hypothetical.

What trouble have you gotten yourself into?

No trouble if you tell me how to open this door.

His growl came out low, angry.

Get your ass back into your car and away from there.

No can do. Help or be quiet. The buzzing of my phone is distracting.

He sat up, unease pulling at him. Girl might have a spark, but she didn't need to be dealing with whatever was on the other side of a lock like that. A deadbolt of that level said someone was serious about keeping people out, and no one dropped that cash unless what was on the other side was fucking important.

You're at that address, aren't you?

No. Never. That would be crazy.

Her smart ass made him want to paddle her. How could she make him laugh at the same time as wanting to throttle her? He'd spent a year keeping her at a distance, making sure to never risk a glimpse because he didn't know if he could walk away once he did.

Now, though? Well, fuck, now it seemed he'd have to go see the troublemaker in person.

And he might fuck her on the spot for being so damned difficult.

Worse? They'd both enjoy it.

* * * *

Tiffany struggled not to kick the door. She'd taken a bobby pin from her hair, bent it and tried to use it. Turned out searching the internet for how to pick locks was less useful than movies had led her to believe. She'd taken fifteen minutes and had no luck.

It seemed the skill was something she'd have to put some time into if she expected to continue her work as a sleuth. Not to mention that trying to do it with a single hand made the entire thing harder. She'd crouched down to use the fingers of her hand in the sling, but nothing worked.

Worse? Kane had been no help. When he'd stopped responding, she'd buried the hurt. Stupidly, she'd thought he'd come through for her.

Guess not.

Like every other man in her life, he'd given up. She was too wild, too headstrong, too everything. The only men who stuck around were ones like Randy. Ones like the alpha who'd made her to run in the first place.

And what did is say when only psychos could put up with her?

Tiffany ignored the point and huffed, kicking the door when her temper slipped.

"That'll show it." That voice…

Tiffany didn't turn, afraid to do so and find it all an illusion, to find he'd slipped away. "Didn't think you'd show."

"Well fuck, guess I'm a gentleman. Came all the way across town just to open a door for you." Kane's voice came from behind her, his breath blowing strands of her hair. It told her he was tall, much taller than she was.

An inhalation told her something else, too. "You're an alpha."

He reached past her, the picks he'd mentioned in his hands. He slipped one into the lock, then the other, his hands moving agilely. "Yeah, I am. That bother you?"

"Why would it?"

"Because omegas get nervous sometimes." The clicking of his picks punctuated the conversation.

"So, you know what I am?"

"The guy who gave you my number might have given me a heads up."

"Is that why you never wanted to meet me?" Not turning around was hard, her stomach flipping. His voice was even better in person, rough and deep and full of attitude. She wanted to lean back against his chest, to close her eyes and feel his warmth.

"Part of the reason, yeah. You didn't answer me. You nervous, doll?"

Her head shake might have been more convincing if she hadn't released a loud gulp at the end of it.

"What happened to your arm?"

"I fell."

"You fell?" The words came out deadpanned, slow and sarcastic.

She offered the same attitude back. "Yep. I'm pretty clumsy."

His laugh was soft and close, but the click of the lock cut their conversation short. He pushed open the door. "So, you want to tell me what this bullshit is about?"

Tiffany went to turn. She wanted to see him. She needed a face to go along with the voice, with the person she'd spoken to for so long.

A hand on her shoulder kept her back to him, but the action caused her to brush against his front. And, yeah, even with her lack of experience, the hardness of his cock said he was interested. His thumb dug into her shoulder in a firm massage, as though it would make the moment less tense. "You don't want that."

"Want what?"

"To see me. Don't got a clue what you were thinking you'd find, but I'm gonna bet it ain't what I am. Why not keep those eyes forward and let yourself fill in details, huh?"

She twisted but couldn't shake the grip. "Let me see you or leave me alone. I'm sick of this game."

"If this is a game, it's one you ain't equipped to play, trust me." Even as he said it, a rough edge to his voice, he released her and took a step backward.

Tiffany turned. No matter what he said, she wasn't nervous. She couldn't be, not with Kane. Sure, she'd made some mistakes in judging people, but not him. He'd been a rock for her, helped her when no one else could, and it seemed he stayed away because he thought it best for her. Hard to be worried about someone like that.

When she laid eyes on him, she realized she'd been wrong.

She should be nervous. Not that he'd hurt her, but that she'd have no defense. He stood tall enough she had to tilt her head to see him, and he was younger than she'd expected. He couldn't have been older than early twenties. His brown hair was shaved on the sides, the top longer and pushed back. Amber eyes caught the light from the street, intense and hard. A black T-shirt stretched over his chest, tight around his thick biceps, and a pair of blue jeans covered his thighs. From beneath the lines of his shirt, colorful tattoos spread out over his arms. Complete sleeves went from arm to hand, and more ran up his throat, a few drifting up above his jaw. She couldn't tell in the dim light what the tattoos were of, beyond a few details. Some vines with leaves, an arrow, what she was pretty sure was an eagle or other predatory bird. She wondered if they covered his chest, his stomach, his back. Exactly how far down did they go?

"Don't do that." His voice had turned guttural, and it went straight to her cunt.

"Do what?"

"Don't look at me like that."

She pulled in a breath and turned her head, trying to get a hold of herself. Maybe his reaction was all physical. He wanted her because he had to, and that was why he fought it.

She understood that pull of something she didn't want. She'd been ready to beg Randy to fuck her when she'd been mid-heat, no matter how frightened she'd been, no matter how she'd hated him.

That dried up the lust, the thought that Kane might feel the same helplessness. "Sorry," she said, continuing so he didn't have a beat to break into the conversation. "Thanks for getting the door, but I'm good if you'd got stuff to do."

"You think I'm going to turn around and let you walk in there by yourself? Especially since you ain't said shit about why you're here?"

She tucked the thumb of her good arm into the pocket of her jeans, trying to look casual. "It's nothing. I'm trying to get back a sweater my ex took."

"A sweater? You asked me to look up the holdings of a shadowy company, and you try to break into the building at one in the morning, because your ex took a sweater?" He cocked an eyebrow and rested his hands on his hips. The action made his chest impossibly wider so he took up even more space.

"Sounds like as good a story as any other." Tiffany offered a mocking salute before turning and stepping into the darkness of the building.

A heartbeat later, his voice startled her, coming from behind her. How the hell was he so silent he could sneak up on her so easily? "I'm not letting you out of my sight, doll. Better get fucking used to having me on your ass."

Sounds good to me.

Chapter Four

Damn, the girl looked good. He'd had no idea she'd be that fucking pretty. Her light hair was braided but still reached her mid-back. If unbound, he'd bet it would reach to the curve of her ass. Bright blue eyes were framed by long black lashes, far too fucking large and sweet for the things her body made him think.

Black jeans framed her ass, and when she bent forward as she crept down the hallway, he held in a groan. His hands itched to reach out and grab her. He wanted to take her hips in his hands and grind against her. He wanted to strip those jeans off her and slide right into her. *Fuck.*

He forced himself to stay in control, to not touch her. Standing so close while he'd tried to focus on the lock had tempted him. Worse? The way she smelled. Arousal fit her well.

She hadn't even fled at the sight of him, but after seeing her?

He didn't come close to deserving a girl like that. He could see her now, in her perfect fucking house, her perfect life. Blonde hair, blue eyes, a body to die for, but him? Tatted up, a delinquent at the best of times, muscle for hire? Yeah, they didn't fit.

Not that it shocked him. He'd gotten used to his life, to how he looked, to it all. Never stung quite as much as when he saw her, but everyone had their place in life. His? It was to keep her safe, but not to fuck her, not to have her.

Fine by me.

Besides, her arm? Didn't that drive up his urges? All of 'em, too. He wanted to fuck her, to strip her down and check her for other injuries. He wanted to fuck up whoever had caused it. *Fell my ass.* He knew her well enough to know when she was lying, especially because she was terrible at it.

She hadn't fallen, but he didn't have a clue past that. He'd be at the hospital the next day looking into it, figuring it out, making sure she wasn't in any danger.

Well, any more danger. Breaking into a place like this in the middle of the night wasn't the epitome of safe behavior.

A creaking had him reacting on instinct. He wrapped a hand around her mouth and yanked her against him, going still to listen.

Nothing. Damn, he was too seasoned to jump at every sound like a paranoid child. Still, he'd never had to try to keep someone alive.

Before he removed his hand, once he'd accepted no danger lurked close by, he noticed exactly what was happening.

Tiffany's lush body was pressed against him, his cock pinned to her lower back, one arm of his wrapped around her to hold her close and the other over her mouth. Her breaths warmed his hand, but he didn't smell any fear.

No, the girl was on fucking fire. Her pebbled nipples strained against her shirt and begged for his attention. How easy would it be to toy with them? He could slide a thumb against those tempting buds, teasing her, plucking them. Then? It'd be too easy to move that hand over her stomach and into the waist of her pants. He'd find her soaked, and she'd ride his fingers until she was screaming, until the voice he'd heard over the last year broke in gasps and moans around his name.

Her head fell back on his shoulder, like the sweetest surrender.

And that woke him up.

The fuck was he doing?

He'd spent the last year telling himself he couldn't do this, so what in the hell did he think he was doing?

Kane pulled away, movement slow, awkward, not wanting her to trip backward if he were suddenly gone.

Tiffany straightened, a shudder when her thighs brushed each other, when her shirt shifted over her still erect nipples. Damn, that temptation was too much.

"Look—"

She lifted her hand, palm out. "Don't. If you're insisting on coming, let's go." She moved away, her gaze anywhere but him.

As much as he hated that look on her face, he reminded himself it was for the best.

She deserved far better than him.

Walking caused the fabric of Tiffany's pants to rub against her swollen clit. She had no underwear, since they'd been ruined when the doctors had cut off her clothing in the hospital. The jeans and shirt were from

Claire, things to hold her over until she got back to her own place the next day. The jeans tugged at her hips, a bit too tight, but she'd made do. Still, each step caused them to stroke against her, to remind her of what she wanted, of what no one wanted to give her.

How do I end up here every damned time?

She had other things to worry about than her lack of sex life, though. Hell, even her desperate clit needed to be ignored right then. She could deal with that later, in privacy, after taking care of the current problems.

They went down the hallway, Kane on her heels, never more than a breath behind her. A scent struck her on the fringes of her mind.

She couldn't ask Kane. He wouldn't scent it.

As she moved further into the building, as they took the stairs to the next floor, it strengthened enough to make her sure.

Omega.

Not a lingering whiff, like when she walked into a restaurant and knew another omega had been there. No, this was strong. The sort of scent that happened when at least a few omegas had spent time there — a lot of time.

"What is it?"

Tiffany didn't respond, following the trail until she turned a corner and entered a room. The door pushed open, hinges creaking against the movement. Inside, the scent bombarded her.

Fear. Pain. Anger. It all saturated the omega scent, twisted it into something ugly. It drove the air from her lungs.

Kane caught her when her knees buckled, when the scent overwhelmed her. "Fuck," he snapped, hauling her against him. A slow inhalation and he snarled. He wouldn't smell the omega, but he'd sure as hell smell the rest. It had soaked into the walls.

She pulled in a full breath when he helped her back into the hallway, when he let her sink to the floor. Tiffany smoothed her hands over her hair to ease the tension. Instinct took one whiff of that room and told her to get the hell out of there, that danger lurked.

"That room's been empty at least a week." He rubbed his hand over her back, slow motions from shoulder to tailbone. "That what you were expecting to find?"

She shook her head, which hung down. "Not exactly."

"Well, about now is the fucking time you to tell me what you were looking for. Because this shit? This is ugly, and I need to know what it is you're after before it bites us both in the ass."

A hard swallow kept her from throwing up. The room smelled like she had smelled after Randy had drugged her. It reminded her of how helpless she'd been, of the snap and tearing pain when her shoulder had pulled from its socket.

Is that what they'd suffered? She smelled no heat, but that was almost worse. It meant nothing had dulled the pain for them, nothing had eased it. They'd endured each spark of terror, each movement with no reprieve, nothing to dull the reality.

Kane's hand went to the back of her neck, a heavy weight. "Come on, now. Girl I know doesn't have panic attacks."

"Girl you knew hadn't been drugged and attacked, yet." Just the words threatened her, but she pushed them down.

No. She wasn't there. She wasn't the trapped omega in this room. No matter what Randy had tried to do, he'd failed. She was free, and he was dead.

The reminder helped her swallow and regain her equilibrium, at least until she met Kane's gaze.

Fury filled those eyes, the sort of threat that signaled someone's death. "The fuck are you talking about?" His gaze moved to her arm. "So, you didn't fall, did you?"

She shook her head, unable to force a word through her tight throat.

"Where's the fucker now?" The words came out in a rumble so low she had trouble understanding them.

"Dead." Saying that eased the tightness in her chest. He was dead, and from her understanding, he hadn't died an easy death. Claire had torn his throat out, and he'd deserved nothing less. "He's dead."

Kane's gaze moved over her, slow and possessive. "He hurt you?"

"Not like you mean. It's fine, really. I…" She breathed slowly. "The smell in there, it reminded me of it. Guess maybe trying to run off the next day was stupid, huh?"

His face softened, shoulders lowering. "This just happened? Doll, the fuck are you doing out here?"

"I didn't want to stay still. I felt helpless sitting in that damned house. Trapped, again, and I couldn't do it, couldn't sit there all night on my own."

"Should have called me."

"I did." The smile she offered was weak, but hell, it was all she had energy for.

"I mean to talk, not to break into shit. Where are you staying? Not alone, right?"

She drew herself to her feet, using her good hand for leverage. "No. Not on my own for a while." At his look, she continued. "Seems my past came back to get me. To avoid being registered, I have to stay with an alpha for a year for some bullshit training."

"And the first thing you do is sneak out to break into a place like this? Ah, fuck, you are so my kind of girl. I'm thinking you might not be acing the whole training shit." His laughter drew hers. Not a chuckle, not something little, but a full laugh that had her gasping for air at the end.

Which, she'd needed. She'd needed a normal moment of fun more than she'd needed a meal or medication. She'd needed a second of 'life could still be okay.'

"Well, let's finish looking around, then I'm making sure your ass gets back where you should be. Don't need you pulling any more stunts like this."

"Don't try to complain. Imagine how boring your night would have been without me." She moved forward and felt his gaze on her ass like a caress.

"Pretty fucking boring," he growled out.

Tiffany moved through the upper level, glad the scent of omega had lessened. Seemed they'd been kept on the second floor, twelve if she counted right. Each locked in a different room, alone. No blood, no struggles, a dirty mattress and the lingering scent. What had happened to them? She'd expected to find something, but not that. The place was on the books of a company that kept coming up in connection with missing omegas. She'd thought she'd find a clue, but nothing so overwhelming as this. The whole reason she'd come was because of what Kane had found on it.

A desk drawer rattled as she closed it, searching for something. Not that any of it meant a thing to her. After finding no sign of anyone else, Kane had left her to her own work, choosing to look in the rooms smelling of omegas instead. It didn't affect him like it did her, so she counted herself lucky. Plus, some space was a good thing. It gave her the chance to take a breath and regroup.

That helped. As it turned out, Kane was even more overwhelming in person.

Over the phone he'd been funny, charming in an odd way, tempting, but none of that was close to how he was in person. In person, his eyes bore into her. The width of his shoulders and the stroke of his voice was more than she trusted herself to resist.

She didn't want to resist it.

Rejection wore on her. Playing it safe hadn't helped anyone else. Claire had suffered, and she'd always played it safe. Every omega she knew who played it safe still lost. What was the point?

If she was going to get taken out, she'd damn well do what she wanted before then.

And what she wanted was sex.

That sounds shallow. Maybe it was. However, she was nineteen and her instincts had pulled at her for years. She wanted to press her thighs into the hips of another person, wanted to feel something more than her fingers spreading her open. She needed it, waking up drenched from dreams that never quenched that thirst.

No matter what she did, it never seemed to work out. She'd taken her time, been cautious around alphas. No need to be stupid. Still, those she'd been forced near had pulled away. Kieran. Kane. Even Marshall had all but run out of the room at the slightest sign of her wanting him.

After yet another dead-end, she stepped back from the desk. *No computer, shelves empty, most things gone.* Seemed when they left, they'd done so in a hell of a hurry.

She headed for the stairs, ready to catch up with Kane on the next floor down.

When she turned the corner into the hallway, however, she ran into a large chest that did not belong to Kane.

The scream from upstairs had Kane moving before it had fully stopped. It didn't sound like and sound from Tiffany he'd ever heard.

His feet ate up the distance as he took the stairs two at a time. He shouldn't have left her alone. There hadn't been any sign of anyone else in the building, however, and he'd need to check the rooms the omegas had been kept in. The scent had played havoc with Tiffany, but he'd hoped to gather some information from the dark rooms.

At that moment, though, he cursed the choice. Tiffany was impulsive, never understood the danger to herself, never cared. She threw herself into situations without thinking, and while he'd enjoyed that spark, it now terrified him.

He turned the last landing of the stairs to find Tiffany and a man dressed in black. She brought her knee up and into the man's junk, and the grunt that came out had Kane wanting to hold his jewels in sympathy. The man stumbled backward, then turned when a low snarl spilled from Kane.

Seemed the coward only beat on women, since a single look in Kane's direction sent him running toward Tiffany. He used his bulk to knock her to the side, her head cracking against the wall. He moved fast, but fuck if there wasn't a limp to his gait.

The desire to chase rose up, the need to track the fucker down. Tiffany's body on the floor smothered it, though.

Kane dropped to a crouch beside her. He tilted her face up and checked her eyes. "You're always getting into trouble, doll."

She smiled, a dribble of blood from her re-split lip running down to her chin and to his fingers. "It's part of my charm."

"No doubt." He didn't wait for an offer, didn't ask, but hefted her up beside him. He'd have rather carried her, but he had no idea if the man was still there, and Kane wouldn't risk being encumbered. So, he slid an arm beneath her good shoulder to help her up.

A yank from her sent her back to the ground.

"We've got to go, doll."

She nodded, but she only slid her hand along the floor, beneath a box. "He dropped something." When she pulled her hand out, a silver necklace hung on a long chain from her fingers.

"The fuck is that?"

She wrapped her fingers around it, then brought it closer to her face. "It's a necklace, and it smells like an omega." Her lips tipped down before she stuffed it into her pocket. "It must have belonged to one of the omegas they kept here. I can't believe he'd steal it."

Kane grasped her good arm and hauled her to her feet. "Whatever the fuck it is, it doesn't matter right now. Let's get out of here."

No sign of the other asshole through the building, nor when he got her into his car.

"What about my car?"

"I'll get it later."

"I can't leave it here."

He reached past her to buckle her seatbelt. "You sure as fuck can, especially since I ain't letting your ass out of my sight until you're somewhere safe." He shut the door before she could argue, and she damn well planned on arguing. It was written all over her face, lips already open to spit out a complaint.

Kane took a deep breath as he circled the car, then slid in. The engine roared to life, and he threw it into reverse before she'd caught her breath to start back in.

Soon enough, though, there she went. "I don't need a babysitter."

"Ain't that why you're living with an alpha?"

She leaned back, kicking her feet onto the dashboard. "I figured you for being more understanding. In fact, I kind of expected you to go all white knight and offer to help me escape."

"Then you don't know me at all." He tossed her a smirk. "If I think the guy's a fucker, I'll kill him."

It took a second for the words to sink in, but after a moment, she let out a snort of laughter.

Kane shook his head at the horrifying sound before asking for the directions and letting it drop, because he wasn't kidding.

If he didn't like the look of the asshole alpha she was staying with, he had no problem gutting him.

Chapter Five

Kieran pulled the door open before the headlights of the car turned off. It wasn't Tiffany's car, but when the interior lights popped on, her blonde hair came into view.

He'd install bars on her windows by the next day. The sneaky omega had slipped out, taking off well before he'd had a clue. He'd tracked down murderers, professional assassins, drug dealers, but a hundred-and-twenty-pound omega got the jump on him?

He couldn't see the driver, only knew he was male. So, some man had driven her home?

She hadn't had sex, but he hadn't stopped to consider she might be seeing someone. Sure, she'd dated Randy, but women did date different people. Was this a boyfriend?

His lip lifted, partly out of frustration at the situation, and partly because he should be too old to be annoyed by such a thing.

Plus, he'd already said nothing could happen between them. Why be jealous if she found someone else?

The car doors opened, the click as they shut loud in the early morning. Tiffany walked up first, thumb hooked in her jean pocket, far too casual for having snuck out and been gone for hours.

"If it isn't my wayward ward."

She shrugged, but the corners of her mouth had turned up. "I'm a very busy person."

"So it seems." He shifted to the side to let her pass, but the outline of the male figure came closer, still in the darkness of the driveway. "Are you going to introduce me to your new friend?"

"Not so new." The answer came as the man stepped into the light of the porch.

Kieran held his temper as only decades of practice could manage. Tiffany had been out with Kane?

Of all the people she could have spent time around, *this* was her friend?

Kane didn't bother to ask for an invitation before sliding past Kieran as well, the arrogant asshole.

A moment to collect himself as he shut the door, then he turned to Tiffany. His mouth opened to ask, but the blood that leaked down her chin caught his attention. "What happened?"

Tiffany didn't react to the violence in the question. "Don't you growl at me."

Kieran turned his gaze on Kane, eyes narrowed. If he'd done something to Tiffany...

A shove to Kieran's shoulder from Tiffany halted the line of thought. "Knock that off."

Kane either had more mercy or enjoyed annoying Kieran, because he answered. "I got a message a few hours ago from her asking for instructions on picking a lock."

"Turns out it's harder than I thought it would be," Tiffany chimed in.

Kane kept speaking as if she hadn't interrupted. "Doll broke into an apartment building, north end of town."

Doll? The affection in that word raised the hairs on the back of Kieran's neck. How well did the two know each other?

Kane wasn't the sort of person Tiffany should associate with. Kieran had worked with Kane a few times, though 'with' seemed a generous explanation of the jobs.

Kane didn't work *with* people. He was hired muscle. He didn't care about the job, about what was at stake. Instead, he breezed in when the pay was good enough and took care of problems others didn't want to get dirtied by.

Need information beat out of someone? Need something stolen? Need to get in touch with someone shady? Kane was the man to go for.

So how the hell had Tiffany gotten herself tied up with him to be called *doll* like they were best fucking friends?

It took a moment to realize Kieran had zoned out of most of the conversation, too busy with his own questions to hear a word of what was said. He went back to paying attention, to gathering the pieces of information offered. The omega cells, the man who had attacked her.

Before the conversation finished, Kieran had his phone out, sending a message to Dr. Brown.

"I don't need a checkup." She went to cross her arms, but the sling ruined the movement.

"You got knocked around. For all I know, you could have a concussion from the wall. There's no chance you're getting out of this without a checkup and consider yourself damn lucky that's all you'll get out of it, girl." A message on his phone had him checking. "Dr. Brown will be by before his shift in about ten minutes."

"Trust me, the other guy's going to be far sorer than I am." The smile would have been adorable if it hadn't caused another drop of blood to seep from her lip.

"Seems this omega likes to go for a man's goods," Kane said.

"Remember that the next time you piss me off."

"Count that as a reason you ain't getting anywhere near my goods."

The banter had Kieran gritting his molars and trying to talk down his possessive instincts.

He had an omega in his home, one he'd seen through at least part of her first heat. She slept beneath his roof, under his care, and some other alpha had flirted with her? Some other alpha had touched her?

If either of the other two noticed Kieran's struggle, they said nothing, like either he didn't matter, or they hadn't seen it.

He wasn't sure which was worse.

Kane took a seat on the kitchen table as though the thing was a sofa. "So, doll, tell me what this is about." He gestured toward Kieran. "He's got a stick up his ass, but I won't gut him, so might as well talk in front of him. You were shocked as fuck to find the holding cells for those omegas, so you weren't looking for that. What were you looking for?"

She hadn't sat, standing between him and Kane, her uneasy fidgeting saying it wasn't a conversation she wanted to have.

Kieran pushed. "Whatever it was, you felt it vital enough to sneak out of a window in the middle of the night. What's it about?"

Her shoulders slumped. "I've heard the company name a few times over the last couple of months. Some of the omegas I've known have mentioned it, and a couple haven't shown back up."

"What do you mean, 'haven't shown back up'?"

"I figured it was a dead end, another thing to mark off the list. I didn't think we'd find anything."

Kieran's temper slipped, his voice coming out in a low demand. "Get to the point, girl."

She pulled in a deep breath, then spoke quickly. "A few omegas I know have been contacted by a company saying they're looking for volunteers to try out a new suppressant. I warned the girls not to return the call, but, well, some of us get desperate. Medication can be hard to come by. When I looked at a few online groups, same thing, omegas getting calls. Some of them are in hiding, some aren't, but it's the same thing. Then? Well, some of those omegas went missing. I didn't know if it was connected or not, but I asked Kane to look into it a few weeks ago."

Kane jumped in. "Looked into it and found that place on their payrolls. Wasn't easy to find, and in my experience, the harder someone tries to hide something, the more interesting it is. Had no idea what she was walking into, though."

A knock on the door halted the conversation before Kieran could get into a lecture. He turned away to open the door and found the doctor standing there, looking far less professional than he had at the hospital.

"Is she okay?"

"I called you to find out." Kieran waved him in, then gestured at Tiffany. "She hit her head on a wall, from what I understand, and probably jostled her shoulder a bit. Why don't you examine her while I step outside with Kane?"

Kane hopped off the table to follow, and Tiffany's chuckled "Play nice" followed them.

He had no intention of playing nice.

Marshall sighed as he took in the blood running down Tiffany's face. "It's been less than twenty-four hours."

"Kieran is overreacting."

"Perhaps." He approached, then gestured for her to take a seat at the table.

Tiffany sat with a huff, as if the little act of rebellion made her feel better. He'd let her have it. She looked as if she could use a win.

He slid his fingers along her scalp to feel the back of her skull. "Kieran said you struck your head?"

"Someone knocked me into a wall."

"Does it hurt?"

A wince answered the question when he found a spot that had started to swell. She'd have a lump by the end of the day, but that was all.

Marshall pulled back. "The medication for your shoulder will also help with this." He went through his examination, checking her pupil dilation, her heart rate, her shoulder. "Everything seems okay, but you need to be much more careful."

"So everyone keeps telling me."

Marshall should have left it at that, but the voice inside him, the one he'd spent his life ignoring, pushed him onward. He dragged the pad of his thumb over her full bottom lip, avoiding the split on the left side. "I've only met you twice, and both times you've been injured. You have a poor track record."

"Or maybe a good track record of attracting cute doctors?"

The come-on had him smiling, but the fall of her lips said she read it as the rejection he'd meant it to be.

He inhaled, and the sweet scent of her cunt distracted him. It was better than when she'd been in heat because he knew *he* caused it, instead of mindless lust. She wasn't craving just anyone. She wanted him.

Despite all the reasons why he shouldn't, he was tempted. With Kieran and Kane outside, he could have done anything. He could have pulled her against him, taken the kiss he wanted and slipped his hand into her pants. Would she be as soft as he imagined?

He'd touched her during the exams, when he'd put her shoulder back into place, but those had been with professional detachment. It hadn't been the time to enjoy or explore.

Tiffany leaned forward, her hand going to his knee. With her even closer, he could see the blue of her eyes, the way it was dark around the outside iris. *She's stunning.* How easy it would be to take what she offered.

Why not?

As quickly as the question occurred to him, he shook it away. There were too many complications, too many reasons he should keep his distance. He'd spent his life avoiding such entanglements with omegas, and the one before him gave him even more reason to resist. She had been attacked, hurt, and now trapped beneath a contract that controlled her. He'd never seen a clearer case of 'keep your distance' than this.

Still, when she leaned closer, her lips brushing his, the snarl of his instinct made his hands clutch. He would grab her and yank her in. He'd hold her down, strip her bare, and —

No.

He stood and moved away, trying not to let on how close he'd come to losing control and how much that frightened him. "Take your medicine, and Kieran can call me if you have any problems."

She shook her head, then muttered "Coward" beneath her breath.

Marshall ignored the barb, letting her have her power by tossing it. He deserved it, didn't he? Yeah, so he was pulling away for her own good, but at the end, it was his own weakness, his own cowardice.

He'd seen what alphas could do, and he wouldn't let his get anywhere near Tiffany, for both their goods.

Kane didn't bother hiding the grin at the aggression rolling off the other alpha. Kieran always saw himself as better than him, as more fucking noble or some shit. Him was having a pissy moment over Tiffany having been around him was too much fun.

Kieran crossed his arms, jaw tight, cheek twitching. "How exactly do you know Tiffany?"

Kane wanted to say something else. He wanted to tell the other alpha something that would set him off, make some innuendo that would make those molars grind tighter.

But…he didn't need that shit to get put on Tiffany. Last thing he wanted to make her life any harder than it was already.

"I started doing jobs for her about a year ago when she'd first been on the run. Sent shit to her parents, hooked up special deliveries, taught her how to stay hidden, things like that. She got my name from the guy who did her papers. We hit it off."

"What does hit it off mean?"

"What do you think it means?" Fine, so he couldn't stop from taunting Kieran. *Turns out I'm still a petty twelve-year-old.*

"Well, this ends now. She doesn't need the trouble you'll bring her. Do you have any idea what she's been through?"

The words gave him pause. "Said something about someone drugging her. Also said the fucker was already dead."

Kieran didn't answer right away, cutting his gaze to look down the driveway. "Got his throat ripped out by an omega in a rage. You hear about that alpha killing omegas?"

That had Kane tensing. "How did Tiffany get in his sights?"

"She doesn't see how dangerous people are." Kieran sent a withering glare at Kane. "She was dating him. He used a drug that sent her into a heat and bound her until she dislocated her shoulder."

And there went the leash he'd had on his temper. "And she was out the next fucking day?"

"She's willful. But can you understand why I don't feel this friendship is in her best interest? After what she went through, are you any good for her? We both know the sort of people you deal with, the things you're involved in. I don't want any of that within a mile of that girl."

"Why? What are you in it for? Because don't think I missed all the things you're throwing out there."

"I'm helping her."

"Oh yeah? You help her through her heat, too? Let me guess, you're hoping she's gonna start smelling so good, the way she does when she's wet, and she'll let you between those thighs?" Kane was pretty sure he pissed himself off as much as he did Kieran, but still took it as a win. He was used to being pissed, so if he got to rile Kieran, he'd take it.

Kieran drew his hands into fists, but instead of throwing the punch he clearly wanted to, he folded his hands behind him. "So, are we thinking a slave sale?"

The switch in topic took him a moment to catch up. *Right, the building.* "Yeah, had to be. Each door had a lock on the outside, windows boarded up, found some shackles. Scent alone said it was ugly. I'd guess we missed 'em by a week, maybe."

"Damn it. It's not that I don't know this happens, but I'd hoped it wouldn't be in our town." Kieran's tension slid from his shoulders as he rubbed his fingers against the bridge of his nose. "First the whole thing with Randy, now this?"

"Tiffany says a few omegas went missing. Seems like they're hunting in town, too."

Kieran sighed. "That's not good. I'll see what I can find out."

Kane would do the same, of course. Kieran had a certain type of people he talked to, and Kane had a different one. The sorts of people he got info from would have given nightmares to Kieran.

Kane nodded, then took a step back. He'd done his job, delivered Tiffany safe and sound to Kieran, hadn't even punched the fucker. That was it, right? He'd never planned on meeting Tiffany, but now that he had, it made it even clearer that he needed to stay away from her.

Kieran caught his arm before he made it off the porch in a tight grip. "I don't want to find you around her again. Are we clear?"

Kane looked down at the hand on his arm, and all the reasons he should stay away fled. He wasn't willing to let the fucker get the upper hand. "Seems to me she does whatever the fuck she wants. Ain't my fault if that's me."

The hand on his arm cranked down, and again he expected a punch. Nah, not Kieran, not the level-headed prick. He released him, walked into the house and slammed the door on Kane.

Damn if that didn't make it more tempting.

Tiffany sat alone in the house, unsure what to do. Should she head back to her room? Wait and talk to Kieran? He was sure to have a lot to say.

He'd kept his temper in check while Kane and Marshall were there, and she had no fear that he'd haul off and hit her. She still wasn't looking forward to his lecture.

The sound of one car leaving, then a second let her know they were alone. Still Kieran didn't come back inside. Was he standing in the small entryway?

Waiting was the hardest part as her mind raced about what he could have to say, about what he might do. He could throw her back. He could decide dealing with her wasn't worth the trouble, and that he'd rather let the system take care of her.

Then again, she'd be no worse off than she'd been already, right?

What surprised her the most was her disappointment. She didn't want him to throw her back.

Tiffany jumped when the door opened, when Kieran's heavy steps filled the living room. She got to her feet, the position feeling slightly stronger than sitting. Not that it mattered since he still towered above her.

"I didn't mean to—"

Kieran pointed a finger at her. "I suggest you listen for a minute."

Her lips snapped together, the hard tone of his voice new. He'd never spoken like that to her.

He kept going. "I am not an unreasonable alpha, but I have a few expectations that you will follow so long as you live in my home and under my care. The first is pretty damn simple. You do not leave, especially in the middle of the night, without a word."

"I wasn't going far—"

His narrowed gaze had her words falling short. She felt like when she'd break the rules at her parents' and they'd give her that same look. No matter what she said, she'd only dig herself deeper into trouble.

Though she'd never learned her lesson then, either, so she gulped and pushed on. "I didn't want to sit in that room anymore."

"So, you go for a walk. You talk to me. You do not head to an abandoned apartment building, having no idea what might be there. Do you realize no one knew where you were? Anything could have happened to you and I would have had no leads as to where you might have gone."

When he put it like that, the guilt grew. He sounded pissed, sure, but beneath that? The worry broke through. He barely knew her. Why would he worry about her?

Instead of asking, because the last thing she needed to hear was obligation, she tried again. "I haven't had to tell anyone where I am in a long time. And the last time I had to, I wasn't good at it."

"Too bad. Get used to it, girl, because that is how things will happen from now on." He jammed a finger toward her. "You are my responsibility, whether you like it or not. You signed the contract, you chose this, and while I'm easygoing, you will not put yourself in this sort of risk without even a word to me about it."

"I wasn't at—"

Kieran came forward with a speed that made Tiffany's head spin. She jerked backward, but it didn't help. Before her mind had cleared, he had her pinned to the wall behind her, his body against hers, his hand in her hair to tilt her face up to his.

His lip curled up, eyes bright and furious and full of passion she'd never tasted. "You were attacked. You were at a place where they kept slave omegas. Do you have an idea what they do to them? They kidnap them and they have auctions and sell them off to the highest bidder. If Kane hadn't been there, you could have ended up one of them. Don't you dare sit there and tell me you weren't at risk."

She opened her mouth, but a tug at her hair silenced her.

"I suggest you be very careful with your words, because believe it or not, this is me being reasonable.

Push me much further and you will find yourself bent over my lap with a hell of a sore ass, omega."

"You wouldn't dare."

"You want to bet?"

He would do it. The line of his lips, the tic of his jaw, they all said he had no problem doing exactly what he said. *Why the hell does that idea turn me on?* Why did the image of her trapped, pinned over his lap, make her cunt tense? It made her gasp, everything too warm suddenly.

And Tiffany? Like she always did, she pushed. "You wouldn't."

The snap of his control echoed through the room, nostrils flaring once before he moved. He hauled her by her good arm to the couch, and even if she pulled, his strength outmatched her by a far cry. Everything spun, and she found herself bent over his lap.

Her good arm came down to support herself on the ground, her bad one cradled against her chest, her body far enough forward that the position didn't hurt it. Still, it put her ass up, and even when she kicked her legs, she could do nothing but accept it.

He reached beneath her to undo her jeans with one large, strong hand, then slid the pants over her ass. He didn't remove them, only moved them to the tops of her thighs, and since she wore no underwear, it exposed him her pussy to him, even with her legs pressed together.

Her cheeks burned at the sight he must have, but he only stroked his hand over her ass once, then squeezed. "I'm expecting an apology, girl, and I suggest you mean it. I can do this all day if I need to, but I doubt your ass can take that much."

She opened her mouth to smart off, but the first strike drew a started yelp. It wasn't sensual, it wasn't the moaning women did to sound sexy. Not even close. It came out frantic and startled like a trapped animal.

Tiffany thrashed on his lap, but he pressed a hand to her back to hold her still, and the pants around her thighs meant she had no leverage to get up. "What the fuck do you think you're—"

Smack.

"I swear when I get up—"

Smack.

"This is insane, you—"

Each hit of his strong palm against her ass, as he switched from cheek to cheek and to different areas, made her skin burn with an awareness she'd never had. She'd gotten off on the idea of spanking before, but had always pictured it as something sensual. She'd pictured sweet little taps that she'd giggle about, that she'd moan and offer up fake 'no's to, that never pushed her limits or even came near them.

That wasn't what he gave her. Instead, each strike came down hard and fast, his fingers catching her skin so hard it stung, and yet that sting woke something else inside her, something primal and hungry. He handled her as though he had a right to do so, and she responded by melting into that confidence.

The first sniffle surprised her as she gritted her teeth. Another hit, and she gave into his demand entirely, and into the part of her, no matter how little she understood it, that wanted to submit to this man. "I'm sorry!"

He paused, the thumb of the hand on her back rubbing against her. "I don't like you in danger, Tiffany. I don't want to have to identify your body because you put yourself at risk. Tell me you understand."

"I understand." Her words turned into an embarrassing moan when his hand stroked over her ass.

He didn't pause even when the sounds she made drifted between moans and whimpers. Some areas he stroked would make her skin burn, but the burn had transformed even more, shifting from something painful to something that made wetness cover her thighs and her hips squirm.

The unease from being bent over his lap and him having a perfect view of her cunt failed to matter anymore, ether. He could look all he wanted if he just kept touching her.

All she could feel was the stroke of his strong hand over her sore ass.

Kieran couldn't tear his gaze away from her ass. The skin had turned pink, a few spots red, a few in the shape of his fingers. She had curves to her, which meant each strike made her ass shake, and the movement transfixed him.

Yes, he'd done it because she hadn't listened, because she was so busy fighting him, she'd refused to stop and hear him. Nothing like a moment of insanity to force someone to take a breath and consider.

He should have known better. The moment he'd hauled her over his lap, punishment had turned into a far distant concern.

"You're not wearing underwear, girl." How had his voice turned so rough?

"I didn't have any," she whispered.

His cock jerked at that, and he knew damn well she felt it pressing against her, poised as she was over his lap. His hand shifted, sliding closer to her tempting cunt, to all the scent and wetness and heaven he saw there. The overhead light made the juices sticking to her thighs stand out, made his mouth water with want to taste her. "It isn't a smart idea to go walking around with alphas near when you're not wearing underwear. Later today, when we get your things, we'll make sure you have some."

His words fell clumsily from his lips, as if they were having a normal conversation. He tried to keep control, even as his gaze traced all he could see. Her cunt was fucking perfect. Plump outer lips pressed tight from how her legs were pinned together. She shaved, so nothing obscured his view. He wanted to press his thumbs into her, to spread her out, to see those inner lips, to see her clit nestled between the pliant folds and ensure she had no secrets from him.

Instead, he contented himself with the sight as his fingers dared nearer, brushing against her slit with the lightest touch.

Tiffany didn't bother to answer, her struggles having died off, so she offered herself up to him. He could drive a thick finger into her waiting cunt and she'd only moan and beg for more. He knew it from her scent, from her body language, from the filthy, broken moans that left her lips.

He wanted to show her all the things she didn't know about yet. He wanted to break her apart beneath his hands until she clawed and begged for rest.

He allowed himself a more solid stroke, from the top of her cunt, where her hidden, swollen clit lay, then up her slit without pressing in, and to her tight little asshole.

Ah, that got her going. She squirmed at the strange touch, but Kieran was in no mood to give in to anything she wanted.

He gave her a quick swat to settle her, then went back to his own exploration. He circled her ass, a single finger light and coaxing. Perhaps one time, when she misbehaved as seemed sure to happen again, he'd fuck her ass. He'd use lube, ensure she was prepared, but he'd wrap his fingers in her hair, put her on all fours and take her snug ass for worrying him. He'd never been an easy alpha to put up with, demanding and strict, but he had a feeling Tiffany could use such a thing. A little punishment might just make the wild omega slow down and think before she did things that risked her life.

His finger pressed against her as she clenched, as she fought him, before he stilled.

What the fuck am I doing?

Kieran pulled his hand away, a hard swallow at how close he'd been to losing control, to taking her. Sure, she'd have allowed it, but that wasn't the point.

He pulled her pants up, ignoring how delicious her disgruntled whine was when the jeans rubbed against the red skin of her abused ass. He helped her to her feet, rising himself, needing space. She smelled too close, and he knew her wetness stuck to his fingers.

Her gaze stayed down, stuck, and at first, he thought she avoided him.

No. It seemed she was staring at the way his full erection showed through his slacks, the way they did little to hide how hard he was, how much he wanted her.

He needed her to be a voice of reason, to tell him to back off, to remind him she was too young, too inexperienced. Hell, he'd wanted to fuck her ass, and she was still a virgin. If that wasn't a great example of what a disaster this was, he couldn't think of a better one.

Kieran opened his mouth, but when nothing came out, he snapped it shut.

She looked up at him, lust a living thing inside her, dancing across her blue eyes and in the pink on her cheeks. At least, it did until she met his gaze.

Whatever she saw there dried it up. Her chin kicked up before she stepped back, though she couldn't hide the grimace.

Whether it was from the jeans on her ass, or the rubbing of them against her still wet and hard clit, he didn't know. Did it matter? He found either equally tempting.

"Right," she said. "Just like always."

"Get some sleep. We'll get your things from your place when you wake up."

She offered a look so hard, he ached from it, before turning on her heel.

"Fuck you, Kieran," she muttered as she walked out.

Well, at least they agreed about that.

I am fucked.

Chapter Six

Just go home.

No matter how many times Marshall repeated the good advice to himself, he didn't heed it. Instead, he stood outside the small coffee shop, arguing with himself.

Tiffany worked inside. He'd known it from her paperwork, and he told himself that he hadn't gone looking in order to stalk her. He'd spotted it on her forms and taken notice, since he passed by the shop from time to time.

The reassurances didn't work, however, and he found himself frustrated at his foolishness.

He'd walked out of the house and away from her because he'd known better. Whatever she wanted, he couldn't give to her. So why couldn't he let it go?

Why can't I forget about her?

The soft taste of her lips that he'd gotten had left him stroking his cock during the night, picturing how she'd feel wrapped around him and how he could service her through her next heat. He'd spend an hour between those thighs, and instead of ignoring the moans she'd made, he'd make them louder.

So, rather than going to bed like a responsible adult, he'd spent the night like a teenage boy, masturbating to take an edge off that never dulled.

And worse? After working all that day, after a full night's sleep, after another day at work, he hadn't shaken loose her memory.

Instead, he'd decided that eight at night was the time he had to have a cup of coffee from that little shop on the corner he hadn't tried.

The third time a woman stared at him, unease on her features, he realized he had to either walk away or go in. If he didn't, Sam would end up being called, and he didn't want to explain to the detective why he was standing on a street corner arguing with himself.

The coffee shop was everything he expected it to be. Small, bright and cheery, with a large display case holding the few pastries left from the day. One other patron sat at a corner table, her fingers flying over the keyboard of her laptop, not even looking up when the bell above the door rang.

A swinging door behind the counter opened to show who he'd missed, that blonde hair pulled into a tight bun, blue eyes bright as she searched for the customer who had set off the bell.

When her gaze rested on him, a moment of pleasure flashed in her eyes before distrust took over.

He crossed the small shop to stand at the register, unsure what to say.

"Are you going to say you were craving a cup of coffee?" Her hands went to her hips, all attitude.

Marshall gave her a smile, as though that could wipe away the misunderstanding. "Of course not. I wanted a piece of lemon loaf, too."

The stupid joke ate up the tension between them until she gave him a smile in return. "You're lucky you're charming. Okay, lemon loaf. Do you want something to drink?"

"Cappuccino, please."

She rang up the order, and he slid his card through the reader on his side. Before he'd finished, she turned her back to him to work on the order.

She moved with a grace that said she was comfortable with the shop and the job. She took the food from the refrigerated case and slid it into a bag, placing it on the counter at the end before starting the shots. As they poured, she steamed the milk, a tap in her foot and sway to her hips that made him think she hummed to herself. The entire thing came together like a dance, and she moved like no one else watched.

She set the cup on the counter, the white foam on top in a perfect layer. "So, how far did you come for this drink?"

Marshall picked up the cup and took a sip. "Not that far. It's between the hospital and my house. Though, with how good this is, I think I'll make a stop more often."

She washed her hands, dried them on a paper towel before tossing it, then came around the counter to his side. A nod at the small table across the shop from the writer had them sitting.

"What are you doing here?"

"You're not wearing your sling."

"I tried, but I couldn't work one-handed. Besides, it's feeling better." She leaned back in her chair. "You're not here to dispense medical advice, though."

He picked off a piece of the lemon loaf and offered it to her. "You're right. I wanted to see you."

She took the offered bite and popped it into her mouth. "You weren't interested in seeing much of me the other day. In fact, I've seen people flee natural disasters slower than you ran."

He wanted to argue, but she had a point. Instead, he cupped the cappuccino in his hands for the warmth. "I didn't think it was smart to indulge in anything. After what you went through, and your current troubles and situation with Kieran, allowing anything seemed unwise."

"I'm a little tired of alphas deciding what's best for me. I can make my own choices."

"You can, but I don't want you suffering for choices I make as well. Kieran isn't someone who shares, and since you've committed to staying with him for a year, it doesn't seem ideal to start anything."

She released a low laugh that lacked any humor. "Yeah, well, I don't think you have to worry about that. Kieran and I aren't happening."

The attraction between the two was obvious. The way Kieran had snarled at people, the tension that had run through him as he'd waited for her to wake the night he had stayed at the hospital all said he hadn't been there out of obligation.

It meant he suspected confusion. Was Kieran trying to keep things professional? Was she? Sometimes physical attraction wasn't the only thing that mattered. Perhaps they'd found themselves incompatible in some other way?

Instead of saying any of that, he let the untruth remain. "Even if you two aren't romantically involved, he still has a large say over you and your life. I thought I would be a complication, a point of conflict between Kieran and you." He sipped the hot drink, let the warmth soothe the tension in him from the conversation. "I thought that, in a year when you were free from the contract, perhaps something could happen."

"But you're here now."

He huffed a soft laugh, then shrugged. "I have less self-discipline than I thought. I couldn't stop thinking about you, and after arguing with myself outside, I finally gave in. You're hard to forget."

She didn't answer right away, and disbelief played across her features.

"Why is that so hard for you to believe?"

She reached over, stole his drink and took a sip. "Because I've gotten used to men not actually wanting me. Seems like my lot in life."

Foam sat on her top lip, and Marshall stopped resisting. What had resisting got him so far? He leaned over the table and traced her lip with his tongue. He cleared the foam, then stole the kiss he'd craved since he'd first seen her.

Tiffany moved with him, no hesitation at all. If anything, she pushed forward, aggressive. His hand went to the back of her neck, pulling her closer, ready to toss the table out of the way and take her —

A loud clearing throat broke them apart. The woman in the corner had stopped her writing long enough to toss a disapproving glare their way.

Marshall fought down the growl he wanted to answer with. Tiffany didn't need him causing her problems at work.

Well, more problems.

He pulled back, took the lemon loaf and nodded at the cappuccino. "Delicious, but I think my heart rate is fast enough." He reached into his pocket, fished out his business card and pushed it across the table. "Call me?"

She picked it up and tucked it into her back pocket, a grin across her lips. "Oh, I will."

* * * *

The lock clicked as Tiffany twisted the key. Her feet ached and her shoulder burned. She should have left the sling on, it seemed, but she'd never admit that. Not to Marshall, and not to Kieran who had frowned when she'd left it at his place.

Still, doing what was normal had centered her. She'd returned to her life, to what she knew. She'd spent the day seeing her regulars, lost in the mindless motions she knew so well.

Being a barista worked for her. She had flexible hours that didn't require her to wake early, and the tips helped her make ends meet. The work was tiring, since eight hours on her feet could wear anyone out, but she loved the constant moving.

Tiffany had always bored easily, hated sitting still, waiting. The movement of the coffee shop, all the little steps that made up the orders, kept boredom at bay.

Her first day back had gone the same way, though Marshall's appearance had surprised her. Try as she might, she couldn't quite get a read on him.

He seemed interested, and that kiss of his... She bit her bottom lip as she thought about it, as she remembered the fleeting taste of passion that had crashed over them both before they'd moved apart.

Still, the few times she'd seen him, he'd always stayed out of reach. He'd speak, but always with a pause, as if he had to measure his words. She got the sense he held things back, that he played the part he thought he should.

The kiss was the only part that had felt real.

Real, and as frightening as it was wonderful.

She'd never have thought something could be both, but it was like getting on a roller coaster, those moments of terror combined with the moments of exhilaration.

The only problem? That car.

The black sedan she'd spotted when she'd opened and again during her break. By the third time she'd watched it drive down the street, she'd been shaken.

Then she'd scolded herself for allowing paranoia to get the better of her.

Randy would not turn her into a coward. No matter what he'd done, she'd not turn into a woman afraid of her own shadow. Fuck Randy, because he couldn't have her confidence. It was what he'd wanted, for her to be afraid, to think she needed some alpha to take care of her, to give up everything to him.

And she refused. Even dead, he'd win if she did that, if she let him have her in that way.

So, she'd gone on with her day, reminding herself she wasn't running for once. She was legit. With the contract signed, the registry wasn't looking for her. She could use her real name without issue.

So why couldn't she shake the feeling something was coming for her? Why couldn't she relax?

She walked down the sidewalk toward the parking lot alongside the building. When she turned the corner, however, parked beside her car was the same black sedan.

Tiffany halted, a hidden, dark figure in the car.

It couldn't be the same car, right?

But, in a parking lot with no other cars, he'd parked next to her. He hadn't chosen the twenty other open spots closer to the street, but had instead parked so close she'd have to slide by that car to reach her driver's-side door. While she refused to be paranoid, she refused even more to be stupid.

The head in the car lifted, silhouette moving, and even though she couldn't see him, every muscle in her went rigid when he looked at her. Whatever instinct inside her that worked to keep her alive told her to run.

Instead of giving in, Tiffany struggled for calm. She patted down the apron wrapped around her. "My phone," she said to herself, but loud enough for the car to catch it. She let a muttered curse leave her lips before pulling her keys from her pocket and turning back toward the coffee shop.

Let him think she'd returned to grab her phone.

She passed the door, though, rushing around the corner and out of sight. She yanked her phone from her pocket. Her first impulse had her finger hovering above Claire's name, but Claire had suffered enough for her.

Instead, she scrolled down and pressed the tile reading 'Kieran.'

"You never call me."

"I think someone's following me." Her words came out choppy, her breathing heavy despite her not having walked far. Nerves alone stole her breath.

"What? Where are you? What happened?" His voice moved away from the phone. Was he putting on his shoes?

"I saw the same car three times today and now it's parked next to mine. I don't know who it is, I can't see, and it's probably nothing—"

"Breathe slowly, girl, or you'll pass out. You did the right thing." The phone shifted, his voice coming from farther away as if he'd put her on speaker phone. "Your work is fifteen minutes away, but I know someone closer. I'll text them. Where exactly are you walking?"

"Down Fourth, toward Hibiscus."

He made a soft sound as though he focused on something else but didn't want her to think he hadn't heard her. "Okay. I want you to make a left at the next block, then a right. If the person comes looking for you, I don't want you on the same road."

"Fucking Randy."

"What? He's dead."

Her fingers numbed from gripping the phone, from the way her heart pounded against her ribs. "I know he's dead, but I was never scared before. I'm probably running from shadows like an idiot, all because of him."

"It's okay. Better to be safe, right? Better to make a mistake and be safe than to ignore the signs and end up hurt."

She wanted to argue it, but what was the point? He didn't understand that she'd never been scared before, that she'd always prided herself on being someone who could stand on her own, who didn't need to rely on someone.

And what happened? At the first sign of anything wrong, she'd called up an alpha like the stereotypical omega she'd sworn not to be.

He ended the call as the engine to his car roared to life. Not having his voice made her edgy, but she followed the plan he'd set. She turned right, one foot in front of the other. He'd show up, and... Then what? She walked quickly as she told herself off for her foolishness.

As she was ready to call back and apologize, to tell Kieran she'd made a mistake, that she'd overreacted, she turned another corner.

And ran into a large body.

Tiffany lifted her knee, but the body twisted to avoid the strike, letting her leg slide up the outside of his thigh. "Settle down, doll," a familiar voice said. "I've seen that little move before, and I'd like to keep my balls in one piece."

She dropped her shoulders and lowered her knee. She pulled in a deep breath, her chest loosening. It wasn't that she expected Kane to fix it all, but knowing she wasn't alone helped. Before she realized it, her fingers that had shoved at his chest curled in to grasp him.

Until she realized, she had no idea how he'd gotten there. "What are you doing here?"

"Kieran texted me. I live right over there, so I was closer than he was. Said someone was following you?"

She hesitated, the words feeling silly. "I don't know for sure. I saw the same car a couple times, and the car was parked next to mine, and maybe it was all—"

His soft, chastising growl quieted her. "You did good."

"Are you going to go look?"

"I wish. I'd like to see who it is and explain it ain't a good idea to fucking scare you, but I can't exactly leave you here while I do it."

"So, what now?"

"I'm gonna take you over to my place to wait it out, and Kieran'll take a look. If someone is following you, it's best to get you off the street."

The words hit her along with the reality of being in a closed space with him, in his space. "Your place?"

"Scared?"

"Should I be?"

Kane laughed before tossing his large arm around her. "Yeah, you probably should be."

Leaving the man who had frightened Tiffany behind tore at Kane's pride, at his feeling of possessiveness. He wanted to go to that car, to pull the asshole out through the window and beat some manners into him. Sure, figuring out why he was there mattered, but dealing with having frightened her seemed paramount.

The wide, frantic set of her eyes had torn at him. She'd faced off against the attacker in the apartment building without a second of thought, without hesitation or fear. So, that someone had caused this reaction in her?

He tried to keep it off his face, but doubted it worked.

He threw the deadbolt on his apartment, closing them in together. Having Tiffany off the street helped him regain his temper.

Until he turned to find her in the middle of his studio apartment, standing beside his fold-out bed with its shitty comforter. Girl didn't belong in a place like that, and for a man who didn't give a shit what people thought, the idea of her seeing how he lived bothered him. He'd never needed much, so most of the money he made got saved.

When she looked like she was about to say something, Kane took the initiative. "The fuck were you doing out alone, anyway?"

She took a step backward. The moment her heel hit the floor, however, she stopped as if the idea of backing away chafed. "I have a life, you know."

"A short one if you pull shit like that."

"*Shit like that?* I went to work, Kane."

He went to argue but couldn't find a single thing to say back. She was right, but he hadn't bitched because she'd endangered herself. He'd bitched because he'd rather she be pissed than see how uncomfortable he was.

Instead, he gave her a snarl and moved into the tiny kitchen. He opened the fridge, pulled out two bottles of water and tossed one to Tiffany.

Girl caught it with ease, though her look could have gelded him.

Seemed she held grudges.

Still, she twisted the top off and tipped it back. The bob of her throat as she swallowed drew his stare. Without meaning to, his brain took a nose-dive down the gutter. He pictured the way her throat would do that when he slid his cock down it, when he used that long blonde hair of hers like a leash and had her take every last inch of him. She'd swallow around him to help with the gagging, just like the way she swallowed down that water.

He realized she'd lowered the water, and her gaze locked on him. *Caught.*

Kane shrugged and drank his own water, trying to downplay the way his dick throbbed and how his body threw off pheromones.

"Thank you for coming." The words ripped from her like a consolation prize as she sat on the edge of the unmade bed, the only place to sit since it served as his couch as well.

"Course. Should know me well enough to know I'd fucking help you."

"Why?"

He sat on the bed beside her. "What do you mean?"

"Why help me? Why do any of this?"

"We're friends, ain't we?"

"We're going with friends? Because what you had pressed against me didn't feel like just friends."

"Maybe you don't have the right sort of friends, then."

She stretched back, setting her water on the nightstand. "So, you're going to keep lying? I'm so sick of you alphas. You like to pretend you're tough, but the bunch of you are cowards."

"I ain't a coward, doll, and I suggest you rethink calling me one."

"Why? You want something, but you're too afraid to go for it. I might not be as big as you are, but at least I actually risk things."

He growled low in his throat, a rumble to warn her off the conversation.

The more she pushed, the more he wanted to push back, and neither of them needed that. Hell, they were already on a bed, and it wouldn't take much to get further.

"Growl all you want — it doesn't scare me. You sound like a yorkie having a hissy fit. Your bark is bigger than your bite."

"You ain't never seen my bite."

Her gaze dropped down to his crotch. "Well, maybe your bite is big enough, but you have no idea how to use it."

That was it.

Kane was on her in a heartbeat, taking her lips with his. He slipped his tongue into the warmth of her mouth, because fuck foreplay and teasing. She'd challenged him and he was all up for proving himself to her.

He swallowed down her startled gasp, his weight on his elbow as he pinned her and shifted his other hand down her side. He moved over her ribs, over the curve of her waist where it dipped in, over her sexy hips where they flared out. When he reached the waistband of her black jeans, he undid the button. The zipper flew down next, and he found her warm skin above the line of her panties.

Soft lace separated him from his goal. He nipped her bottom lip as he pulled back to gaze down, to see the strip of skin between her open pants and her shirt.

Pink? Her panties were fucking pink lace. It drew a laugh from him because of how not surprised he was.

Of course she'd go with something so ridiculous. She wasn't a simple girl, and no matter how tough she kept proving herself to be, she managed to look like sheer temptation.

He moved down to curl his fingers into the waist of her pants, then met her gaze. "You ready to throw in the towel, doll? Ready to admit this shit is a bad fucking idea, like I been saying from the start?"

Her blue eyes hardened, and instead of an answer, she wriggled her hips to work the pants down in his hands.

That spark of fire inside her had him growing harder. He yanked the jeans down, tossing her shoes fuck-knew-where before letting her jeans join them. Her spread her out beneath him in nothing but a shirt and those tempting panties. He wanted to remember it forever, to look back on it once she'd realized how stupid it was, when she'd dropped him flat on his face and he'd need it for those nights.

He'd never had much patience, though, so the first roll of her hips had him pulling free the panties, too. Drenched, and smelling so sweetly of her.

Her legs parted as she let him pull them off, but it caused him to catch sight of something.

Kane grasped her hip and rolled her, getting a look at her ass despite her yelp of confusion. "You want to tell me who left marks on you?"

Her body tensed when he stroked over the red finger marks left on her ass. He'd fucking take apart the asshole who—

She moaned. Fucking *moaned*.

It was the best sound, throaty and loud and breathless. She did it again when he repeated the motion, and that told him, didn't it?

Whoever had left 'em, she'd enjoyed the fuck out of getting them.

His cock jerked, pre-cum leaking from it. Sure, he wanted to snap at whoever had touched her, whoever had gotten to pull those sounds out of her, but at the same time? Damn if he wasn't turned on by the idea of someone spanking his troublesome omega. He pictured her over the lap of an alpha, tears running down that pretty face of hers, ass up and turning pink.

"Kieran."

Of course, it was him. She was living with the fucker, so it shouldn't surprise Kane this ended up happening. Still, he stroked the marks again like he could claim them, like they could become his and not Kieran's, until he rolled her to her back and ran two fingers up her cunt. "So, you two *are* fucking?" He gathered her wetness on his fingers before seeking out her clit, before rubbing it without mercy.

Watching her struggle to think was too much fun.

She shook her head, her back arching up against the rough treatment. "We aren't."

"Really? Because you had a lot of say about what 'just friends' do and spanking your ass ain't one of them."

"He didn't want to."

That had him slowing the touch, gentling it. "He didn't want to?"

Her gaze moved away and fuck the shame that colored those cheeks. "He walked out after he did that. He didn't want more."

Kane grasped her chin in one hand to force her gaze to his, his fingers still working her clit. "He didn't even get you off, doll? Well, ain't that rude?"

"He thinks I'm too young, too inexperienced."

"How much experience is it that you got?"

"None."

The word drew everything to a still. His fingers froze and his breathing halted. None? This delicious, seductive girl beneath him was a virgin? How the fuck was that possible?

Suddenly all the ways she gave in, the longing, the surrender, it all made sense. Girl was beyond needy —

she was fucking desperate. She had instincts inside her going crazy, craving something she hadn't yet tasted.

"Are you going to stop now?" She didn't try to hide as she asked, a challenge in that voice, but all the bravado didn't change the truth.

She expected him to stop.

Hell, maybe I should.

It'd take a stronger man than him to pull away with his finger on her cunt and her taste on his tongue.

"Nah, doll, I ain't going no fucking place until I have you screaming my name."

Chapter Seven

Kane's words made Tiffany lift her hips and force his fingers harder against her clit.

She curled her fingers into his shirt to pull him down, but he bypassed her lips. Instead, he kissed along her jaw, licking her racing pulse. Between the kisses, he nipped at the skin, and raised goosebumps in their wake.

Each stroke of his fingers against her clit made her hips roll and her cunt pulse. She dug her nails into his sides, yanking at his shirt, needing more of him. He was giving her a glimpse of the passion she'd dreamed of, and she had to have more.

Kane took his lips away and leaned up to strip off his shirt. Tattoos covered his chest and his stomach. She only got a moment to see before he blanketed her with his solid body, before his weight trapped her and he latched his sinful lips to a single spot on her neck. He sucked hard, the skin stinging after a moment. She might have objected, but he chose then to slide his fingers forward, pressing one long, thick finger into her soaked hole. The action made his palm catch her clit, and her breathing labored.

She'd used her own fingers on herself before, even tried a toy or two, but it wasn't the same. Those things had been extensions of herself. She'd know what she would do, how it would feel.

Kane's fingers weren't her own. When he twisted his wrist, dragging his knuckles against her tight walls, she couldn't expect it. When he curled those fingers in to press against the front of her pussy, when her thighs twitched and closed around him from the shocking feeling, she couldn't prepare. She wasn't in control of any of it, and that reached a part of her that masturbation never could.

He released her neck and pressed a kiss to the spot that no doubt held his mark. "Fuck, your cunt feels good. It's so fucking needy, ain't it? Bet I could get my dick into you and knot you and you'd want more."

She might have hated his words if they weren't so true. Even the mention of his cock, the thought of how it would grow at the base, how it would lock them together and stretch her in a way nothing else could had made her tighten around his finger.

"Like that idea, huh?" He offered a lick up the outstretched column of her throat. "Well, you're gonna have to be happy with my fingers, doll. Ain't got time for fucking you the way you need it right now. You wanted this, been about begging for it, so I want to feel that pretty cunt of yours grip my fingers. I want to see you come because you're that desperate."

Her hands moved to his cheeks and pulled him down. She wanted his lips to hers when she came, wanted to taste him in whatever way she could, needed a connection beyond the way his finger fucked her.

He groaned, deep and masculine, as if the kiss was even better than being buried knuckle-deep in her pussy.

The world shorted out as she came, as all that tension snapped free, as everything crumbled down around her. It washed over in, spreading out from her core until every muscle in her froze, overwhelmed.

Even as it happened, his lips never stopped, gentle against hers as his fingers dragged out each sensation. When he finally pulled from her, she whimpered at the closeness and sensitivity.

His dark chuckle didn't reassure her. "You'll look amazing stuck on a knot, doll. So sensitive like that? You'll squirm, and you'll cry, and you'll come over and over again, but you won't be able to do a fucking thing about it." He nuzzled her throat, another lick to the still stinging spot he'd marked.

When he pulled back, his gaze still ravenous, Tiffany got her first good look at him.

The colorful ink spread over his chest mirrored his arms, but was more tightly packed, covering each tiny inch of space. When she looked closer, she frowned.

Running on the edges of the tattoos, where colors changed and pictures shifted from one to another, rough skin sat. Without thinking about it, she reached out.

Her fingers stroked over one, raised and uneven. *Scars.*

The more she stared, the more she realized how many sat on his chest—some thin, some thicker, some short and some nearly a foot long. They hid in the ink and the beauty of the pictures.

The moment she touched him, he jerked back. All that hunger in his eyes drifted away and left something cold and empty staring back.

"What happened?"

He reached for his shirt, yanking it on so hard she feared the seams might give. "Nothing."

"You've got scars."

"I fucking said nothing!" Waves of anger rolled off him, the seething something she'd never seen in him, never heard in his voice. He stood and panted as if trapped, as if she were the enemy trapping him.

A phone went off, and Kane turned his back to grab his cell off the table. "Hello?"

Tiffany slunk off the bed, movement slow and unsure, two things she never was. She slid her jeans on, then slipped her feet into her shoes. In the pocket of her jeans, she found her phone and the missed messages from Kieran.

"Yeah, she's fine. Nothing. Fuck you, asshole. Why don't you come get her, huh?" Kane's side of the conversation came rushed and angry.

He still hadn't turned back to her when he ended the call and slid the phone into his back pocket. "Kieran'll be here in about ten minutes."

The idea of sitting in the room with him turned her stomach. Kane still hadn't faced her, still wasn't talking to her. His quick withdraw made her uneasy and empty. After something she'd never done before, with her body out of her control, she felt adrift.

"I'll wait downstairs."

He turned but her gaze stayed down. "The fuck you will. You're not sitting out there when someone might have been after you. You'll sit your fucking ass down until Kieran gets here."

She went to move past him. "I don't want to spend another minute here."

He took a step to the side, blocking her path. "Don't be stupid, doll."

Tiffany planted her hands on his chest and shoved, even though it only moved her backward. "Don't you call me that! I'm not staying here, not when it smells like sex."

"So, you regretting what we did? Only matter of time before that happened, I guess."

"Fuck you, Kane. You're the one who all but leaped away the second it was over."

His body didn't move, and all she could see in her mind was the way his eyes had grown so cold. "Look at me, Tiff." His voice softened, coaxing.

She shook her head, arms wrapped around herself, heart pounding as if it hadn't quite come down from her orgasm. "I want to leave."

A sigh, but he moved aside. "Fine. Ain't gonna force you, ain't gonna stop you."

She said nothing else as she rushed from the room, from the way their scents had mingled together, the way she'd thought she had something for a moment.

She sat on the bottom step of the lobby of his building, waiting for Kieran. Anger faded away until hurt filled the space, but she only wrapped her arms tighter around herself as she told herself she didn't care.

Even as the weight of Kane's gaze, the way she knew he watched over her from somewhere, pissed though she was, reassured her, she swore she didn't care.

Caring was too painful.

* * * *

Kieran glowered at the dark ceiling.

Tiffany had showered when they'd gotten back then retreated to her room.

They hadn't spoken since he'd found her in the lobby of Kane's building. The moment he'd spotted her, his frustration had grown at the idea of her out there alone. Only spotting Kane at the top of the stairs, watching over her, kept him from taking it out on the other alpha.

The look on her face said something was wrong, but the moment he'd spotted the mark left by Kane, he'd spent all his focus on not reacting.

He didn't own her.

Maybe if I say that enough, I'll believe it.

Worse? Upset hung on her. He didn't think Kane would have hurt her, but something had happened. If her face hadn't showed it, her silence would have.

Tiffany hadn't done silence well since he'd known her, not unless she was angry.

He should say something. He should ask her what was wrong, see if he could help, talk it out. The problem appeared to revolve around sex with another alpha, and thinking about that sent Kieran's temper slipping, but he couldn't let that affect him.

He'd taken her under his protection. He'd agreed to care for her, to watch over her, and that meant more than his jealousy. It had to.

The next morning, he'd talk to her. He would sit her down, talk it out, resolve whatever it was. They had three-hundred-sixty-three days left together, and they couldn't last with this sort of tension between them.

Not to forget, he had to speak to her about the car. When he'd arrived, he'd found no one in the parking lot. He didn't doubt she'd seen someone, only that it had been anything more than coincidence. Black sedans were common enough. She'd done the right thing calling him, but all that had happened had to weigh on her. After what Randy had done, anyone would worry, would see danger that wasn't there. He'd have to ensure she felt safe, perhaps start the self-defense sooner, anything to help her not to worry. She deserved to feel safe, and while he could keep her safe, it wasn't the same thing.

Just as he prepared to roll over, to force himself to sleep, his door creaked open. In the doorway stood a small figure, obscured by the dark hallway.

She hesitated there, her fingers curled around the door frame, tension thick.

Guilt pulled at him. She had enough problems in her life without dealing with him.

"Come on, girl," he said.

The bed dipped as she crawled in, but she didn't leave space between them. Instead, she curled around him, placing her head on his naked chest, her soft hair spreading out over his skin.

So much skin teased him, it was clear she hadn't worn much. A thin tank top had her nipples pressed to his arm, her breasts flattening. The blanket over his lap meant he had no idea what she wore on her lower half, but he'd bet it wasn't much more.

Best not to think about it. *As if I'm not already.*

Kieran curled his arm around her, pulling her closer. "You okay?"

Her cheek stroked his chest, her warm breath falling against his skin. "I couldn't sleep."

"You've had a couple of hard days. It makes sense sleep might not come so easily." He stroked his fingers over her bare arm. "Is it about what happened earlier?"

"With the car?"

"No, afterward, with Kane."

She didn't answer right away, only shifted closer. A sigh blew warm breath over him. "I didn't think you'd want to talk about that."

"You're living here. You're upset. That's all there is to it, so tell me what happened."

She wrapped her arm around him tighter. "I'm tired of having things slip away. Every time I think I've got something, I can't get my hands around it." She paused, then slid her leg over his as though she still couldn't get close enough. "What is it about me? I know I'm a lot to handle, but is that it?"

He brought his hand over to brush the spot where the hickey was. "Seems like you're not too much."

"Yeah, men are interested until they get an offer. Is that it? Am I too forward? Is there a smell I'm unaware of?"

Her spiral had him ready to laugh at the insecurities. Instead, he caught her chin, lifted her face toward him, and brushed his lips to hers. The kiss was slow, teasing. Without the frustration from before, with her so sweet and trusting against him, he tried to use the kiss to reassure her.

She leaned up, shifting forward to deepen the kiss. Even so, it stayed slow, leisurely. She squirmed, messing with the blanket until she could get beneath it. It left them with nothing but their clothing between them, and yeah, she'd worn only underwear on her bottom half.

Her leg maneuvered between his, her thigh wedged against his cock through his boxers.

He normally wouldn't have worn anything to bed, but since she slept in the house, he hadn't wanted to risk it. With her warm thigh against him, he was both glad for it and cursing it.

She shifted, moving her leg to the outside of his hip to leave her straddling his lap, the two scraps of fabric between them.

Kieran slid his fingers into her hair and used it to break the kiss. "You sure?"

"If you turn me down, I swear…"

He moved his hands to her hips, thumbs sliding below the waist of her underwear to press at her sharp hip bones. "Take what you want, girl."

A soft shudder ran through her, her hands on his shoulders as she lifted her body up. Her hips rolled, grinding on his lap. It made his cock nestle against the heat of her slit.

She made a hell of a sight above him, thin shirt doing nothing to hide her breasts as they swayed with her movements.

It wasn't the tight fit her cunt would be, but the wetness that spread from her underwear through his boxers had him ready to come already. He gritted his teeth and refused, wanting her to have what she needed, first. *I can damn well wait.*

She arched her back, a lusty moan leaving her lips. It pressed her full breasts out farther, and Kieran couldn't resist.

He cupped her breast, noting the way it fit into his hand, the nipple pebbling into his palm. He closed his fingers until he could toy with the point through the fabric, tightening to add a delicious sting. Meanwhile, he moved his hand from her hip to her ass, grasping to guide her hips as she rode him. He rubbed over the skin of her ass he'd bet was still sore.

Sure enough, her blunt little nails dug into his chest, and she ground harder against him. It made him want to offer more, to show her how much she could take. He wanted her to discover what she enjoyed, when she needed.

Kieran was almost there, so he released her breast, caught the back of her neck and pulled her down into a kiss. Gone was the sweetness of before, drowned away by their need. She didn't return the kiss, her attention locked on the movement of her hips, on the way his cock stroked her hardened clit through their scraps of clothing.

He rubbed her ass, using it to pull her harder against him.

She came with a gasp and a shudder, eyes closing, lips parted, hips still rocking with barely-there motions.

Kieran broke the kiss to press one to her throat, and before he could think better of it, he'd bitten down on the same spot as the hickey. That set him off, the sense of possession when he covered Kane's mark with his own as he came.

She squirmed from the bite, and her cunt pulsed against his shaft even without him being inside her. It made him wonder how it would feel to be buried deep inside her when she did that.

He released the bite, leaving a teasing lick like an apology, or it might have been if he felt the least bit sorry.

Tiffany collapsed down, her body draped over him, her chest rising and falling roughly. She pulled her head up enough to peer at him. "So, no smell?" Even in the dim light, the quirk of her lips showed.

"No smell." He laughed before letting her settle against him.

She kept that leg between his, her weight braced on him, body sprawled out over him. He ignored how his cock ached and pressed hard against her, and the scent of her cunt. He could get off some other time.

Instead, he shifted back on the pillow, easing into the sensation of her against him, the warmth, the way it made a part of him that usually remained tense to relax.

He stroked his fingers through her hair mindlessly as he closed his eyes, as her breathing evened out and she drifted off.

Maybe he'd fought it too hard? Maybe he'd convinced himself it couldn't work, but maybe he'd written it off too fast.

Was there a future between them?

Chapter Eight

Tiffany shoved her phone into her purse. Kane had sent her messages, but she'd ignored them all.

He wanted to apologize, at least in the only way he did it. He'd never cared for saying sorry, but instead liked to make a joke as if they could move on without discussing the issue.

She didn't know how to move on, though. It was the way he'd retreated, the way he'd pulled away and snapped. Whatever those scars meant, whatever they'd come from, he curled around the story like a wolf protecting a wound.

So, despite the way he'd tried to coax her into talking to him, she'd refused to play.

She didn't know what to say, anyway. Had she ever felt so conflicted? So confused by the three men who filled her mind?

She'd lost herself in Kieran's strength, in his steady hands and drugging kiss. He'd been there when she hadn't had anything, stepped in to help her when he hadn't had a reason to. The silver at his temples, those dark brown eyes that seemed to know everything made her want to give in. She wanted to surrender, and somehow, she knew she could with him.

Kane had befriended her when she had been at her lowest, and he'd never failed her. That bond had only grown when she'd met him and gotten a look at his rough appearance. While he doubted his appeal, she'd appreciated every tattoo, the way his muscles stood out without any fat above them. He was like fire, crackling around her, like a wild thing she wanted to touch.

And Marshall? It was new, unexplored, but she couldn't stop thinking about him, either. He was reserved, careful, thoughtful, and it made her want to come closer. Where Kieran made her want to retreat and be chased, and Kane made her want to tease and tempt, she wanted to ease closer to Marshall. She wanted to see where it would go, wanted to play the game with him. It seemed so uncomplicated.

The one thing she didn't want to do was choose. She didn't want to pursue one and not the others, and that made guilt eat at her. She felt as though something was wrong, as if she was cheating each of them out of what they deserved.

Claire had ended up with three alphas, but they'd been a trio already. She'd added to a group of alphas looking for single omega. That was a different situation than three alphas who barely knew each other at the best of times and actively hated each other the rest.

Should she back away? Stop going after what she wanted? *What do I even want?*

As soon as she asked herself, she pulled her phone out and hit the number she'd saved.

A few rings before Marshall answered. "Dr. Brown."

"Hello, Dr. Brown, I have a serious medical problem."

"What's wrong? How can I help?" His voice kept the professional tone, slightly distracted. What was he doing? Clearly, he hadn't recognized her voice, yet, giving her time to play. She did love to play.

"I've been sweating, my heart is racing, and I'm feeling faint."

"Go to your nearest hospital. You should be seen."

Her lips pulled into a grin at the fact that he hadn't pegged her voice yet. "I was hoping for a check-up from you. A very personal exam, since I slept through the last one."

There was silence before Marshall's warm chuckle said he'd caught up with her game. "I should have realized it was you. Give me one second." His voice became muffled, as if he'd covered the receiver as he spoke to someone else. A moment, then the closing of a door. "Sorry. I'm glad you called."

"Even with my terrible humor?"

A creak, then another of those laughs that made her think about his charming smile. "Even with it. How are you?"

"Good. Are you busy? I didn't mean to interrupt. I don't want anyone dying because you're distracted by me."

"Don't worry, I'm only mid-heart surgery, but they can wait." At her pause, he kept going. "I'm kidding. I was between cases. What are you doing?"

"I paid someone so I could punch people."

"I think maybe we need to limit your time with Kieran."

She leaned against the wall, cheeks aching from the grin. Somehow, that effortless back and forth, that flirting, felt so natural. "Well, it is his fault. He said I needed self-defense lessons."

"Probably a good idea. Besides, if he annoys you too much, you'll have options."

"So, are you going to take me out some time?" Tiffany asked it with the same forwardness she usually had.

"After you learned how to punch people? I don't know, it seems risky."

"What if I promise not to use those new skills on you?"

"I think we could work that out. I'm off most nights by seven unless there's an emergency. Why don't you send me a message when you've seen what works for you? I'll pick you up from work, if you want."

That would mean avoiding Kieran, which would be good. She wasn't hiding things from him, or going behind his back, but she also didn't need him to see her leave with another alpha.

"Yeah, I'd like that."

By the time she'd hung up, Tiffany couldn't hide her grin. The idea of doing something so ordinary as going out on a date with Marshall made her wish she had someone to call and tell, a girlfriend to go out for coffee with and gush to.

Since that wasn't available, she turned and headed into the martial arts studio where her class was.

She supposed punching things was a good second-place option.

* * * *

Kane wanted to lick the sweat from Tiffany's neck. Maybe that was weird, but fuck if his body cared. The sweat caught the light and watching her pummel the punching bag had him hard as stone and trying not to show it.

The last thing he needed was someone calling the cops because some man was walking around with a boner.

Still, that passion? The strength and the grace in her movements? It became clear Tiffany had taken lessons before. He supposed that helped explain why she'd reacted with the knee strike so quickly.

Though, it also made him wonder if they wanted to teach her more. She did enough damage with that wit and sharp tongue. Not sure they wanted to add broken bones to the bruised egos she could dish out.

Still, when she'd refused to respond, he'd damned well tracked her down. Hadn't taken much, since he'd worked out she wasn't at home, wasn't at Kieran's, wasn't at work. She'd mentioned the self-defense, and he knew Kieran worked with this studio.

She shook the hand of the teacher before walking out, tipping her water bottle back to take deep gulps.

"Ignoring people is rude, doll."

She jerked back at his voice, water sputtering from her lips as she leaned forward and coughed.

Fuck, drowning her hadn't been his plan.

Kane slapped his hand against her back to help her cough up the water that must have gone down her windpipe.

Great job, idiot. Nice start to making things better.

She pulled in a gasping breath before tossing a glare. "What are you doing here?"

"You were ignoring my messages."

"And you got from that that I wanted to see you?"

"No. I got from that that you needed to see me."

"Trust me, I don't." She turned and started to walk away, moving quickly.

Which he found adorable in a way that would probably get him used like one of the punching bags inside, so he kept it to himself and fell into step with her instead. "You gonna ignore me? You can't keep that up forever."

"Want to bet? I ate a watermelon that made me sick when I was three and haven't touched one since."

Fuck, she's stubborn.

"Where are you going?"

"To my apartment."

"Why? Honeymoon with Kieran over?"

She cast him a withering side-eye. "I need my address book."

"You living out of fucking boxes for a year?"

"Kieran hired movers for next week. They'll put everything in storage, but I forgot my address book."

Mention of the other alpha had Kane shoving his hands into his pockets, trying not to recall anything about the man. Like his nice fucking house, or his stupid perfect face. Who cared about him?

Who cared if Tiffany was living with the fucker, or if a new bite mark rested over the hickey Kane had left, or if Kane knew there was no competition between them?

Nope, don't care at all about any of that.

They walked at a brisk pace, the conversation drifting off. Kane didn't do apologies. He'd never had people he cared enough about to offer them. Most of the time, it was easier to snap first than risk anything else.

The idea of losing Tiffany over that had brought him there, though. Sure, they didn't have a lot between them, but he'd prefer something to nothing.

Still, admitting shit wasn't something he liked to do. He didn't want to tell her about the scars he'd spent thousands of dollars in ink to cover up.

When she'd touched them, when her face had fallen, he'd gone back to default asshole-mode. He'd regretting it the moment she'd walked out and he'd realized how deep his words had lashed. A quick 'sorry' wouldn't cut it.

She wouldn't let him get off that easily. No, she'd want the truth. She'd want him to fucking reopen those wounds and share shit. If not the whole story yet, she'd at least expect some tidbit to explain why he'd acted the way he had.

They turned the corner to her apartment building, and he didn't need help finding it. He'd known where she'd lived already, not to stalk her, but because he'd needed to drop packages at times. The idea that she wouldn't live there anymore left a sense of loss.

Kane pulled open the door for her before she could reach it, but at least her glare had lost some of its bite.

"So how long are you planning on being pissed?"

"I don't know. How long are you planning on being an asshole?"

He shrugged as he stepped into the elevator beside her. "Being an asshole is my natural state, so I don't think it's ever changing."

She faced the doors as they shut, and he took the opportunity to slide behind her, a breath between them.

His lips neared her ear to whisper. "Besides, I think you like me this way."

"I don't think I like you at all right now."

"No? Because you liked me when my finger was inside you. Want to try it again? Could hit that stop button and take as long as we want."

A tremor ran through her despite the way her hands gripped into fists as if she could fight it. "Why would I want to try it again? As I remember, it didn't end that well."

His lips brushed her ear, his tongue snaking out to flick the lobe. "I remember it ending with your cunt squeezing down on my finger as you came. Seems worth trying again."

She crossed her arms, stance defensive.

He nipped her lobe, daring her to keep ignoring him. "You think crossing your arms scares me off? Ah, doll, all it does it press those tits together. You think I can fuck 'em sometime? Because you'd look pretty beneath me, tits pressed together around my cock."

And there went her chest when she inhaled on a harsh breath.

The ding said they'd reached their floor, but neither moved.

Tiffany didn't pull away, and Kane had no intention of giving in first. He'd fuck her in that elevator if she let him. The opinions of random neighbors didn't mean shit to him, not when pitted against the temptation of her body.

He dragged the tip of his nose up her throat to behind her ear. "You smell so fucking delicious. Tell me yes, doll. We'll go into your apartment, and I'll make it worth your time."

She leaned backward, the move so subtle no one would have noticed if they watched. The elevator dinged again, the doors starting to close, and it must have woken her up. "Thanks, but I like my orgasms without a chaser of regret."

She walked away, and like an idiot, he stood there dumbstruck long enough that the doors started to close again.

He slid out before they could, following that hellcat of an omega down the hallway. He'd had enough of this, and the throbbing of his cock said he needed to fix it.

Kane caught her and turned her, her back sandwiched to the door of her apartment.

Tiffany tried to knock his hands away. "Don't you push me around."

Kane pinned her to keep her still. "Listen up, doll. I'd rather get over this by fucking you until you ain't pissed anymore, but that ain't your style. So, let me be clear. What happened? I'm sorry, okay?"

When she tried to hold on to her anger, when her eyes didn't soften, Kane leaned forward and pressed his forehead to hers. "Don't ask about the scars, please? I don't like talking about 'em, don't want to discuss 'em, okay?"

Those blue eyes of hers lifted enough for him to pull back, and there it was. Yeah, Tiffany was tough, and she was a ball buster, and she was a snarky little asshole when she wanted to be. She was also fucking sweet. He might have snarled at the pity in her face, but it was better than anger.

Plus, if she felt bad for him, it meant she had to care a bit, right? He'd take what he could get.

Her hands, pressed against his chest, softened and slid to his sides. "And you won't snap at me anymore?"

"Oh, I'll probably still snap, but you might like it when I do. Why don't we go on in there and you let me make it up to you? You could try to ignore me during if you want, see who breaks first?"

Her fingers tightened around his waist and pulled him closer. "Okay, but trust me, I'll win."

He leaned in for a kiss, but she twisted so his lips landed in her hair as she unlocked the door, then turned the knob.

They tripped forward when the door opened, and Kane wrapped an arm around her waist to steady them, ready to lift her against him, set her on the first surface that would hold her and get his mouth on her.

When they turned, though, they both froze.

Everything sat in disarray in the apartment, with furniture turned over and the contents of drawers strewn about.

Someone had ransacked her place.

The wreckage of Tiffany's apartment sat before her, and she didn't know what to do.

Kieran and Sam were on their way over, Kane having called them after checking to make sure the house was clear.

"Fucker came in through the fire escape. Broke the latch on the window." Kane didn't sit, gaze moving around as if still on alert.

Then again, the last time they'd thought themselves safe, they'd run into someone, hadn't they?

"I'd say you could pick some of it up if you wanted, but Sam should take a look first."

Tiffany shrugged, staring at the remnants of her life. "It doesn't even look like my stuff anymore."

"What do you mean?"

"It's like someone ruined it all, like they changed it all." She shook her head and leaned forward. "I don't even want to touch any of it, to be honest."

He set a hand on her shoulder, a gentle squeeze. "It'll be okay. Probably some asshole who realized no one had been here in a couple days. I know everyone who sells anything, so once Sam gets a look, once we realize what went missing, I'll find anything they took and get it back." The offer was sweet, Kane's attempt to make her feel better.

It didn't, though.

Randy had come through and uprooted her life, changing everything. She'd gone from her simple days to living with Kieran, being under contract and at risk of registration, and now? Now someone had destroyed the tiny bit of normalcy she'd had.

The sofa she'd picked up at a yard sale and reupholstered sat flipped over, cushions askew. The desk she'd organized, that she'd put silly fabric-covered corkboard squares above had its drawers open and papers spread about.

The life she'd created, that she'd worked so hard for, and other people kept tearing it apart. How many times could she pick up and start over? How many times did she have to weather people ruining everything for her before she got what she wanted?

The door opened, no knock, but she didn't startle. The space wasn't hers anymore, wasn't a sanctuary where she could let her guard down.

Sam walked in, already in detective mode. Kane squeezed once more before moving over to speak quietly with Sam.

Kieran dropped to a knee in front of her, his fingers setting beneath her chin. "Hey, girl. Are you okay?"

Tiffany gave him a weak smile. "Yeah. Just tired of everything I have getting torn apart."

His lips tipped down. "We'll find who did this. Between Sam and I, we will figure it out."

"And me," Kane added.

Kieran turned, gaze going hard. "I think you've done more than enough."

"Like fuck. If someone stole her shit, we both know I got a way better chance of finding it than you do."

"Criminals stick together, I suppose." Kieran rose to his feet, and the testosterone in the room could have choked a person.

They crossed the space between them with sure but slow steps, the tension crackling in the air.

Great. After everything else, now they were going to fight? Hadn't she dealt with enough?

This was exactly why she'd worried about this, because even if she didn't want to choose, they'd force her to.

She rose, not wanting anyone hurt. Territorial alphas could do a lot of damage, and they had both tried to claim her. "Settle down."

Neither noticed her.

Kieran's lips were peeled back, his voice low. "Why are you even here? She's dealt with enough without slumming it with you."

"Oh, and you, who had to get her in a fucking contract to have a shot? You think you got any room to bitch at me?"

"You aren't good enough for her, Kane. You can try to leave marks on her all you want, but you will never have her."

An answering snarl tore from Kane's throat, so feral and primal Tiffany's blood froze. "What are you going to do about it?"

"Stop this!" Tiffany tried to rush forward, to get between the men who stood chest to chest, a breath from violence.

A strong arm wrapped around her, yanking her back. Sam's voice rose above the snarling. "Don't get close. They might not even realize it's you, and no matter what they might do to each other, if they hurt you on accident? Well, that would be far worse for them."

The alphas broke whatever leash they'd had, and the power behind the first punch shocked Tiffany.

She'd never been around violence. She'd sparred, but she'd never seen alphas fight, never witnessed any real conflict. Kieran and Kane didn't play around, didn't circle slowly. They hit, countered, blocked and dodged with a speed and strength that turned her stomach.

"Knock it off!" She yanked against Sam's grip, but he wouldn't relent.

Instead, he twisted to push her behind him, then leveled a finger her way. "I'll get between them if you stay back. I don't want you getting a stray punch on accident. It'll be my head if it happens, and I happen to want to keep my face this pretty. Stay back, okay?"

Tiffany nodded, and Sam turned, hesitating as if trying to figure out how exactly to get between them.

As the fight went on, Tiffany worried her bottom lip. This was all her fault. Kieran and Kane were fighting because of her, because she hadn't made a choice, because she couldn't make a choice. They hadn't been friends, clearly, but they hadn't thrown punches, either.

Again, everything was being torn apart. Her life. The futures she wanted but couldn't figure out how to get. Her apartment.

Even two of the alphas she'd come to care for didn't listen to her at all, too busy trying to win her, to claim her.

It overwhelmed her, and she struggled to breathe through it. She couldn't sit there, not as blood sprayed from Kieran's bottom lip after a hit from Kane, as it splattered over the side table in her living room. She couldn't help clean up her place, or either of the men, after it all calmed down.

The idea exhausted her. She needed a break, needed time to think, to close her eyes and be still.

So, as Sam threw himself into the fight, Tiffany slipped out of the door.

Maybe if she left, they'd stop this.

And if they didn't? At least she wouldn't have to watch.

Chapter Nine

"She isn't yours!" Kieran drove his knee into Kane's side, to be rewarded with a grunt from the other man.

Their skills being evenly matched both pleased and irked him. On one hand, beating on a man who couldn't defend himself never gave Kieran any joy. On the other, if only a good beating would make the other alpha back off.

Each time Tiffany left his sight, she seemed to end up around Kane. Each time she ended up with Kane, she either returned reeking of the alpha, or she got herself in danger.

Either way, Kieran had grown sick of it.

"She ain't yours either, you stupid fucker." Kane's coarse words grated, the slang, the way he didn't care if he sounded like low-bred trash.

It was one of the millions of reasons they'd never gotten along. While they had to work together now and then, he had no desire to spend any time with the other man.

Kane wanting to screw Tiffany only made it worse.

Sam got between them, trying to shove them apart. Even after getting grazed with a hit meant for Kieran, Sam didn't back off. "You idiots are going to scare Tiffany if you keep this up. I don't think either of you wants that."

Kane's lips showed teeth covered in blood, but he didn't seem ready to end the fight. Good, Kieran wasn't in the mood to give in, either.

"Just leave her alone."

"She wants me gone, I'm gone. It ain't up to you, though."

Sam shoved once more at their chests. "Don't think I'm above using my stun gun on the two of you. Let's see how much that omega wants either of you after you piss your pants from that, huh?"

Kieran's eyes narrowed, but he lifted his hands and took a step backward. Bloodying the idiot wouldn't help, wouldn't change a damn thing. He doubted the other alpha had enough brain cells to get sense knocked into them anyway.

"Where the fuck is Tiffany?" Kane's voice shifted, the tension out of him as if the fight hadn't mattered at all anymore.

Sam twisted toward the front door, which sat ajar. "She was right here. I told her to stay back so she didn't end up getting mowed over." He went to the door of the apartment, stuck his head out and called her name.

Kieran and Kane stared at one another, their peacemaker no longer between them. Neither spoke, though the snarls said all that needed saying, Kieran supposed.

Sam came back, face unusually hard for the normally cheerful man. "Well, good job. You two scared her off."

"Nothing scares that girl," Kane said.

"Then you pissed her off enough that she left. What the hell was that? You two aren't teenagers. You know better."

Kieran crossed his arms, straightening his back, which had already started to grow sore. Seemed he'd passed the age where a fight made him feel alive. Now it hurt. "Where could she have gone?"

It seemed Sam hadn't finished his talk, because his voice kept the *'you fucked up'* tone. "Wherever it is, let it be for right now. You need to work *this* out first."

"The fuck you want from us?" Kane pulled his phone out, thumbs moving over it. *Texting her?*

"I want you to act like she's more important than your egos!"

"Fuck you." Kane's voice lacked any real anger, attention on the phone and not on the other alphas. "Ain't my fault he won't back off."

"She's living with me. You're a passing fascination. She'll tire of your soon enough."

"You think? Because that's not how it seemed when my fingers were in her."

They sailed toward each other again, but Sam got between them before they could start in again, the alpha's growl vicious in a way Kieran had never heard from him.

Sam was always happy, always steady. If he was still as difficult as he'd been when younger, he'd have enjoyed getting beneath the unflappable man's skin.

Still, it wasn't Sam who pulled them apart. Instead, the ringing of Kieran's phone separated them.

"Hello?"

"Hey, Kieran."

He frowned at the voice. "Did you need something, Marshall? I'm a little busy."

"Yes, beating on Kane from what I understand. I wanted to call you so you didn't worry about your missing omega."

If Marshall knew where she was, had she gotten hurt? She couldn't have been gone more than ten minutes, so what did that mean? Even for someone as troublesome as Tiffany, getting injured already would have been impressive. "Is she okay?"

"She's fine. I wanted you to know she's safe and will be spending the night at my house. It seems she needs a break from the both of you."

"At your house? Exactly how well are you two acquainted?"

"Since I don't want to be a part of whatever conflict you and Kane have going on, I'll choose not to answer that. I didn't want you dragging Sam in to track her down. I'll ensure she calls you in the morning, once you and Kane have settled down and cleaned up."

"You expect me to accept that?"

"Yes, I do, since we both know she could run as far as she wants if pushed. So, have a nice evening, and please stop this little fight with Kane. I'll ignore any calls for the rest of the evening, so you two can find someone else to stitch you up." The line went dead, leaving Kieran to stare at his phone as if that would create an answer.

How did she know the doctor? He had treated her twice, but Kieran hadn't realized anything else was between them. Just friends, perhaps? More?

It didn't have him reacting like he did to Kane, the idea less frustrating.

He turned toward the other alphas, noting the damage to Kane's face. Blood leaked from his nose and he sported a few nice bruises. Kieran would bet his face looked the same. "She's safe. She's staying with Marshall."

"The doctor?" Kane's brows furrowed.

"He treated her twice. I guess they've become friends."

Sam knelt beside the window in the small open bedroom. "Why don't you two go get some sleep? I've already called this in, and we'll look into it."

Kane hesitated. "She thought someone was following her the other night. She said she saw the same car a few times, and when she went to leave work, the car was parked next to hers."

"When I got there, no one was there. I think everything with Randy made her paranoid." Kieran ran his forearm over his lip, wincing at the sting.

"And what's this? More paranoia?" Kane held his arm out at the room.

"It's a break-in. They happen, especially when an apartment has been empty for a few days."

Sam waved them both off. "We can guess all we want, but it won't make any difference. Go home. I'll call you in the morning."

Kieran wanted to argue. He wanted to demand that he'd stay, that he'd help, that he'd do something. It wasn't that he didn't trust Sam to take care of it, because the man was an exceptional detective.

It was that the idea of going back to his own house alone, of how quiet it would feel without Tiffany already made him want to growl.

He refused to say such a thing, and especially not around Kane. Instead he nodded, then left.

All he could do was hope she'd only be gone for a single night, because if she left for good? He was pretty sure it would hurt more than he was willing to admit.

* * * *

Opening the door for Tiffany made Marshall nervous in way he wasn't used to. He worked in a high-pressure profession, used to being sure, to making choices that could save or end a life.

Why did inviting an omega into his space make him uneasy?

If she noticed, she said nothing, walking in with dragging feet. Poor girl.

"I'm really sorry about this—"

He cut her off before she could go further. "It's fine. I've got spare rooms, and you could use the break."

"It's not quite the date we had planned."

"Well, I can't offer you a blockbuster new movie and fine dining, but I do have trashy television, a large couch and microwavable popcorn."

She looked at him, and the smile was worth anything. "Sold."

Two hours later, Marshall had his arm over the back of the couch, the popcorn bowl in his lap and Tiffany curled up against his side.

As they binged on reality TV, she'd started beside him with a bit of space between them, but each time she'd reached for popcorn, she'd scooted closer. By the start of this episode, she'd moved into the space beneath his arm as if it were made for her.

Though, to be fair, it pretty much was. He'd left the space open, hopeful she'd choose to move closer, and he'd ignored the way it made him feel like a fifteen-year-old on his first date when he had no idea how to talk to a girl.

It seemed classics never went out of style when they worked.

Marshall looked down, ready to tell her they should probably get some sleep. He had to be at the hospital early, and as much as he enjoyed the quiet moment, showing up exhausted wasn't a good plan.

Only, it seemed she had the same idea. Her eyes had closed, her body gone lax and turned toward him. Her chest rose and fell in easy breaths, the hem of his shirt she'd worn as pajamas showing off her upper thighs, her legs folded beneath her.

While it hadn't been her looks that had attracted him at first, he had to admit, she was stunning. Her long blonde hair and those striking blue eyes all made her look like some innocent doe. Though, mistake her for such a thing and she'd show just how sharp her teeth were.

He should wake her up and send her to bed, but he didn't want to lose the moment. Who knew if they'd get another one? Tomorrow they'd wake, they'd go back to their lives.

She might have needed a night off, but that hardly guaranteed she'd feel that way again, that she'd want anything else from him. She'd have to return to Kieran, to whatever was happening with Kane.

Not that those things bothered him. Marshall had never been a jealous man, had never expected to be interested in an omega. Hell, he'd spent his life avoiding them.

He could still remember the nights as a child when he'd fallen asleep to the sound of his father's snarls. He'd wake to the bruises on his omega mother's face, the broken hunch of her shoulders.

One night, when he'd gotten old enough to think about standing up to him, he'd asked his father why he did it. All seven-year-old of him had gotten between them, had tried to cover his mother's body with his own tiny one, as he'd hurled the question at his father.

His father had grabbed him by the collar and hauled him from the house despite his mother's screams. He'd gotten a black eye for the interference and his answer.

'It's what we are. You can't see it yet in you, but I see it in those eyes, prowling around. You'll see when you get older, you'll understand. Being an alpha is like having a monster inside you, and you give that fucker whatever it wants, because the power you feel? Best feeling in the world.'

Marshall shuddered at the memory, at the fear that swamped him as it had since he'd first realized he was an alpha, when at sixteen he'd recognized the signs of his designation, and he'd worried his father's words were right.

Tiffany huffed an unhappy sound, twisting closer, her arm thrown around him hard enough she smacked him in the ribs.

He shoved the memory away. He'd spent his life making up for what he was, and in all that time, he'd hidden that side of him. He'd controlled it, leashed it.

Tiffany will never see that side of me, never be risked by it.

Sleep came easily, as if the scent of the omega calmed a part of him he hadn't realized was so tense. He spent so much time worrying about his alpha side, so much time trying to control the snarling monster that lived beneath his skin.

Somehow, that side of him relaxed with Tiffany against him. It always prowled, always sat beneath the surface. Right then, though? Right then it eased enough of him to close his eyes and rest.

Hours later, something woke him. He lifted his wrist to find the time. *Three-fifteen.*

A glance around let him remember why he had slept upright on the couch. The stretched-out omega against him was the blame. She'd gotten even closer, his legs on the table and her body draped over him.

Still, what had woken him? The uncomfortable position?

A soft sound from Tiffany told him no. She twitched, her legs slung over his thighs, and the sound happened again.

A moan, soft and gentle, that dissolved into a purr.

Despite the fact that he'd never taken an omega, had never heard the purr of one, instinct alone let him identify it.

Her hips shifted forward, her lips parting so her next moan came out louder.

Marshall's cock ached. Huh, guess he'd been hard already, as if even asleep he'd risen to the occasion for her, to the call of her mouthwatering scent.

The temptation to reach a hand down and stroke his cock to those pretty sounds she made had his arm moving. Before he'd moved more than a hair, he stilled.

No. That was instinct, and it was disgusting. He wasn't going to masturbate to her sleeping body.

Her fingers curled into his side, and the warmth of her bare cunt rubbed against his thigh.

Well, it seemed she'd worn nothing beneath his shirt. It shouldn't have shocked him, since she'd tossed her clothes in his washing machine so she'd have them clean by the next morning.

Still, a deep growl rumbled from his throat as if crawling out itself.

A louder purr was her response, her hips grinding her cunt against him and leaving a wet mark on his sweats.

He had to stop it. It wouldn't be right to let it go on, to let her do this without meaning to.

And the other part of him feared he couldn't control himself if she didn't stop.

"Tiffany," he whispered.

At the sound of his voice, she dragged her soaked pussy against him again, slower and harder, as if his voice turned her on more.

He repeated her name, louder, almost frantic. If she didn't wake up, he was going to pull her closer, spread her thighs and slide into her.

She jerked up, a hand to his chest, darting her sleepy gaze around the room. It took her a moment before the panic slipped away and she seemed to remember where she was.

A shift of her hips brought her cunt against his leg again, and this time her moan was loud and surprised. The moment she did it, the moment she realized what had happened, she shoved backward. "Oh, god, I'm sorry. I didn't mean to—"

That sort of rambling would take her a bit, so Marshall caught her hand before she could retreat far. "It's fine."

"It's not fine. I was…"

He stroked his thumb over her wrist as he tugged her back. Maybe letting her go was the smart choice, but the pink on her cheeks and the shame in her voice had him wanting to fix it. Not to mention he feared that if he let her go, she might not return. "You were asleep. It's fine."

She let him tug her back beside him, but this time when she folded her legs, when the hem of the skirt rode up, he could only picture the way she must look beneath it. He thought about how wet she was, how hot her cunt had felt against his leg. He'd never knotted an omega, and since an alpha's knots only grew when taking an omega, he'd never experienced it.

His knot would ache when he masturbated or when he took a beta. It would pulse at the base of his dick like a reminder, and even after he came, that ache never went away.

What would it feel like?

"I'm sorry. I didn't mean to put you in a position like that. You've been so nice, and you let me stay here, and I do that to you?"

Her words had him frowning. His cock had been hard before she'd even started, so it wasn't as if he hadn't enjoyed it. It wasn't as though he wasn't desperate for her. Marshall nodded down at his crotch, his embarrassment better than her guilt. "As you can tell, I didn't exactly mind."

"So why did you stop me?"

"Because if anything like that happens, I want you awake for it. I want you doing it because you want to. For all I knew, you were dreaming of someone else. I wouldn't want you to wake up and regret anything."

She twisted to look at him. "So, you're wanting something to happen?"

"Of course." When she settled back in beside him, he pushed his luck. "Were you?" When she didn't answer, he clarified. "Thinking about someone else."

Her laugh was soft, embarrassed, but sweet. "Don't tell me you're another jealous alpha."

"No. Jealousy would be me being mad about your answer. I'm not worried about you wanting anyone else, I need to know if you want me in that way as well."

Her fingers played over his leg, stroking the wet spot her cunt had left. Did she realize what it was? It sprang forward, the idea of having her lick her own wetness from his fingers, of forcing her to taste herself, of sharing what he was sure was a taste that would drive him crazy.

Finally, she answered. "Yeah, I was thinking about you."

Her admitting it drew a possessive growl from him, one he cut off as soon as it started. "Maybe you should go to bed." He forced the words out even though they were the last thing he wanted to say. He'd do about anything for her not to leave, not with the way she smelled, and that he knew how little separated him from the sweetness between her thighs.

"Do you want me to go?"

His head shook before he could think about it. "No, but maybe you should. You've got to tell me what you're wanting, because you have a lot going on, and maybe this whole thing is too much?"

She slipped her hand to the inside of his thigh, pressure there as she gripped him. "I want this."

"What is it you want?"

Her chest lifted against the shirt she wore, as though she was hyping herself up with a deep breath before she slid from the couch and to her knees. She said nothing, but the look in those eyes was enough.

She was on her knees begging, and he'd give her what she wanted.

Marshall's thighs spread out around Tiffany's shoulders, so close that they brushed her when she shifted her weight.

Each move turned her on more, and her clit begged for attention. She'd woken up mid-dream with his voice in her ear, and her body hadn't forgotten it. It still hummed with unspent energy, awake and wanting and uncaring that it had been wound up on something not real.

Marshall undid the tie of his sweats, then slipped his fingers past the waist. "Look at me."

She tore her gaze from the outline of his thick, tempting cock and moved up his body. He wasn't as muscular as Kane or Kieran, having lived a life that didn't require it. His body was large, as all alphas were, but it had a softness the others lacked.

"Tell me about your dream."

Nothing came from her, but the tilt of his lips got her moving. "It was when we met in the hospital."

He shifted his hips up to pull his sweats down far enough to free his hard dick. It was thick, surrounded by dark, neatly trimmed public hair that followed up in a line to disappear beneath his shirt. "Do you have a bit of a medical kink?" The question didn't make her uncomfortable, not with the heat in his voice. "Tell me more. What did I do?"

Tiffany pressed her thighs together as she recalled the dream. "You were examining me, running your hands over me. Your fingers kept brushing over my breasts, and you asked me how it felt." As she spoke, her hands followed the path his had in the dream. Her nipples peaked against the fabric.

"And what did you say?" He held his hand out to her, and she did what she knew he wanted. She licked up his palm, giving him the lubrication he needed before he wrapped his hand around his cock in a tight grasp.

"I said it was fine. I didn't want to admit it felt good."

His groan had her slipping one of her hands down her stomach, his scent strong from being so close. "And what did I do about that?"

"You moved your hand between my legs. You fingered me while you leaned in, whispering that you knew it felt good, that you knew my body better than I did. You said I needed to come, and that you'd make sure I did."

A low growl filled the living room, something she didn't expect from him. Kane and Kieran growled at everything, but not Marshall. He held himself to a higher standard, always careful, always thoughtful. To see him lose control because of her had her thighs drenched.

Even better? His cock, the way he stroked it so near her that she could have stretched her tongue out to steal a taste of the wet head. Somehow, not doing so was better, the denial, what she wanted so close but out of reach tantalizing her.

"You need to come now, too, don't you? Go on, I want you to slip your fingers into you. I want you to ride those fingers, to do what you dreamt I did."

She followed his rumbled demands, her hands like an extension of his. She dipped beneath the hem of her shirt, her gaze on his hands and the way his fingers struggled to wrap around his cock.

"Lift your shirt, omega. I want to see."

Cold air hit her ass as she stripped it off. It left her bare, but the lust in his voice made it worth it. Hell, she wasn't someone worried about how she looked. His lust-soaked gaze, his husky voice, and his straining erection left little room for doubt.

"You listen so well," he praised. "Go on, now. Let me see those fingers disappear into you."

His words weren't as filthy as others, not as vulgar, but it was the restraint in them that did her in. He spoke clearly, carefully, and that thought made her feel needy and out of control.

Tiffany spread her thighs and stroked her fingers against her clit, her entire slit wet. She twisted her wrist to seat two fingers inside her, then fucked herself in rhythm with his strokes.

"Are you thinking about the dream?"

She shook her head.

His laugh was breathless, showing how affected he was already. "Are you thinking about my dick? Imagining your fingers are it?"

She dropped her head back as she moaned, lifting her hips as she thrust her fingers into herself, moving as though she rode him. "Yes."

"Do you want to taste me? Do you want to wrap your lips around me?"

Tiffany opened her eyes, locking on his length as she leaned forward, drawn by the offer. Yes, she wanted to taste him, needed to. She wanted to feel his hard shaft stretching her lips wide, wanted to feel him throb against her tongue, feel him inching back toward her throat.

Except, when she came closer, he pulled his cock flat against his stomach, keeping her from it. "I don't think so, omega. This has all been fantasy, right? Oh, don't look at me like that—I'm not as soft-hearted as you think." He huffed a rough laugh before reaching his other hand forward and pressing his thumb past her lips. "I can't resist that pouting. Here, see if this won't keep you busy."

Tiffany latched her lips around his thumb and sucked, doing her best to pretend. The thumb was far too thin, but then again, she'd never sucked cock before. The taste was wrong, but she did the best she could to make do. She pulled back, then slid forward, her fingers in her cunt never stopping. She added a third finger, moaning around his thumb at the stretch, thinking about how it would feel if it was his cock instead.

The cords of Marshall's neck stood out from the tension running through him. He hooked his thumb down to pull open her mouth. "You've done so well, Tiffany, so I think you've earned something. Keep your mouth open and don't swallow until I say so."

She kept it open, and however stupid she might have looked, she didn't care, especially when he rose to his feet in front of her. He stroked his cock, now pointed at her open mouth.

His towering body made her feel small kneeling before him, yet it didn't bother her. She didn't feel afraid, didn't feel like she wanted to struggle against the position. Instead, it felt safe, protected, cared about.

She kept her mouth open, her gaze up at him, at the way he stroked his cock, at the lust swimming in those dark eyes.

His guttural sounds never let up, his strokes quick, erratic, desperate, even his hips straining forward. The first drop of cum to land on her tongue was hot, searing her to her core. The first drop was followed by more, but she didn't swallow, just held it as it pooled on her waiting tongue.

The submission in the action and the taste of him had her coming, her body twitching as she tried to remain still, shuddering through her own orgasm. Her breath panted through her open mouth, and remaining still made her so much more aware of how her body tensed and shook.

When he finished, when he'd milked every last drop of cum, he stroked the hot head of his cock against her lips, the only actual contact she'd had with it.

"Swallow," he said, voice so deep, so different, she nearly didn't recognize it.

Tiffany closed her lips and drank down the cum he'd given her, her omega side rejoicing in it, in the scent of him, in the way his pheromones would cling to her afterward.

His lips pressed to her forehead, and she opened her eyes to find him crouched in front of her. The intensity he'd had during, the way he'd looked at her with a wild side she'd never seen before had drifted away.

Or had he chained it again?

She felt like she'd gotten a glimpse of the real him, of something she'd felt from the start but that he'd kept hidden.

The only thing she knew absolutely was that she already wanted more.

Chapter Ten

Tiffany woke to someone pressing a hand over her mouth. She shoved, digging her nails into the hand to get free.

Marshall's whispered voice calmed her. "It's me. Someone's in the house."

That slung off any remaining sleepiness, especially with the tension through Marshall's body. He removed his hand from her mouth, and they both rose from his bed, which they'd crawled into after what had happened in the living room.

He grabbed his phone and tucked it into his pocket.

"Aren't you going to call the police?"

"Security system has already alerted them. They're on their way, but it's going to take ten minutes for them to get here."

Tiffany cursed that her clothing sat in the dryer, leaving her still wearing only Marshall's shirt. She didn't even have her shoes. "Should we go out of the window?"

He shook his head. "We're on the second floor. There's a good chance, if we tried that, one or both of us would sprain an ankle."

"Do you have a gun?"

"I hate guns. Patch up as many bullet holes as I have, and they don't seem so wonderful."

She worked her bottom lip between her teeth, searching for a weapon. "So, what do we do?"

He grasped her arm and pulled her toward the closet door. "We do nothing. You get in that closet, back behind my suits, and don't move until either I tell you, or you hear Kieran's voice." He pushed her into the closet.

Tiffany caught his wrist when he tried to pull away. "There's no way I'm staying in the closet."

The argument went no further, not when the door to the room opened. From her spot, Tiffany couldn't see the intruder, couldn't see anything.

Marshall pulled back, gaze toward the door, his face hard in a way she'd never seen before, his lip pulled up to bare his teeth. "Whatever you're looking for, you aren't going to find it here. I'm sure you already grabbed anything that looked like you could get a few dollars from it, so take that and go. Cops will be here in a few minutes."

The voice that answered was male, but Marshall's body kept her from leaving the closet or from seeing him. "Where is she?"

Tiffany's breath stilled, but Marshall's answering snarl frightened her more.

"Leave, now."

"Not until I have what I came for."

"If it's her, then you're leaving empty-handed." His gaze dropped, but no fear showed in his face. "That doesn't change my answer."

Marshall moved forward, but he didn't fully leave the closet door before he stopped, shoved backward then went forward again.

Tiffany sprang from the closet, finally able to see the fight. A single man sat wrestled with Marshall, a beta from the scent. They moved too fast for her to identify any specifics, but she didn't think she knew him.

Dark hair hung over his forehead, and he wore an all-black outfit. A gun sat on the ground, and when he tried to reach for it, Marshall yanked them clear.

Still, neither gained ground, neither seemed closer to wining the fight. The man again went for the gun, but Marshall rolled them the other way.

Tiffany tried to edge around them. If she could reach the gun, she could at least remove that from the equation. No gun would reduce the chance anyone might get killed. As she moved around them, something caught her ankle.

She tripped forward, her hand catching the gun and shoving it as she tried to catch her fall. Her shoulder screamed when the action aggravated the healing injury. She rolled to find the man's hand wrapped around her ankle in a bruising grip. He yanked, and she slid along the hardwood floors, the shirt she wore providing no friction to keep her still.

She lifted her foot and drove it forward, a crunch as it slammed into his nose. Her foot came free, and she reached beneath the low bed, feeling for the where the gun had slid.

Marshall still fought with the man, but a lucky elbow to Marshall's face meant the man pulled free while Marshall shook off the hard blow.

The man grabbed Tiffany's leg as she squirmed partway beneath the bed, reaching for the gun, her fingers brushing something metal and heavy. He pulled, and her shirt rode up to drag her hip against the floor. She released a hiss at the way it scraped her skin, but even as she swung her foot again, she couldn't make contact.

He pulled her enough that she rolled onto her back as she struggled. He moved up, crawling over her, his hands pinning her beneath him. He didn't grope, didn't try to touch her. Even as his body surrounded her, his thigh falling between hers, hips holding her down, he didn't do anything sexual.

He moved his hands from her arms to her neck, but she lifted her hips to try to throw him. It knocked him forward, but he caught himself with his hand on the ground. Again, he sat back and wrapped a hand around her throat.

A crack ricocheted in the room, loud and sickening. The man's hand fell from her throat and he collapsed forward. His body, still and lax in a way bodies should never be, had her squirming to get out from under it.

She shoved the heavy body off, then stumbled to her feet. Marshall stood beside her as they both stared down at the man who had broken in, who had come for her.

What now?

* * * *

The frosted glass hid the details of Tiffany's body, but Kane recognized her. It was in the blurry curves and the scent that filled the room. Even above the soap and shampoo, he could pinpoint that uniquely *her* scent.

He'd gotten to the house, the big fucking house Marshall owned, with all the cops outside and Kieran going a mile a minute. The asshole had been talking to Sam, going over the details, probably. Marshall stood with them, pointing as he explained.

Kane had caught a bit of it, but they could deal with it later. A subtle nod from Marshall, then he'd gestured upstairs.

Fucking weird. He'd expected the doctor to be as possessive as Kieran, but who the fuck knew.

Kane had taken the stairs, avoiding the cops, avoiding the other alphas, wanting only to see Tiffany, to ensure that she was fine.

The call he'd gotten had made his chest ache. Someone had broken in. When he'd heard that, he'd assumed they'd been after Marshall, or maybe hoped for a lucky score. Only they hadn't been. They'd asked about 'her' and the only her they could have meant was Tiffany.

Was it connected to the warehouse? To Randy? Did she have other secrets she wasn't sharing? Kane had a million questions but no desire to ask them.

Hell, once he'd crept into the bathroom, once he'd gotten the first whiff of her, he'd known all he needed to about his plan.

His pants hit the floor, not caring if they ended up wet. Once he'd stripped down, he slid into the large glass enclosed shower behind her.

Tiffany stood with her front to him, her head back and eyes closed, water pouring down her hair. He hadn't seen it free before, hadn't realized how long it was. His mouth watered at the way her tits pressed forward, pale skin pink from the heat and steam that filled the small enclosed space. The necklace hung down her, nestled in the valley between her breasts. She never seemed to take it off since she'd found it, like some talisman. Funny, since it didn't seem to have helped the last omega too much.

Was it some vigil? Fuck if he knew.

The lust in him sizzled until his gaze found a new scrape over her right hip.

"Aren't you supposed to knock?" she asked with her eyes still closed.

"Don't care for knocking. I need the element of surprise on my side."

"When dealing with enemies, sure."

"You're one of the most dangerous things I've chased, so I think I'll keep the odds stacked my way best I can." He moved closer, then stroked beside the scrape. "What happened here?"

"Slid on the floor."

Kane crouched down to survey the shallow wound. Not too deep, but large enough it'd be fucking sore as it healed. Sometimes scrapes were the worst, the large area of damage enough to make healing a bitch. He pressed a kiss above it, then another to the inside edge. He followed that, lining the entire wound with those kisses until his lips pressed to the top of her mound, beside the inner crease of her hip. Water splashed down on him, kept the chill of the room away.

He was surrounded by her scent, so close that a hard press of his tongue between where her legs hid her pussy and he could taste her.

He bracketed his hands on her hips. "Look at me, doll." Staring up at her, seeing every inch of her luscious body on display had his cock hard and heavy between his legs.

She tipped her head down and opened those pretty eyes. So much hidden there, or at least so much she tried to hide. *Worry. Fear.* Fuck people for asking too much of her, for expecting her to be fine with shit, for not realizing how much she wanted to be fine.

"You did good."

She ran her fingers through his hair, pushing it away from his face. "I don't know what I'm supposed to do."

"Right now? Lean back against that wall and let go. You're thinking too hard, worrying too much, and I don't much like it."

"I've got to figure this out." She scooted back at the urging of his hands.

Once her back hit the tile, he tapped her ankles so she spread them wide. "You think people ain't already working on that? You're gonna walk out of this shower in twenty minutes, and you're going to have to deal with whatever's going on. That ain't changing. You won't know shit more than you do now, but you'll be worked up, and you'll be tense and you won't be thinking straight. So, knock it off."

"I don't know how."

He pressed a kiss to the top of her slit before using his thumbs to tilt her hips forward, to give him access to her cunt, to let him have everything he'd been thinking about. "Give me a few fucking minutes, and I swear you won't be thinking about shit."

He waited, gaze on hers, asking. He wanted her to trust him, to give in to him, to know that he'd help her and afterward? Well, afterward they'd fucking end whoever had dared to target her. The reasons didn't matter, because they'd picked the wrong girl to fuck with. *With my girl.*

Her fingers, still in his hair, loosened. Kane had his tongue on her before she'd finished her nod.

How could Kane distract her? The worries swirled in her mind, and even after the blood from the man had washed down the drain, even after she'd used water so hot she feared a burn, she came no closer to an answer.

Who was after her? Why? What was she supposed to do about any of it?

She thought Kane would have no chance of what he'd claimed until the first swipe of his tongue made her thoughts blank. His tongue, hot and firm and relentless, licked across her clit in a hard and sure stroke. It wasn't like his finger, wasn't like her own or a vibrator. It didn't feel like anything she could compare it to.

The touch was soft, slippery, and made her cunt grow wet. It probed her clit, tracing along the sides, moving over her in a way she couldn't predict. He explored her, finding every secret, every fold, every tiny crevice of her pussy.

Her hips came forward to meet him, to ask for more. She couldn't think, couldn't worry, couldn't do anything but feel. On a hard stroke upward, she rose to her tiptoes, but his hands kept her in place and spread out.

He tilted his head, using the new angle to get his lips involved. He took her hardened clit between his firm lips and sucked, the sensation causing her to cry out.

Had the shower muffled the sound? Maybe. *Who cares?* He let her go with a noisy pop, then took one hand off her hip.

"You taste delicious, doll, like I knew you fucking would. You got a cunt meant for feasting on, but I know that sound you're making. You empty?" His lips pulled into a promising grin, and even in the soaked shower, she knew the shine on his lips came from her.

Kane didn't wait for her to answer, taking two fingers and shoving them into her with a hard push. The stretch bordered on painful, but that was what she needed. She needed him to overwhelm her so much she couldn't think past the feelings. She needed him to take her so hard, to force her to only react, to live only in the moment.

He must have understood her need, because that was what he gave her. He set a hard pace with those long fingers, fucking her in a way her own fingers hadn't done the night before. He forced her to take them, over and over again.

"You're so fucking tight. Funny that with how needy this cunt is, you're still so tight. Won't be after I fuck you, though. Nah, you'll be stretched out on my knot." His breath spilled over her clit before he blew a stream of cold air that drew a shiver from her. "You got any idea how many times I've come thinking about that? Thinking about all the ways I'm gonna fuck you, and trust me, it'll be a lot. Gonna put you on all fours and mount you. Gonna hold you up against a wall like this and pin you there with my cock, force you to take every inch I got. Fuck, gonna lay you out on a bed, tip that head of yours back, and slide my cock down that throat. You know how tempting that shit is? I want to feel you gagging on me, feel you give in and swallow me down, see the way my cock'll look down your throat, those pretty tears that'll fall outta the corners of your eyes."

Tiffany couldn't breathe as she pictured it, as if she were there, as though she already had his dick between her lips. How would it feel to be so powerless? To give in so fully to him? All that power, all that strength, all above her and using her mouth as he wanted to?

She tightened her hand in his hair, pushing his lips back to her clit as the image overwhelmed her.

He chuckled against her cunt before giving her what she wanted. He licked once more, a lazy stroke that even went down to where his fingers still fucked her, to where her lower lips stretched around him, before he latched around her clit again. He sucked with deep draws, rhythmic and building in pressure. Each pull had her moaning louder, had her fingers tightening and her hips rolling toward him.

He set her off when he pulled back and shoved a third thick finger into her. Any other time she'd have said it hurt, but right then? The burn, the sting, the too-damned-much sensation melted into something wonderful inside her.

Her legs shook as she came against his lips and around his fingers. He didn't stop, fucking her harder if anything, taking every sound she made as an offer to keep going, to take more, to give more. Each drag of his large knuckles against her spasming walls made her yank his hair to stop, but he didn't.

He growled, loud even above the falling water, but he didn't release her. His gaze flashed up to hers, and he reminded her of a beast with a meal. He was a man with no intention of letting it go.

He scraped his teeth over her swollen clit and curved his fingers inward, toward her front wall. Before the first orgasm had even faded, before she'd caught her breath, he shoved her head-first into another. It crashed over her, dragging her beneath the enormity of it. She gasped in greedy lungfuls of air, but it didn't cool her, didn't help.

Especially because he still didn't stop. He still didn't give her a break.

"Please," she begged, her legs trembling and weak.

"One more."

"I can't."

"Yeah, you can. One more and I know you won't fucking worry about shit. Plus? This thing in my head is screaming to not let you go, screaming to fuck you against this wall. You got any idea how hard it is to deny it? To not shove my dick so deep into you that you won't ever forget it?" He nuzzled her thigh, never letting his nose drift far from her, as though he still needed the scent and planned to tattoo it on his DNA. "You keep getting hurt, and you keep smelling like these other alphas, and now that I got you to myself for a minute, I ain't wanting to let you go. Since I'll have to, give me one more. I want to see you over-fucking-whelmed and crying and shaking for me."

Tiffany wanted to say no. She wanted to tell him she couldn't.

The lust in his dark eyes, the need that went deeper than anything she'd seen before had her nodding.

He traced his tongue up the crease of her thigh, the pink against her skin like a reminder of where that tongue had been and where it was going again. He offered a nip to her hip bone, a sting that was like him — unpredictable, uncomfortable, too much.

As quickly as it had happened, he returned to her pussy. His lips surrounded her clit, a nip like the one he'd done earlier, but to her clit? She bucked her hips forward. For more? Less?

She didn't know.

He pressed three fingers deep into her, then pulled one out. The loss had her whining, but the whine turned startled when he twisted his wrist and pressed that same finger to her ass. The pressure made it clear what he planned.

He didn't coax like Kieran had when he'd done that. No, this wasn't a game, this wasn't him testing to see if she liked it. He pressed against her hole with purpose.

He was going to fuck her ass with that finger, while his other two took her cunt, and he planned for her to come while he did it.

The tightening of her stomach said she would.

Tiffany's mouth dropped open, her hand flinging to the side, catching the shower handle to ground herself against the unfamiliar pressure of his finger.

He growled low. Not a purr to reassure her, but a sound to scold her. Even without his voice, she recognized the meaning, could hear it as well as if he'd spoken out loud. *Stop trying to keep me out, doll. I'm gonna fuck your asshole and you're gonna love it. You'll only feel it more if you keep clenching, but it won't stop me.*

He scraped her clit with his teeth again, causing her to clench everywhere, and as soon as she loosened again, he pressed hard. His finger, soaked from her wetness, sank into her ass.

It wasn't much. He had only pushed in to the first knuckle, and only one finger, yet the feeling went straight to her cunt. It was wrong and weird and new and so much more than she could process. She wanted less and more at the same time, wanted him to pull out and yet the thought made her clutching hands curl to pull him deeper.

His growl transformed into a wild snarl, one she felt through where his mouth pressed tight to her, and she lost any fight she might have had.

As he withdrew the finger and fucked her again, all fingers moving at once, his lips adding pressure to her clit, she came.

This time he eased her through it, softening his touch so he offered light flicks of his tongue and a gentle rocking of his fingers, enough to prolong it, to bring her down, to soften the effects. His lips left her clit, instead showering affection on her cunt, her thighs, her hips. He caught any drop of her juices he could find before withdrawing his fingers.

The pull against her sensitive ass as he left her made her cry out, something between pain and pleasure.

"Easy," he whispered as he stood and placed his forehead to hers.

Tiffany leaned up to kiss him, but the moment she tasted herself, she lavished the same affection on him. She used her tongue to clean her cunt from his lips, to taste her own need on him. He only groaned and allowed it, his fingers carding through her hair.

When she'd finished, when her lids felt too tired to lift, with her body worn out and buzzing at the same time, he pulled her flush against him for a kiss.

And Tiffany knew, whatever was going to happen, she couldn't lose this.

* * * *

Kieran held his temper even as Kane sat beside Tiffany. When she'd come down the stairs beside him, reeking of the other alpha, Kieran had ground his teeth so tight his jaw ached. He'd said nothing, not wanting to worsen the situation.

He didn't own her. She'd been through enough without worrying about him flying off the handle.

With all the risks and unknowns involved, the smartest thing seemed to go somewhere unexpected to talk.

It left them all at Bryce, Joshua and Kaidan's home. Well, theirs and Claire's, their unexpected omega. The feminine touches showed where she'd left her mark on the home she'd claimed. The woman had once held a gun on Kieran, making it clear that despite how fragile she appeared, she'd been created with tougher stuff. Not that he held grudges.

Marshall sat at the kitchen island beside Kaidan. Joshua and Claire sat on the floor by the table, and Kieran and Bryce paced while Sam leaned against the armrest of the couch.

"Do we have an ID on the man who broke in?" Bryce halted his pacing long enough to toss Sam the question.

"Yeah. Bradly Howard. Two-bit criminal who does others' dirt work."

"But if he's dead, it's over, right?" Tiffany asked.

Kieran and Bryce exchanged loaded looks. Her voice held so much hope he'd have liked to tell her yes, to say it was over and she could sleep easily.

He couldn't lie, though. "No. Someone like him wasn't after you for himself. Whoever he is working for is the problem, and since he failed, they'll send someone else."

"Someone for what, though? I haven't done anything!"

Joshua answered. "You did something — we just don't know what, yet. I pulled the cameras on Kieran's house. Same two cars have been passing it and parking down the street. They didn't realize his security cameras could zoom that far."

"They've been watching me there, too?" Ah, there was that spark of anger Tiffany had. She didn't sound so frightened anymore, with anger taking over. Good, he'd rather she be pissed.

Sam stepped in. "My guess is they tossed your place looking for something. They tore it apart too well and didn't take anything, so they had to be searching it. I'd say that man did it then waited for you to show. Marshall's cameras didn't show anything, so he probably followed you from your place to Marshall's."

"For what?"

"People only track down someone for a couple of reasons. One, the person knows something. Two, they have something. Three, they can get something. Since he searched your apartment first, I'd guess they think you have something."

"But what?"

He shrugged. "If I knew that, I'd already have this closed up. The timing is strange, though. It all started after Randy, after the hospital. So far, we're looking at it involving Randy, your old life or what happened at the warehouse."

"That's a lot of options," Tiffany offered.

Kane squeezed her knee. "We'll figure it out, doll, but we can't go back to any of our places. Whoever the fuck we're dealing with is well connected and knows where we all live."

Kieran hated to agree with the asshole, but he was right. "I need to take her somewhere off the grid, something unconnected to anything."

"You? Fuck that, I'm going, too," Kane said.

Before Kieran could argue, Marshall spoke up. "I'm going, too. I've already talked to hospital and told them I'm taking some personal time. And don't argue, Kieran. Are you going to tell me she wouldn't be safer with three of us watching than with just you?"

Kieran wanted to argue—he wanted to tell them they could all fuck off, that he wanted that time with her on his own. Except Marshall was right, and her safety was more important than his jealousy.

He snarled low. "Fine. That doesn't tell us where to go."

Tiffany sat up straighter, meeting his gaze. "I've got somewhere in mind. It's a few hours out of town, in the middle of nowhere."

"Any connection to you?"

"None. I know the omega who owns it under another fake name, and she hides out there all the time. There's no way they could know about it."

Kieran nodded, the idea sound. Away from town meant no accidental sightings, no credit cards to follow a trail, or hotel rooms. "Sam, you'll keep working the case from this side and keeping us updated?"

Sam nodded. "Of course."

Bryce spoke up from his spot. "We're doing everything we can, too, digging into the man's past, trying to find some connections."

Kieran took a deep breath. Running wasn't something he liked to do, but damn it, Tiffany's life meant too much. Until they knew who was after her, knew what they were dealing with, the best plan was to get her as far away from the danger as possible.

It seemed all four of them would be going on a trip together.

He had no idea if any of them would survive it.

Chapter Eleven

Kane looked around the cabin, impressed. He didn't know much about the omega who owned it, but she had set up a hell of a safe house. Enough food to feed them for months lined shelves of the large pantry. In the freezer, fruits, vegetables and meats rested frozen in neatly labeled vacuum-sealed bags.

Four bedrooms sat ready, each decorated the same no-frills way as the others. A security system ran through the house, a large closet in the hallway housing the equipment. It didn't hook into a central company, but instead ran self-contained. Each window and door was wired, the gate at the bottom of the private road and a sensor on the fence to alert them if it were cut.

Most impressive of all? Beside the security equipment, in a locked safe Tiffany knew the code to, sat an arsenal he'd have been proud to own. Pistols, rifles, shot guns, blades all meticulously cared for and clearly used.

Alison hadn't said much when they'd arrived before she'd shoved the keys into Tiffany's hands and fled.

Seemed she had something in need of doing, and the woman didn't seem inclined to spend time with them. Fine by him.

The trip had taken a few hours, and they'd used an SUV Bryce had supplied so no one could follow them. A quick run through a store to pick up supplies — new clothes, necessities — and they'd reached their destination.

Kane shut the door to the closet, turning to face Kieran who stood behind him. "So, how is this going to work? We going to keep beating on one another until one of us gives in?"

"I would bet we'd both end up in the hospital. Giving in isn't either of our styles."

"True enough. So, what then? Because this was ugly when we weren't sharing a fucking cabin with an omega who smells like Tiffany does."

Kieran's shoulders dipped, and for the first time, Kane noted the exhaustion on the other alpha's face. Then again, Kieran wasn't as young as he was. Why didn't that please him as much as it should have?

"I don't know. I know that I don't intend to back off, not unless she tells me she wants that. You refuse to back off, either. Maybe we should stop trying to fight one another and allow her to choose."

The option seemed obvious enough. Tiffany could make the choice on her own. Besides, it wasn't as if Kane would want her to pick him to discover she'd done so because he'd knocked Kieran out of the picture. He wanted to be her first choice, not her last option.

Kane huffed a soft laugh at the simple solution. "So we each try to win her? That's your big idea?"

"Afraid you're not up to the task?"

Ah, that arrogance. Why was it that every alpha possessed it? It was something that seemed to be written into their bones, something they couldn't escape. Alphas could be spotted well before they showed symptoms in their teenage years, before their scents changed or the markers showed in their blood. They were more aggressive, more territorial, more stubborn. Kieran showed every sign, tempered by age and experience as they were.

"Oh, I'm up for it, old man. I just don't want you crying foul later when she picks me."

Kieran didn't react to the jab, didn't spit back an insult. He only shook his head and took a step back. "It will take more than confidence to win, kid, but sure, give it your best shot. It'll be easier for her to see that you're no good. You may have fooled her at first, because she didn't know any better, but you won't be able to keep this up full-time. Once she gets a look at you compared to other alphas? She's as good as mine."

Kane kept his smile easy, offering a mocking salute with his middle finger before walking down the hallway.

He wasn't a man to play many games, but fuck if he didn't plan to win this one.

Tiffany packed her things into the drawer of the room she'd taken. All the rooms opened off a long hallway, making it easy to pick. She'd taken the one in the middle, with Kane on one side, Kieran on the other and Marshall across the hall.

"Do you have enough?" Marshall nodded at where she placed the jeans in the dresser.

"Yeah. I won't be winning any beauty contests in it, but it'll be fine until we can get back to my stuff."

Marshall's hungry gaze drew her attention as though it brushed over her skin. Sure enough, he stared, that edge to him peeking out. "I think you'll look great."

How did he do that? She could see whatever he hid, yet it didn't show in his voice. Did he know how close to the surface it lurked, or did he assume he'd buried it deep enough?

What would it be like if he lost control of it?

Why did he hide it in the first place? Most alphas thrived on that primal side of themselves. They loved the strength, the power, the privilege their designation bought them. Few hid it, so why did Marshall?

Instead of asking, because the answer terrified her, Tiffany slid the drawer shut and tore her gaze away. "Do you think this is a crazy idea?"

"Hiding from whoever is after you?"

"No. Bringing Kane and Kieran out here. They haven't had a great record of working well together."

He chuckled, the tension sliding away. "They'll figure it out."

"I doubt it. Seems to me they're pretty set on acting like possessive assholes."

When Tiffany went to put her backpack on the top closet shelf, Marshall took it and put it in place for her. "Men in general, and alphas specifically, aren't good at adjusting. We tend to like things our way."

Tiffany sat on the bed, then flopped backward, arms spread out and legs hanging off the end. "Yeah, I've noticed. I think alphas are spoiled and used to getting their way, so they throw tantrums when they have to change."

Marshall shifted the bed when he sat. "Fair enough, though I suggest you not tell Kieran he's having a hissy fit. He seems the type who might take that personally."

The memory of Kieran putting her over his lap rushed over her. It hit her so fast, her skin warming, her pussy growing wet, that she pulled in a shaky breath. "I did once, and no, he wasn't a fan."

Tiffany expected a growl. She expected Marshall to react to what was clearly arousal aimed at another alpha. It was what Kane would have done, what Kieran would have.

Instead, his soothing chuckle came as he stretched on the bed beside her. "That doesn't surprise me. Neither does that blush on your cheeks. I'm going to guess whatever his response was, you weren't all that opposed to it."

Tiffany rolled to her side, needing to read him. "Why aren't you jealous? You said you liked me, but you don't get upset over them."

He rolled toward her, mirroring her stance. "Because I'm not the jealous type. Maybe it's because of my job, because I've seen how fast everything can get taken away. I guess it makes me wonder what the point of jealousy is." He set a hand on her hip. "The fact is that a body isn't a consumable. It isn't something that gets used up or ruined. A person isn't less because they're shared."

Shared. It created scenarios in her mind so fast she couldn't help the way her heart sped.

Shared made her think about lying flat while Kane leaned over her, while he pressed her breasts together to create space for him to thrust into. Kieran would spread her thighs wide and take her cunt, deft fingers on her clit. And the man beside her now? He'd slide past her lips, feeding himself to her inch by inch.

Even the way he spoke made her think he enjoyed watching, that as he fucked her mouth, his gaze would take in the sight of the other men taking her, using her.

"Your scent is irresistible," Marshall whispered. "I know they might be fighting this, they might be stubborn, but I think you like the idea more than you let on."

Tiffany placed a hand on his chest, pushing back enough for her to take a breath and clear her head. "Dealing with one alpha seems like a lot of work. Three would be insanity. Claire might be crazy, but I'm not."

"What have you always wanted?"

"Not three cocks."

His chuckle warmed her cheeks. "Come on, think about it. If you could have any future, what would it be?"

Tiffany frowned as she thought about it, her foot sliding over Marshall's calf. "I want to be happy. I want a family, and a life with a mate."

"And you think you could only have that if you pick one mate?"

She opened her mouth to say yes, to say that she hadn't intended to collect alphas like trophies, that screwing three different men seemed wrong and like a lot of work.

Except the future he mentioned started to form. *Would it be so bad?* Kieran would be gruff, strict. He'd never let her get away with anything, but the way her ass and her face had burned when he spanked her said she might not mind it. Kane would help her get into trouble, but also help to get her out of it when needed. And Marshall? He was steady, dependable, and a thinker. He planned, carefully.

She pictured dinners together, all four of them around a table. She heard the fights over the remote when they watched TV, when they all wanted something different on.

She thought about having kids, about the support of three to lean on, and what sort of family that would create.

"Maybe," she admitted.

"Life doesn't always go the way we expect or plan, but that doesn't make it wrong. Give it some thought."

Tiffany slid her hand down his chest, tracing the buttons of his shirt, pressing against each as she passed. "My parents were happy. It seems like you don't see many alphas and omegas who make a good life for themselves, but I had that. No man loved his mate more than my father loved my mother. When he'd get home from work, he'd sneak up behind her, grab her hips, plant her on the counter and kiss her. I knew never to interrupt, because that was important. It was their ritual, like this sacred thing that I got to watch." She slipped her fingers beneath his shirt, stroking his heated skin. "It was like watching magic, the way he'd stare at her, the way a touch of her hand could calm him. I wanted that. I still do. Claire told me when I ran, when they were going to register me, that relationships like that don't exist, but I know they do."

"And that's why Randy was able to trick you, wasn't it?"

She sighed, not wanting to remember. "I wanted that life so badly, I made myself believe he could give it to me. I've always been willing to rush to get what I want. Stupid, I guess."

Marshall groaned when she slipped her fingers below the waist of his slacks. "Not stupid, just hopeful. You know what you want, and that's more than most people can say."

"And what do you want?"

"Peace. I want to go to bed at night knowing I have what matters to me, that it's not going anywhere, that I won't lose it or ruin it or risk it." He answered in a low voice, as if he didn't want to answer at all. The words came out halted and full of things she couldn't unpack, that she didn't know him well enough to understand. Marshall wasn't done yet, though. In a hollow voice, he added, "I guess we all learn things from our parents."

She went to ask him what he meant, especially with the shadows that crossed his eyes, and the way time and memories clouded his words.

Instead, Kane's voice barreled through the door. "Get your asses in here to eat or there'll be nothing left!"

Tiffany jerked back as if caught. Funny that, even alone, she felt guilty. She didn't want to pull away, but she didn't want anyone fighting, either.

Marshall shook away whatever haunted him, his eyes regaining the ease he normally wore. Again, the quick change made her wonder how much he hid and why.

He gave her no time to ask or pry further, a chuckle at the way she'd pulled away. He yanked her back to him and took her lips with a kiss so good, she couldn't think clearly enough to remember why she'd pulled away in the first place.

The idea of anyone fighting, of shame or guilt or worry mattering struck her as insane. Who cared about any of that? As long as Marshall didn't stop kissing her like that, the rest of it could go to hell for all she cared.

Too bad kisses always ended eventually.

Chapter Twelve

Kieran laced his shoes, pulling them snug before tying them. "It doesn't matter if you're used to running alone. Doing so when you're in danger would be foolish."

Tiffany bent forward, reaching for her toes. The round of her spine, the way her tank top rode up to show the delicate curve of her lower back, the agile lines as she placed her palms to the ground had him wondering what other positions he could put her into.

Her head lifted, drawn by the deep sound he'd made. That it wasn't fear that sprang up in those beautiful eyes but lust reminded him again why he liked her.

Liked?

Way to downplay it. Even without having fucked her yet, the bond had started to grow. His alpha side wanted her for his own, and while his own feelings grew, he knew the pull had more to do with that bond.

Not that he cared the reasons behind it. If he wanted her, did why matter?

She didn't straighten, only gave him a smirk before spreading her feet out and repeating the stretch, a position even more tempting.

"You are a brat," he said.

She didn't deny it, reaching toward one foot then the other. "I never pictured you as a runner."

"I wasn't always a network engineer."

"Oh yeah? What did you do before?"

"I served. The military instills the importance of physical training."

She stood, her gaze on him, thoughtful. "I could see that. You've got that order and regulations attitude. Why'd you leave?"

"I got tired of pulling the trigger from someone else. After I got out, I started my company. Bryce got out a few years later, and we started doing some work together as well."

"Do you miss it?"

He crossed his arms and gave himself a chance to consider. "I miss the community aspect, the feeling of someone always having your back. That's something civilian life doesn't offer. Bryce, Joshua and Kaidan remained together, a strong unit, but I didn't have the same experience. My job had been largely solitary, but I still had a group. After leaving, I've lacked that."

Even admitting it had his skin itching. He didn't care for advertising shortcomings or weaknesses. What was it about her that made him open his mouth and say things he'd never dare to tell another person?

Whatever it was showed when she looked at him. She didn't mock him, didn't laugh, didn't make light of the confession. Instead, she took a step forward and wrapped her arms around him.

Funny that despite how small she was compared to him, or that her arms barely wrapped around his wide frame, that she didn't even clear his shoulders, her hug made him feel something.

Like he had a place? Like he could have a place? Like that sense of belonging he'd missed might still be possible?

He let the thoughts linger for only a heartbeat before pushing them away. A kiss to the top of her head was the only thank you he could muster, and as if she knew he'd reached the limit of where his emotional ability reached, she stepped back.

"How fast do you run?" he asked, changing the subject.

She lifted the other knee to stretch the leg as her gaze moved over the tree line. "Faster than you."

"I doubt that."

Her laugh had him smiling back, the fun odd but welcome. She set her leg down then hopped, one foot to the other, shaking her hands slightly. Everything she did seemed adorable, a fact he doubted would go over well with her. It was true, though. The way she warmed up, the way she laughed, the way she moved, it was all something he'd never dealt with.

He'd dealt with angry omegas, with sweet and quiet omegas, with broken omegas. Had he ever dealt with one so feisty? One who enjoyed life with such a passion?

For a man who had little passion in his life, hers intoxicated him. He had tiny tastes of it from her, glimpses into a life lived to a fullness he didn't know how to achieve, and it made him ache for more.

The fact that she'd kept that sort of feeling despite all that had happened only reinforced the point that she was special.

Her smile turned mischievous. "Well, let's see if you can catch me." She took off from the porch of the cabin, toward the tree line, feet quick but loud.

Kieran gave her a head start, but not long. Thirty seconds was all he could hold himself back for before giving chase.

He had an omega to catch, and when he did?

His cock hardened at the thought.

Tiffany's breath came out in heavy panting no matter how much she tried to slow it. She wasn't a long-distance runner, and judging from the state of Kieran's shoes, from the wear marks, she'd guess he was.

It made sense. Kieran was a long-haul man in general. She could see him lacing up his shoes and going out for a ten-mile run, where he wouldn't go fast but he'd eat up mile after steady mile. He was a marathoner.

Tiffany was a sprinter. It was how she ran and how she lived her life. She went all out for a short time, almost frantic with excitement, then would rest.

It meant while she couldn't sustain any real effort, especially against him, she had speed on her side.

Still, twenty minutes into their game and she got the sense he was toying with her.

He'd cornered her twice, but each time she'd slipped away. Did he not want the game to end?

The lust in those eyes said he wanted to catch her, but the way his running shorts had pushed out said he enjoyed the chase, too.

The drenched state of her underwear made her admit, so did she.

She lowered, crouching in the dirt, fingers against a pine tree beside her. The cloud coverage meant there was little in the way of moonlight, so she strained to find any movement, to spot his figure closing in on her.

Nothing.

It gave her time to catch her breath, to coax herself to rest, to bring her heart rate back down. She closed her eyes, breathing slowly. *In. Hold it. Out. In. Hold it. Out.*

Before she could think of her next plan, of how to outmaneuver Kieran again, his voice danced across her ear. "I've caught you, girl."

"Not yet." She bolted forward but didn't make it a full step before he caught her hips in his strong, dragging her down.

They wrestled, both careful to keep it a game, but his bulk won out. In close contact, Kieran outmatched her.

"Fine, you win. Now what?"

His hips fell into the space between her thighs and rocked forward, his teeth catching her bottom lip hard enough to earn a yelp. "Now, I plan to enjoy my catch."

His cock caught her clit through their clothing, and Tiffany let her head fall back.

Finally.

* * * *

Kane set his feet on the table, the kitchen cleaned after dinner. He'd put together the meal, some stupid part of him wanting to show off that he knew his way around a stove. They'd finished off every last bite, which meant either they'd been starving, or the food was good.

Kane figured it was the latter. Besides, fucking up spaghetti was pretty hard.

After Tiffany had helped clean up, she'd wanted to go running. Kane could have gone with her, but he hated running. It bored him, the rhythmic motion of it all, the steady pace. Nah, he tended toward things with a bit more fun. He could handle hiking, and he loved rock climbing — not that he had a chance to go often. Still, he figured him complaining the whole time would have put a damper on the event, meaning he let Kieran and Tiffany head off for their run.

He could concede a battle to win the war. Let Kieran take the run, and Kane would find another activity he and Tiffany could do. This wouldn't be a fast win, so he settled in for the long haul.

Marshall sat at the desk on the far wall, laptop and piles of papers in front of him. He hadn't said much, and Kane didn't know the other alpha well, but at least he didn't hate him. Made for a better stay, he figured.

"Are you gonna work this whole time?"

Marshall finished typing something before lifting his gaze. "No. However, I left on personal time so quickly, I wanted to review these files and assign the best doctor to take over each case."

"I figured doctors had their shit better worked out than that. What if you got hit by a car? You don't have someone already to take this shit over?"

Marshall flipped to the next page, speaking as he wrote. "Yes, I have someone who will step in if I need them to, but I prefer to hand cases over individually. I deal with sensitive cases and patients."

"I heard you work with only omegas?"

Marshall nodded. "Yes. I get work from the police department and the federal level. Often omegas in cases of abuse or violence require special treatments. Their bodies don't respond to many medications like others do, which means a specialist is helpful. Add to that the delicate nature of abuse victims, and I'd rather pick who takes what." He tapped a page. "For example, I have a patient with a history of abuse from an alpha. However, her panic attacks are calmed by an alpha's presence. That means that she would do best transferred to a trained alpha doctor. Another patient, however, was raped by a male beta, so she would do best with a female doctor taking her case, beta or omega. They'll all do better with the right doctor handling the case."

Kane frowned as he listened, as he was reminded again of how easy it would have been to have Tiffany ended up like them. Fuck, it was lucky that Claire had been involved, that Kieran had gotten there in time. The only thing he could give that asshole was that he'd helped Tiffany, that he'd gotten her through it in one piece. Sure, she wasn't perfect, but she'd come out of it a lot better than if Randy had won.

Fuck, if Randy hadn't decided to go after Claire, he'd have murdered Tiffany. Would Kane have even known? Would he have found out?

Eventually, he would have. If she'd stopped responding, he'd have gone looking for an answer. Still, what would he have done?

A world without Tiffany seemed cold, dark.

He offered another question to Marshall, willing the silence to stop. "Why do you do it? Why work with omegas like that? You, you're a fucking bleeding heart, so this shit gets under your skin. Why do it?"

"Because it needs to be done. These omegas, they'd suffer no matter what, but at least I can help. I can lessen it."

"But why you? Out of anyone, why do you think it's your job to do it? Bet you wake up at night seeing their faces, so why?" When he didn't answer, Kane pushed. "Come on, we got fuck knows how much time here, give me something."

Marshall sighed and set down the pen. "Very well. My mother was an omega. My father killed her. I do what I can to help others not suffer the same fate."

Kane tapped his fingers against the armrest of the couch, letting the words simmer. Sure, that was something, but there was more.

Marshall wasn't selfless only to be selfless. Fuck, few people were. They did things because they got something out of it, a feeling, a payoff. Some people did good because they liked others to see it, they liked the praise. Some did it to please a magic man in the sky, and some did it for that rush it gave them when they got to say they were a good person.

What was Marshall's reason?

The firm set of the man's shoulders, the buttoned-down attitude, the 'I'm in control of shit' attitude gave it away.

"You think you can make up for what happened? Think that if you do good, that the fact your alpha dad killed your omega mom means you ain't the same as him?"

Another alpha would have sailed across the room at such a blatant guess, but not Marshall. His eyebrow twitched, the only outwardly reaction, before he gave a quick nod. "You're more observant than I'd have given you credit for. However, if you're tearing open wounds and ignore basic privacy, why don't you do the same? How long do you plan for this nonsense with Kieran to continue?"

He almost told Marshall to fuck off, but the turnaround was fair play. He shrugged. "As long as it takes for her to pick me. With the fun-sucker Kieran is, shouldn't be too long."

"So, this is a game to you two? You'll keep pulling her in different directions until she breaks?"

"Ain't a game. Game implies I don't give a shit about the outcome, but I do. It's less a game, more a war, and I don't plan to lose."

Marshall shook his head before picking the pen back up. "Trust me, push too hard, you'll both lose her."

"Surprised you ain't jumping at that chance. With us out of the way, she's all yours. Don't think I can't smell you on her, don't think I'm stupid enough to miss all the eye-fucking you're giving her."

"I never claimed not to want her. However, I'm not trying to win."

"You're playing with her?"

"Not at all. I tried to explain this to her, but you all seem equally stubborn. There is a reason there are fewer omegas than alphas. There's a reason so many alphas settle down with betas in the end."

"Survival of the fittest. It's a way to force alphas to fight over mates, so the strongest passes on their genes. I did learn some shit at school."

Marshall huffed a soft laugh but didn't comment on the jab. "Some people think that, but I don't, not anymore. I don't think the reason there are more alphas is because we are supposed to fight over mates."

"What is the reason then, *professor*?"

Marshall dropped his gaze to his paper, returning to his work as his final statement sat between them. "I think we were always meant to settle in groups. I think alphas were always meant to share omegas."

Chapter Thirteen

Tiffany squirming beneath Kieran only made him harder. The more she moved, the more she struggled, the more he wanted to bury his teeth in her neck and his dick inside her. The chase had thrilled him in a way he'd forgotten, the hunt, the kill.

When he'd finally cornered her, when he'd taken her to the ground and pinned her, he'd known.

He had to have her. While Kane might have talked about the game, about winning or losing, Kieran now understood he had no other choice. The more of her he touched, the more he discovered, the surer he was that she was his, that she had to be his. He wanted to take her as his mate, wanted to breed her until she bore his children.

He didn't want this for a year. He wanted it forever.

Funny that the moment of clarity came when only instinct ruled him, when he couldn't think beyond the demands of his nature. It pushed aside all the rest. It made him forget that she was too young, too inexperienced, made him forget all the omegas he'd helped who had run off on him.

Those things failed to matter to his baser side, so he reveled in the simplicity of the moment. When it ended, he could work.

He scraped his teeth over her pulse, sating himself with the small sting it would offer as he gripped the flimsy leggings she'd worn.

Those fucking leggings...

The chase might have lasted half the time if she'd not worn them, but each time he caught a glimpse of how they hugged her ass, he'd damn near tripped.

He gave up his annoyance with them when he tore them free with a single jerk. The flimsy things had their usage.

"Hey! I only have a few things to wear." Tiffany hit her palm against his shoulder.

"So now you'll have one less. Be thankful, because if I saw you wearing them again, I'd have had to fuck you right then." He reached between her thighs to find no underwear, nothing hiding her pussy from him.

To think he could have stroked her at any time during their game?

Next time he would pin her, cup her cunt through a pair of those thin leggings, then let her go again.

Catch and release with her cunt sounded like a game he could get behind.

Perhaps they'd play as a group, herding her. Kane would—

Kieran froze at the unwelcome thought. No. Whatever had him even considering such a thing could go to hell for all he cared. He didn't share, and certainly not with that idiot.

Tiffany pressed her heels against the dirt, lifting her hips toward him, forcing his fingers to move.

Right. Focus.

Kieran found her folds drenched. At least he knew she'd enjoyed the game as much as he had, and it was a good thing. He doubted he had the patience for much foreplay. The chase had woken every instinct inside him, and they all screamed to knot the omega beneath him.

Still, as he forced her thighs wider with his body, as he buried two fingers in her, he held back. "I'm going to fuck you, girl. Are you going to tell me no?" His tongue darted out to taste her lips as he waited for an answer, his breath frozen. What if she said no? What if she wasn't ready?

He'd stop, even if it fucking killed him. He groaned at the ache in his cock. *It just might kill me.*

"Hurry up, then," she whispered against his lips. "I've waited long enough."

His shoulders sagged at the truth that she wanted him, that she wasn't going to turn him down or push him away.

"Have you and Kane—"

She silenced him by nipping hard at his bottom lip. "Even if I have, I'm not going to feel bad about it." Her words came out strong, but a waver through them showed a deeper hesitation.

"I'm not trying to make you feel bad. I need to know if you've done this before."

She shook her head.

Possessive need roared through Kieran at the idea she hadn't had sex, that his dick would be the first to take her untouched cunt. He nudged himself against her sex, against the heat and wetness that demanded he plunge into her, that he fuck her the way he'd imagined since he'd first met her.

Still, he waited as much as instinct and need would allow. He rubbed the head of his cock against her slit, savoring the tightness that tempted him, the shudders and wanton gasps she let out.

Kieran sank his length in her wet, hot heat, filling her in one solid thrust, knowing she'd adjust, that her soaked pussy would accept every thick, hard inch of him and still want more. Even when her nails gouged into his sweat-dampened skin, even when she cried out, her cunt pulsed around him in needy waves.

He closed his eyes at the way she gripped him, the way his knot ached, wanting to swell and trap her to him.

Not yet, though.

He planned to savor each second, to commit each to memory, to swallow whole every sound she made, every taste he had of her luscious body. He held still, letting her cunt adjust to the way he'd stretched her open, to the space his shaft claimed inside her.

Except no, Tiffany wasn't the sort to wait for anything. Her breath came out in harsh panting that broke on moans while her heels dug into the dirt to thrust up. She couldn't move much, not with his weight pinning her, but she still writhed for the friction she needed.

Kieran released a harsh laugh at her desperation, at the needy, hungry way she moved, before reaching down for one of her thighs. He hauled it up, spreading her open for him, wide enough he could tilt his body and see how her pussy lips stretched tight around his dick.

He'd never seen a better sight, even in the darkness of the night, than the way he looked sunk into her tight body.

The first time he pulled back, when he slowly slid himself from her tight body, she twisted like a caught animal beneath him. Her hips raised, her back arched and she tried to get him to return.

When he'd pulled almost all the way out, so only the head of his dick rested inside her clutching cunt, he shoved back into her, filling her all at once.

"Fuck!" Her filthy curse accompanied her nails in his skin. Her mouth parted, head back as her neck, arched like an offering.

Kieran took the offer, leaning down to dance his lips across the column of her throat. He loved that space, the delicate curve of a woman's throat, the submission it took to offer it to someone. He glided the tip of his tongue up the center of her throat, then set a hard pace.

His abs curled as he fucked her, as he pulled out and plunged even deeper. Maybe her first time should have been slower. Maybe she'd hoped for candles and romance, but Kieran didn't have those things to offer.

He had this to offer, his hard cock and his willing body and a promise to take care of her. He showered her with the only affection he knew or understood as he released her leg to grip the neckline of her tank top and rip it down the center.

Tiffany's leg stayed put, her thighs spread wide when she grasped the knee herself. The tiny rolls of her hips were like pleas from her lips, a begging for him to keep going. Hell, she didn't even complain about her shirt, which told him how far gone she was, how lost in the haze of lust.

Good. He didn't want her thinking. When she thought, she second-guessed herself and worried about things she shouldn't. Worse? Maybe she'd change her mind. *Maybe she'll start thinking about —*

Kieran snarled. Kane had no place in this moment. This was Tiffany and Kieran, and he'd damn well have it without the other alpha. No matter what happened, no matter who she chose, he wouldn't let the asshole sully this moment.

The thought of his competition had Kieran snapping his hips harder, had him fucking her as if he could reach deep enough to scour away the memory of the other alpha. He wanted to take her so fully she had no room for Kane, had nothing left untouched or unclaimed by Kieran.

The aching in his knot, the tension that ran through his thighs, his ass, his lower stomach — it all said he neared his end. He yanked her sports bra up to free her full breasts. He leaned down and feasted on the hardened nipples, using his tongue and lips to tantalize them.

Tiffany's knuckles brushed his stomach, and he released her breasts to look between them. He found her hand moving toward her clit.

"Good girl," he whispered against the soft skin of her breasts, against the full under-curve he traced with his tongue. "I want to see you come. I want to *feel* you come on my cock, want you so desperate you get yourself off because you can't wait another second."

She dropped her legs farther open and reached her clit. The way she'd graze his cock on some rubs had him gritting his teeth to hold off. The throbbing of his knot refused to be ignored, but damn it, he'd wait.

He sucked at her breast, near the top, high enough that a low-cut shirt would show it. The mark would sit on her skin, and he knew he'd grin each time he saw it. Well, grin and think about this moment, about how he'd fucked her on the ground because neither had been able to wait another moment.

It was the bite of his teeth on that spot, however, the gave him what he wanted. When his teeth closed down, her body went wild. She bucked her hips, taking his dick deeper still, like a feral beast who didn't want to be caught. Her cunt cranked down on him, tightening like a fist until neither moved, and she went entirely still, not even drawing breath. A deep red flush sprang up over her chest, her face, her hands drawn into fists and chest pushed forward.

The sight of her so defenseless and at his mercy lost the fight for any control. Kieran let himself come, let himself spill into her like he'd needed.

A building pressure inside Tiffany allowed fear to creep through. Kieran's thick cock already felt as though it tested the limits of her pussy, like it filled her until she had no room for anything else. When the base swelled, when it wedged behind her pelvic bone and kept growing, spreading her walls more than she'd thought possible, she whimpered against the strange sensation.

Kieran's voice dipped low and rough as if it slid across sandpaper. "Take my knot, girl. You can do it."

She pushed his chest, but nothing moved him, even as he rolled his hips forward to lock himself inside her already over-full cunt.

Her moment of panic didn't last long, and it couldn't stand against the crushing pleasure that overwhelmed her at the first jerk of his dick inside her. She could feel his hot cum fill her in quick jets, as though it soaked into her body, and it didn't give her the chance for fear. Instead, as if instinctual, she came around his heavy knot, the pushing of her hands turning to clutching, like the source of all the exquisite sensations might get away. She ground her hips forward against him, seeking more, body behaving as though she had no control over its frantic movements. It wanted, and she was powerless to stop it.

Dirt dug into her back, but she hardly felt it. The ground beneath her, the way the scraps of ripped clothing hung off her limbs, none of that mattered compared to the way Kieran's length stretched her pussy, the way his body imprisoned her and the way his demanding lips moved against hers even if her own pleasure kept her from responding.

After the last hard kick of his cock, all the tension that had strung his body tight drained away. His weight rested on his elbows and his knees, which sank into the ground between her thighs. Still, his pelvis pressed against hers, not a whisper of space between their bodies.

The closeness of the moment, the way his fingers mindlessly danced over her jawline, grew nervous energy inside her. She squirmed, wanting to get up, to put distance between them, to gather herself. Only, when she shifted, a universal 'get off me' sign, Kieran's massive knot held her tight.

He wrapped a hand around the nape of her neck to keep her still. "You can't go anywhere yet, Tiffany. We've got at least ten minutes before I can pull out of you."

Ten minutes? He expected her to lie there trapped for ten minutes? Didn't he understand how uncomfortable that was? Forget the way his dick would still shift inside her, sending sizzling streaks of pleasure to her clit, even though what she wanted was to sleep for at least twelve hours. Forget that even the tiniest of movements caused his hard knot to pull against her, making her toes curl and goosebumps rise over her skin out of need.

Sex was new. It was different. She wanted to get away and feel like herself and —

A sting in her lip had her refocusing on the alpha above her, his brows furrowed. "Whatever you're thinking, whatever you're telling yourself, stop it."

"You don't get to tell me what to think."

"Well, I am, so get used to it."

She narrowed her own eyes at the commanding tone in voice. "What do you think gives you that right?"

Kieran's abs contracted, bringing his hips forward so his pelvis ground against her clit before he pulled back enough to tug his knot against her pussy. He didn't pull out of her, couldn't, but the point was clear and forced a whine from her. "I think being knotted inside you gives me that right, at least while you can't get away. Besides, I'm not trying to control you, but whatever was going on there? It was nothing good. If you insist on entertaining it, I expect you to at least share it with me."

She parted her lips, but no words came out. It seemed that explaining she needed space was even harder than wanting space.

Kieran used his other hand to caress her bare side. "You're going to be with me for a year. This won't work if you can't even talk to me."

She released a sigh as if that would help her figure it out.

When nothing else came out, Kieran gave a soft growl, an oddly playful sound, before repeating the gentle bite to her bottom lip. "Let me try. You're overwhelmed, because you've never had sex before, and you were hoping to escape and build up your defenses again. You wanted to do this, but it ended up being more than you expected, and you end up knotted and stuck against me, and you want nothing more than to think about what you want away from me?"

"How did you know?"

"You're not the first omega I've dealt with. There's a reason the judge was willing to let me take you for the year."

The words sucked the lust from Tiffany. Was she just a job to him? An obligation? Another omega in a line of ones he liked to knot, train, then release?

The idea prowled inside her, like an ugly stain on something she'd grown to like. She'd foolishly thought about a future, but they had an end date, didn't they? Kieran had never implied he'd want her for longer than the required year.

In fact, he'd admitted he wouldn't have taken on the contract at all except circumstances required it.

Sickness churned in her stomach, and she fought the desire to shove at him again. It would only show him the ache inside her, the stupid part of her as childish as he'd claimed, that had thought for a moment she could have more.

He stroked harder against her side as if to try to coax her back to their conversation. "What did I say?" He asked the question with honesty, lips tipped down.

Tiffany swallowed thickly and shook her head. "Nothing. I'm just tired."

His shrewd eyes searched her face, but he'd find nothing there. She hid the worry and the hurt so far beneath the surface even he couldn't find them.

She'd learned her lesson, hadn't she? Even knotted as she was by Kieran, he didn't want her.

Chapter Fourteen

Kane sat on the bed he'd taken, too much energy running through him for sleep to come. He couldn't get over the sight of Kieran and Tiffany walking in, her wearing his shirt, his scent clinging to her.

Why would she fuck him? What's wrong with me?

Kane caught sight of his arm, the tattoos that ran across so much of his body. From waist to neck hardly an inch was left uncovered, like some addiction he couldn't help.

Stupid question, ain't it? Too many things to list.

He rolled his shoulders, trying to keep from doing anything, because anything he did would be bad. He'd bounced around the idea of waking Tiffany up with his tongue as deep in her cunt as he could manage. He'd bet a few more orgasms and she'd see reason, give him a chance.

But, a chance? He snarled at nothing, like the sound would scare off the ugly thoughts. There was no chance. She was so far above what he could hope for, so why the fuck did it sting? Why care? She should be with someone she could be seen with, someone who could give her what she deserved.

Fuck Marshall and his whole idea. Alphas had been slaughtering each other for thousands of years over omegas. It had always helped to decide who was strong, who could claim those prized females. The idea that a group should settle by sharing one?

He waited for disgust at the thought, but none came. *What the fuck?*

A soft sound traveled through the wall he shared with Tiffany. He stilled, leaning closer as though that would do shit to help him hear.

It happened again. Was it pleasure? A soft moan from her taking care of herself?

Maybe Kieran hadn't been up to the task. Old age could fuck with someone's dick, and no matter how petty, Kane grinned at the thought of Kieran trying to get it up.

He rose, slipping from his room silently. Do as many shady things as he had and moving without making noise became instinct. Her door creaked as he pushed it open, shutting it behind him.

She lay above the covers, that long hair of hers unbound and spread out. At least she'd changed out of Kieran's shirt, something that brought down the desire to claim her, to prove his own possession of her.

Instead, she wore a tank top and a pair of sleeping shorts so tight he could tell from there she wore nothing beneath. The sight of her so unguarded had his dick filling, readying to prove himself, to convince her to pick him.

The sound escaped her lips again, and this time he recognized it.

Fear. Is she having a nightmare?

Kane crossed the room and settled on the bed beside her, placing his hand on her shoulder. "Hey, doll, wake up." He kept his voice soft, not wanting to startle her.

Waking up from a nightmare with someone who looked like him above her wouldn't calm her any.

Her eyebrows twitched, her lips pressed tight together until, through gritted teeth, she let out a more desperate cry.

Kane shook her that time, then. There wasn't anything for him to fight, but she wouldn't be afraid, not when he was there.

Her eyes snapped open, not a speck of grogginess there. No, she woke swinging, small fist flying toward him. It nailed him in the jaw, and while the hit was solid, he didn't react with more than a small jerk of his head.

She twisted, gaze taking in the room in a quick survey until she stopped at Kane. The pink of her tongue peeked out between her plump lips. Her shirt tightened against her chest as she breathed hard and fast.

Neither spoke, neither looked away. Kane wasn't good at talking, at knowing what to say, especially to a female like her. Instead, he offered the only thing he had. His presence.

I'm going fucking nowhere. He thought it like a vow, like he could make her believe it without saying it. Didn't matter what happened, didn't matter if she picked him, he was going exactly nowhere.

A full-body shudder ran through her, the tension leaving her until she leaned forward, head dropping.

Kane took that as his sign. He pressed a kiss to her forehead and gathered her small body into his arms.

She didn't fight him—in fact, she came closer. She plastered every inch of herself to him, doing all but crawling right into his lap. She pressed her nose to his throat, her fingers tight against his sides.

He'd let her hold as tight as she wanted. She could take strips from his skin and he'd smile through it. He'd bled for shit that was a lot less important than this.

"I like how you smell," she whispered.

He huffed a soft laugh. "You can smell me any time, doll."

"He didn't smell like you. He didn't smell right. I knew it, but I ignored it."

Kane tried to move back, tried to see her face, but she wouldn't allow any space between them. "You're smarter than that. You're trouble, and you ain't any good at listening, but you're smart enough to have seen the signs."

He left the question unasked.

Why?

He didn't blame her, but fuck, he wanted to know why, when she knew the alpha had smelled wrong, when she'd damn well known the risks, why had she kept that shit going?

Her breath blew across his throat in a slow sigh. "I was tired. Tired of running, of hiding, of being alone. Claire warned me so many times, but I never wanted to listen. I wanted an alpha. I wanted the life my parents had, that sense of belonging. So, when Randy showed up, when I thought he wanted me for me, I ignored everything else. Nothing else mattered but the fantasy I wanted. Stupid, huh?"

Kane carded his fingers through her soft hair. "Nah, ain't stupid. Everyone wants to belong."

"Not you. You don't care what anyone thinks of you, don't need anyone to want you."

Kane pulled back despite her clutching fingers, risking more than he liked to. "Funny thing is, I do fucking care what some people think. Just ain't that long a list."

Her hands had shifted from his sides so they rested on his bare abs. "How long a list?"

"Pretty much one feisty omega."

Everything stopped when he muttered the truth. Would she let him down easy? She wasn't the sort to laugh at him, too kindhearted for that shit. Nah, she would pat his arm and explain she wasn't interested, tell him that she was interested in someone like Kieran, but that they should stay friends.

What a fucking mistake.

Kane started to move away, to walk out, to escape the room before he had to hear any of it, before he had to see rejection on her face.

She grasped his wrist when he got off the bed, a tight grip that said she wasn't letting him go. "Wait."

He shook his head, gaze down. "Nah, doll, this was a mistake. I'm sorry, okay? Look, I get it. Kieran, he's more your speed, right? This shit is a stupid crush, and I should know better." The excuses poured from his lips, but nothing he said made her loosen her grip.

She lifted her other hand and ran it down his stomach, dipping into the valleys between the muscles of his abs. Each one twitched beneath her steady strokes. When she reached the line of his sweats, she teased her finger past the waist, brushing the head of his cock tucked there.

A growl left his throat, aggressive and pleading at the same time. He wanted to warn her with it, tell her how close he was to the line of his control. He also wanted to beg her to keep going, to want him, at least for right then.

Kane reached out and wrapped his hand in her long hair, pulling it into a tight grasp. "I don't need pity, Tiffany."

She jerked his sweats down, letting his cock bounce free from the clothing. "Pity isn't what I'm feeling."

"Oh yeah? What are you feeling?"

"Let's see if you can figure it out." She dropped her head and wrapped those full lips of hers around his dick in a single motion.

Fuck, this girl is gonna kill me.

The salty taste of Kane filled Tiffany's senses, her lips pulled tight around his thick cock. She closed her eyes to savor the moment, the exploration.

Her nightmare had drifted away as if there was no room for it with Kane. He chased the uneasiness, the fears, the ugliness of the dream until nothing but Kane, his dick and her lips remained. She released his wrist to wrap that hand around his cock but leave it to Kane to not do as she'd expected.

He caught her wrist before she touched him and dropped it to the bed. "Hands down, doll. Let me do this." His words didn't come out smooth, broken instead by lust and need. Each rumbled word stroked through Tiffany's body like a caress.

Kane used his grip in her hair to shift her forward and back again. It made her lips slide over every detail of his length, let her explore it all. She traced her tongue over the raised veins of his shaft, then swirled it around the indent surrounding the head. Even with the pace he set, as his tight grip controlled the speed and depth at which she took him, she played.

She gave in to the fantasy, the new experience. His scent clouded her head and she wanted to bury her nose in his public hair, to inhale him so that between his cock and his scent, she had no space unclaimed by him.

However, when she went forward, when she tried for more, she only pulled against his unshakable grip in her hair.

"Easy, ain't you?"

His words made her whine around him, and despite the soreness of her pussy, she felt gush of wetness against her shorts. *Why does it turn me on when he talks like that?*

He gave her no time to ponder it, to wonder why she enjoyed the way he pushed her, the way he manhandled her even with his words. "Let's see if this fills you up." He yanked her forward, so the head of his cock sank deeper, her lips sliding over his hardness until he neared the back of her throat.

She gagged, unable to help the automatic reaction, but Kane didn't pull back.

He let out a sinful groan, instead. "That feels fucking nice when you do that, but you need a break? You need to stop? Just slap my thigh so I know, huh?"

She tried to nod, but anchored as she was on his dick, she could only open her eyes and cast up a pleading look toward him

What was she pleading for? She didn't even know anymore. She wanted to feel something that overwhelmed her, that made her feel like waiting had been worth it. She wanted him to turn her mindless, to drown her in him and lust until she couldn't think straight.

His steel grip in her hair was at odds with the soft look on his face. Funny that a man who had such a hardened appearance, covered in tattoos and attitude, could give her such a warm look. Here he was, holding all the power, and yet he stared at her like he'd do anything for her.

Tiffany stroked her tongue against the underside of his dick, a clumsy motion with her mouth stretched wide around him, but it was all she could do.

He blinked, as if it woke him up, then gave her that trouble-filled smirk she loved. His gripped tightened again, and this time he held her still while his hips came forward. He tunneled into her hot mouth, his length teasing that point in the back of her throat where she gagged. Still, each time she did, he'd press forward then pull back, tiny, quick thrusts.

Tiffany pulled her breaths in through her nose, taking him deeper each time he forced forward, each time he buried yet another inch into her, taking her as no one had before.

"Your throat is so damn tight," he groaned. "Love the way it grips me when you gag. Omegas are amazing because you are made to be fucked any which way. You took my finger in your ass no problem, you're gonna take my cock down your throat, and you'll love it. You were made for this, weren't you?"

Her moan filled the room, loud because he'd pulled back enough to rub his cock against the inside of his cheek, leaving more of his delicious taste smeared there. His pre-cum covered her tongue and filled her senses, but it only made her long for more.

"One more time, doll. Let's see if I get those pretty lips of yours all the way up." He waited, staring down his body at her, until she offered another almost invisible nod. The moment she gave it, Kane slid his other hand into her hair so he cradled her head, then pulled her forward.

He went farther than before, plunging deeper. He didn't jerk her forward, didn't slam into her. Instead, he delved forward, one deliberate inch after the next. Even when she gagged, when fresh tears ran down her face, he didn't stop. "Swallow," he commanded.

She wished she could see his face, but he'd buried himself so deep, her eyes couldn't see anything but his pelvis, but the bottom line of his tattoos where they sat on his lower stomach.

Tiffany followed his advice, swallowing, surrendering to him and the moment. She relaxed the best she could, gave into the advance of his dick, to her trust that he'd never hurt her. Slapping his thigh, using her out, never even occurred to her.

When she feared she couldn't do it, her lips pressed against his body, his hard abs tickling her nose.

He tightened his fingers against her head and his dick twitched. She expected him to come, to let her have her fill of him, but he didn't.

She released a cry when he pulled back, when he took what she wanted away. Tiffany reached out to claw her nails into his hip, to force him back, but he caught her hands in a steady grip.

"Ain't stopping, but I need a taste of you myself. You've been teasing me with your scent all fucking day." He stroked her cheek, capturing a tear that had fallen from his rough treatment. His smile widened before he licked it from his finger. "Don't pout, doll. I got an idea that I think you can get behind." He leaned in and slid his tongue along her cheek, capturing any other tears there. "Or over. Whatever."

Tiffany was going to ask what he meant, but a heartbeat later, he'd moved her. She gasped as he shifted her, positioning her like he had every right. They ended up with him on his back on the bed and her kneeling above him, her knees spread around his head.

It left her shorts-covered cunt directly above his face, and only inches from his talented mouth.

She scrambled, uncomfortable with the close contact, with the position

Kane grasped her ass, a cheek in each hand to hold her still. He lifted his head and licked the tight fabric over her crotch. The position muffled his voice, but it did nothing to lessen her reaction to it. "Ain't gotta be shy. I'm gonna pull these shorts down and eat you out, doll, and you're gonna forget all about those nerves. Besides, I got something to distract you with anyway." A lift of his hips that made his still solid cock bounce proved his point.

He was right. The moment her gaze locked on his glistening shaft, wet from her saliva and the pre-cum that had leaked over it, that still beaded on the slit at the top, she stopped worrying about how she looked.

Let him see everything. If I can taste him again, I don't care.

Sure enough, Kane pulled her shorts down, angling her body to work them off one leg at a time. The moment he had them off, he spread her knees wider.

The first pass of his pointed tongue through her dripping folds made her legs shake. He didn't stop there, though. Kane wasn't a man to take things slow. Instead, he returned one hand to her ass, fingers digging in, and used his other to spread her cunt wide. It uncovered her clit and gave him access to anything he wanted. "You got one good-looking pussy. I think I'd be happy to die right here, face to face with heaven."

He didn't let the comments simmer before tightening his grip on her ass and burying his face in her cunt.

Tiffany leaned forward, arching her hips for a better angle for him, and sought his cock with her lips. She encircled his shaft with her hand, using it to guide him toward her hungry lips. The taste of him was her reward when she fed him into her mouth, the solid mass of him as reassuring as the growl he let out against her pussy.

She closed her eyes, the warring wants inside her tearing her apart. She wanted to feel more of his tongue, to ride his lips and lose herself in the sensation. She also wanted to taste him, to swallow as much of him down as she could. No matter how she tried to focus on the two sensations, she could grasp neither well.

As if he knew it, Kane took the hand that had grasped her ass and set it on the back of her head. He lifted his hips to fuck into her mouth, shallow and quick. His tongue mirrored the movements, driving deep into her pussy while he rubbed the fingers holding her open against her clit.

The feeling of so many things at once overtook her until she came with a gasping cry. Her thighs trembled as he only forced his tongue deeper, his face so tight against her folds she had no idea how he could breathe. His cock jerked against her seeking tongue before the first shot of cum emptied from it, painting her tongue in his hot seed. Even as he came, as his body tensed and his dick emptied, the movement of his tongue never slowed, never ended.

He devoured her as though he'd never get enough, as if he were drugged by her scent and her taste, like he could lick her dry.

The thick cum slid down her throat as she swallowed, releasing his dick so she could whimper as he kept her at that height.

He didn't let her rest, didn't let the orgasm end. Instead, each piercing thrust of his stiff, demanding tongue only prolonged the pulsing of her body, the waves of tension that snapped almost painfully inside her.

When he finally slowed, she couldn't hold herself up anymore. She rested all her weight on him, bonelessly spread over his body, nuzzling his softening dick with her cheek.

Kane pressed one more kiss to her cunt, even that pulling a shudder from her. He rolled her over, then adjusted her until she was cradled in his arms, their legs entangled.

Her cunt throbbed, sore from Kieran's knot and overworked from the way Kane had feasted on her. Kane reached down and cupped her sex with his large hand.

She squirmed at the idea of more, at the thought of him pushing her worn-out body into yet another powerful orgasm.

He kissed her head, a possessive grasp over her cunt, long fingers toying with her folds while he avoided her clit. "Easy, doll. Ain't doing anything. Pretty sure you need a rest."

"Why are you doing *that* then?"

"Because I like the way you feel, slippery and open and swollen. Because it took me this long to get your cunt and I ain't ready to let it go just yet." He rubbed his cheek against the top of her head before settling in, those fingers fading into an almost sweet massage.

"Now stop bitching and go to sleep, or else I'm gonna assume you ain't finished yet."

Tiffany lifted her head and stuck her tongue out at him, though he only responded with a chuckle before using the petulant gesture for his own fun. He slid his own tongue against hers and stole a deep kiss, rolling his wrist so his palm stroked her oversensitive clit as a warning.

She whined, breaking the kiss, and went lax against him when he left her clit alone. Served her right for trying to play a game with him, she supposed. Still, the warm glow in her body, the way his mass melded against her, the way it kept the chill away, she snuggled in as close as she could.

Maybe this game is worth playing.

Chapter Fifteen

Marshall carried a box of pastries in one hand, a large container of coffee in the other. After waking at five in the morning to check in with colleagues and going into town to collect the files Sam had sent, he'd thought sugar and caffeine would go over well at the cabin.

Kieran had woken when Marshall had left, resetting the security systems. Kane and Tiffany still slept, but it didn't surprise him. Neither seemed like morning people.

At just past eight, he figured most of the cabin should be awake. They needed to go through Tiffany's belongings and see if they held some clue as to who was after her.

The entire thing had hung on Marshall's mind all night, making sleep difficult. She had Kieran and Kane there, so what did he expect to do? Marshall wasn't a fighter—he wasn't like the other alphas in the house. He'd spent his life learning how to heal, and what use was that to her?

What am I even doing here?

Well, that answer was obvious. Marshall was there because he couldn't not be there, because the moment he'd realized the danger she was in, he'd known he had to be by her side. That instinct he hated, the one he'd spent his life trying to downplay, to control, had refused to be ignored for this.

Though, he had proven himself useful in one area. He was less stubborn than the others, and his steady disposition gave some stability to the chaotic grouping. He was able to talk them down, to get them to listen.

Inside the cabin, he found Kieran, a towel over the dining table and a rifle spread out over it. The sight had Marshall stopping short.

Kieran cocked an eyebrow up before returning his attention to his work cleaning the weapon. "Not a fan of guns?"

"I've spent my life patching people up from what those things do."

"I can teach you to shoot."

"I can teach you to sew up the people you shoot."

Kieran huffed a soft laugh. "It wouldn't do any good. I don't shoot many people, but the ones I do? Some stitching wouldn't save them."

Marshall set the food and coffee on the kitchen counter, seeing as the table was occupied. "Do you think Tiffany should see that?"

"She's tougher than you think. Besides, maybe it would do her some good to get a clear idea of what she's up against."

"She's been targeted at least three times we know of. I think she is aware of the danger."

"*She* can speak for herself." Tiffany came out from the hallway, her wet hair braided back and the strong scent of lavender and lemon following her.

Kieran wrinkled his nose. "Why are you using that? I think we're past you needing to hide what you are."

She popped open the lid to the box of pastries. "It's all Alison left. Why? Not a fan of lavender?"

"No. Lavender and lemon cover scents, strong enough to dilute most alpha and omega pheromones. It makes me feel as though someone is covering my eyes."

"Well, we can pick up other shampoo in town if you want. Until then? This is all I've got."

Kieran offered a short, half-hearted growl before opening the case his sniper rifle had come in. "We need to go through the files Sam sent. He's hoping Tiffany can pick out someone she's seen. We can't hide forever, so we need to find out what they want."

Kane came out, stealing the muffin Tiffany had taken from her hand. "Sounds good to me."

"No one asked your opinion." Kieran snapped the rifle case shut after packing the weapon away.

"No one had to."

"Knock it off, you two. I can't take your bickering. If either of don't want to be here, leave." Tiffany left the muffin with Kane, grabbing a coffee mug from the shelf instead.

A glare passed between Kieran and Kane, as though they could settle the fight silently and not piss off the omega in the room.

When she turned back toward them with the cup, both alphas jerked their gazes down like children caught doing wrong.

The entire situation was enough for Marshall to laugh. *Figures it only takes one feisty omega to send two alphas like that running.*

Tiffany tossed a grin Marshall's way, then poured herself a cup of coffee. She added creamer and sipped the steaming liquid. Her eyelids drifted shut as she drew tendrils of steam into her nose. Kieran took a step toward the door before gesturing at Kane. "Come on. If you refuse to leave, you can at least be helpful by getting the rest of the files."

Kane popped the rest of the muffin into his mouth, then brushed the crumbs from his hands. "What, you mean you ain't enjoying my charm and boyish good looks?"

Marshall shook his head as the two walked out. Childish bickering was better than another fist fight.

"Are they ever going to stop that?" Tiffany toyed with the tie at the bottom of her braid.

"Probably not." At her glare, he only smiled. "Boys will be boys, Tiffany. Even if they work this out, even if they decide not to kill one another, I suspect they'll always try to one up one another."

"Men never stop dick measuring?"

"Something like that." He grasped the end of her braid and tugged softly on it. "You look like you didn't get enough sleep."

A blush covered her cheeks. "The lavender smell doesn't bother you?"

He used his grip on her braid to tug her closer, until the front of her body melded to him. "No. Omegas use it in my line of work so often it doesn't affect me. I can smell beneath it." He leaned closer, drawing a deep breath. Sure enough, under the oils that had been in the shampoo, under the sharp lemon and the heavy lavender, he could taste the omega beneath. For such a brash spirit, her scent was soft, sweet.

"How do I smell?"

He pulled his lips into a smile at the breathless way she asked. "Like temptation." As he spoke, his lips brushed hers, a gentle teasing that riled his other side.

For her part, Tiffany closed the distance. She tilted her head to take the kiss he hinted at, sliding her lips against his, the taste of vanilla from her coffee on her breath.

Marshall let himself have the kiss. He grasped the back of her neck to further tilt her head, and when her lips parted, he delved inside.

His cock pressed against her flat stomach, a roll of his hips grinding him against her. He considered the height of the counter behind her. He could move the box out of the way and set her there. A quick shifting of her clothing and he'd have access.

He'd have a willing omega cunt wrapped tightly around his knot, finally. That ache inside him would ease.

Can I keep my alpha side under control then? What if I can't?

Marshall broke the kiss, chilled by the thought. His insistent cock didn't care, but he did. He tilted his head, forehead to hers to keep his lips from hers. "We don't have much privacy."

"So?" She darted her tongue out to swipe across his bottom lip. "I don't care."

"You will when Kane and Kieran get back. They're already at each other's throats. I don't think we need the complication of them finding me inside you."

Her heavy sigh warmed his lips. "Are you always the responsible one?"

Marshall ran his fingers from her neck and down her chest, tracing her sternum between her breasts. "Well, I can't exactly leave that to you, can I?"

She hit her palms against his chest in a playful shove before she muttered, "Smart-ass."

She pulled away, that sway in her step as she collected her cup of coffee and headed toward the living room. That omega tested every limit he had, pushed at all the lines he'd so carefully drawn for himself.

He had to be careful.

Chapter Sixteen

Marshall sat on the couch, the television playing despite him not watching it. Instead, he worked on his laptop.

He wasn't needed for the cases. For each file he opened, he found the doctor who filled in had dealt with the issues as he would have. Each patient appeared to be doing well, to be healing as well as he would have expected.

Still, working made him relax. He understood work, understood his place. When he was elbow-deep in cases, when he helped omegas, when he saved lives, he knew he had a place. The world made sense.

That feeling fled when he was faced with Tiffany, with her sadness. They'd gone through the boxes of files, through the pages of pictures and names and places, but none of it had sparked anything in her. She didn't recognize anyone, had never been to any of the places mentioned, knew nothing. It meant that after their time in the cabin, after Sam's work, they seemed no closer to an answer about who was after her. The stress hung on her, and he didn't know how to help.

"I didn't expect this to be your sort of show," came the voice he'd been thinking about.

Marshall lifted his gaze to the TV, which had switched to some dating show when he hadn't been paying attention. A woman stood there with two men behind her. They argued over which one she should pick.

He huffed a soft laugh. "What? Didn't see me as a trash TV sort of man?"

She sat on the couch beside him, all but collapsing. Some of the sadness had disappeared from her features, leaving that spark he knew already. "Not really. You seem like a documentaries sort of man."

"You think me that dull?" He leveled a grin at her, especially at how wrong she was. He used to watch documentaries, mostly because he'd felt he needed to. He'd thought watching complicated documentaries somehow proved he was smarter, better. Only, as his work had become more difficult, he'd realized that there was nothing better than relaxing, letting his mind shut off while watching pointless action flicks with far more car chases and explosions than was necessary.

"I don't think you're dull," she admitted, twisting toward him.

It wasn't the words he heard, though. Instead, it was the way she said them. It was the lust in them, the lust he didn't think she even knew was there.

It hung in the air, the delicious scent that blossomed in the room. Heady and deep and primitive.

He drew it in, let it soak into him. His body responded as if she controlled it, as if the only thing that mattered was satisfying her need. His cock hardened, the base aching with a desire to knot her, to finally feel blood fill the thick area at the root of his dick, to lock inside an omega and feel her snug pussy pull tight around him.

"Most people would," he said, his voice deep and rough with want. "Most people would think I was boring. Far too boring for a girl who likes to knee men in the balls and gets into as much trouble as you do."

Her smile widened, that flash of trouble and life he so enjoyed. She leaned in closer, pressing her hand to his shoulder. "I think you're way more fun than you want to admit," she said.

His eyebrow lifted. "You think so?"

She took his laptop, closed it, and set it on the table. "Yep. I think you just need some motivation."

"What sort of motivation?"

She rose and peeled off her shirt. He saw the fluid shift over her body, the way one side of her ribcage arched up while the other lowered, the line of her body elongating. She wore no bra, so her breasts came into view, the weight and movement causing them to sway, the nipples pebbling beneath the chill and his gaze.

As quickly, she slid her thumbs into the waist of her sweats and slipped them down her legs. She dropped the cloth to the ground, so it pooled around her ankles, leaving her nude.

As she stood there, hiding nothing, on display, he was humbled.

He would never be able to deserve that girl.

Tiffany slid into Marshall's lap, his hips forcing her thighs to spread wide. It was easy to think of him as safe, as the easygoing one, as the healer. It made her forget he was an alpha, that he carried the bulk common to their designation, larger than most betas but muscles not so defined.

However, when against him like she was, she couldn't forget it. The wide set of his shoulders, the natural size of his body, it all tempted her. He didn't carry the muscle of the others, but that didn't mean he was weak or small.

He set his hands on her bare hips, his fingers against her skin. "You're playing a dangerous game."

She angled her hips so she ground against his lap, against his hard-on that offered a delicious friction for her. "I'm not playing."

A laugh from behind them had her turning to find Kane taking a seat. He let his knees fall wide, jeans showing off his impressive erection. "Don't mind me, doll. Just taking in the show."

Marshall teased his fingers up her side. "Do you mind if he stays?"

Tiffany tilted her head back, surrendering.

A soft bite to her pulse reprimanded her silence. "You need to tell me. Can he stay? If not, we'll go somewhere more private. It's up to you."

The weight of Kane's dark eyes, the low growl he released with every breath, all gave her an answer. He sat there like some silent guardian, his tattoos and his lean frame, and his menace all more attractive than any of them should have been.

"Stay," she whispered.

"Good fucking answer." Kane grunted softly and a rustle of fabric said he'd undone his pants. Even without looking, Tiffany could picture him wrapping his large palm around his dick.

Marshall dragged his hands up her sides to cup her breasts. His touch was strong but restrained, as always.

He pressed the tips of his fingers into the weight of her breasts with a tight grope. Her pebbled nipples stuck out like offerings to him, ones he worshiped by sliding his thumbs against them.

Tiffany moaned at his stroke, at the way her nipples gave beneath his touch. She pulled her shoulders back to stick her chest out, to beg for more. The chill of the room didn't matter against the heat of his hands or the heat the burned inside him.

Another growl filled the room, lower and more dangerous. *Kieran.*

Marshall caught her chin to keep her gaze on him, her attention locked on him. "It's still your choice. Do you want to stop?" His fingers dug into her chin where he gripped her, but he continued the touches to her breast. He closed his fingers around her nipple to tweak it, pulling until she gasped.

The scent of all three males, their heavy gazes and deep growls filling the room and her mind made her cunt clench around nothing, made her want all of them. She needed them to come forward, to feel Kieran's rough hands, to feel Kane's talented tongue. The temptations of them all, the need to feel each of them against her made her feverish with want.

Tiffany undid Marshall's pants, yanking at them with hard pulls, desperate to feel him.

Marshall used his grip on her chin to guide her forward, to take a kiss so deep and passionate she nearly lost herself in it. Only the need for his cock kept her hands moving, had her reaching into his boxers to grasp his hard length.

He blew a warm breath past her lips, masculine and with the same restrained need he always wore, that distance, that holding back.

Still, Tiffany danced her fingers over his dick, tracing around the thick head, the slit at the top, down to his heavy balls. At the base of his cock, she could feel the area where his knot would swell, already thickened with need. To think he'd never had an omega before, that he'd never felt the sensation of locking inside a female, something that had to be as bone-deep as her own heat.

"Are you going to let me have you?" Despite it being a question, the words left his lips like a demand. He lifted his hips, pushing his shaft against her hand.

Tiffany answered by rising on her knees and positioning him against her pussy.

Kane's laugh made her clench. "Fuck, doll, you got any idea how well he's gonna stretch you? You can't tell from your angle, I bet, but those lips of yours are gonna spread wide when he fucks you." The filth he said, the way he said it without the barest hint of shame, had her dripping with need.

Marshall grasped her hip as she lowered herself. His blunt head caught her entrance, her body fighting his thickness.

He wasn't as long as Kieran, but he was thicker, so thick her pussy resisted his demand for entry.

"You can do it, girl." Kieran's words came out less like reassurance and more like a command. Not only could she, but she would.

Marshall set his other hand on her waist and twisted her. The quick movement drew a startled gasp as she tried to reorient.

It left her still in his lap, but now with her back to Marshall's chest and her front toward the room. She faced Kane and Kieran, who sat in the large armchairs across from the couch.

Both had their own pants undone and their dicks out, their hungry gazes locked on her.

Marshall moved one of his hands from her hip and slid it up her body, to her breast. He again captured a nipple between tight fingers. "Lower yourself onto me," he growled out.

The lust in the eyes of the alphas had her reaching forward to finger her clit, the first brush so strong she cried out. Her clit throbbed, and even as she rubbed it, it wasn't enough.

She wanted to be filled. She wanted his thick cock to take her, wanted to feel how his wide his knot would grow inside her. Hell, she wanted to struggle against that fullness, to know she couldn't do anything but accept it, but give in to it.

He put pressure on her hip, a reminder of her task. *Right.*

Tiffany drew in one deep breath before letting her weight settle, letting it press her against him harder. The pressure grew until her body gave in, until the thick head of his cock slipped past her the tight lips of her cunt.

The sounds that came from Marshall and Tiffany competed. Tiffany's were throaty and wanton, whereas Marshall's was aggression — barely leashed and snarling against her ear.

She wanted that grip he had on it to snap. She wanted to feel him not holding back, to not have him keeping some of himself away.

"You're so tight," he whispered to her, low enough it sounded like a filthy secret between them, a funny thing since the other alphas saw everything. "Your body is squeezing me, and I'm only an inch inside."

Kane's thumb stroked over the head of his cock, over the pre-cum at the top. "That's right, doll, fuck yourself on him." He spread his thighs wider, leaning back.

Tiffany did as he said, her fingers still moving as she lowered herself. Each massive inch she took of Marshall's dick stretched her cunt, and drenched as she was, it still was a fight. Every time she lowered her body, when he slid farther into her, she gasped at the fullness.

Kieran leaned forward, his biceps tensing as he fucked into his grasp. He ran his tongue along his bottom lip, a slow stroke as if he could taste her from that far away. "How does it feel, girl?"

When she didn't answer, Marshall delivered a hard pinch to her ass. "He asked you a question."

"Full," she gasped out.

"You can do better than that," Kane said. "Use those fancy words you got. Tell us how it feels to take him like that."

Tiffany closed her eyes and dropped her head back against Marshall's shoulder as she kept sliding down his cock, as each roll of her hips took him deeper. "He's thick, and it feels like he won't fit."

A growl in her ear said Marshall liked the suggestion.

It kept her lips moving, kept the words coming out. She whined as a lift of his hips sent his cock delving impossibly deeper into her. "It stings." She set the hand not still playing with her clit on the one of his, grasping her hip. Her nails bit into it.

"A little more, girl. You've nearly taken him all. The fact you can stretch like that is amazing, that your cunt spreads that wide. It makes me wonder what other fun we could have with you," Kieran said.

Marshall released her breast and grasped her hips in his solid hands. He used them to pull her down as he lifted his hips up, seating the last inch of his dick into her. It filled her so much she could only breathe as she adjusted. He tightened his grip and released, the tentative grasping of a man who still held himself back.

Tiffany reached forward, setting her hands on his knees for balance, her body spread out over his lap. She lifted and sank down again, a shallow movement that caused his thickness to stroke against her. Each place where he teased her walls drove her higher.

A more vicious snarl came from behind her, then Marshall jerked her down on his length.

"Yes," she gasped out at the roughness, at the way it felt real. *That's what I need.*

Marshall did it again, using his grip to lift her then pull her down. He used it to fuck her, taking her at his speed, taking her the way he wanted to. He didn't wait, he didn't ask, only took. Being used like that stroked her deeper than even his heavy cock, reached into her in a way that melted her defenses. Even the sound he made had turned primal, and the thickness at the base of his cock, already swelling, said what he needed.

"You feel that?" Kane's gaze was locked between her thighs as he spoke. "Bet his cock is already thick, like he's already got a knot. It's because he ain't never knotted an omega before. Bet it's been swelling a bit every time he smelled your pretty cunt, getting thicker, waiting. You gonna let him knot you?"

Yes. Please, yes.

Tiffany wanted nothing more. Well, she'd have rather Kane and Kieran be closer, to feel their hands and their lips and their breaths on her while she was knotted by Marshall.

Only, the pressure didn't grow. That possessive snarl from Marshall cut off, and he went still behind her. He held her hips so tight it brought out a whimper.

As fast as it happened, he moved her again. Not down, not against him, but instead he pulled her off him. The quick withdraw shocked her, the sudden emptiness as he pulled out of her cunt, as he shifted her over onto the couch beside him.

Marshall rose, tucking his still hard cock into his pants.

"What are you doing?" Tiffany twisted to sit on the couch, pulling her legs toward her chest.

Marshall avoided looking her in the eye as he buttoned his pants. "Nothing."

Kane and Kieran had stopped, gazes darting between Tiffany and Marshall but saying nothing.

"Nothing? Then what the hell was that?"

He took a few steps backward, as if he needed distance between them. "It was nothing."

"So what? Am I not good enough for you? Do you have other wonderful options out there?"

"It's not you." He turned and nailed her with an empty, haunted look that was nothing like he normally wore. "I won't ever knot you, Tiffany." The words came out with such certainty, they were like a slap to her. He left no room to discuss it, to come to an understanding.

Suddenly, everything crashed in on her. All those stupid fantasies she'd had where she thought a future would happen with the three males became clear. She was sitting there, naked, with three males who refused to give her anything real.

As if he could see it on her face, Marshall's expression softened. "Tiffany."

"Don't you try to be nice to me. I don't need you pretending."

"I'm not pretending."

"Of course you are! You're pretending all the time, pretending to be something you're not, pretending we might have a future, pretending you'll give me something you have no intention of following through on."

Tiffany didn't stop there, though. She was invigorated by letting out the truth she'd hidden, that she'd buried deep down. She turned a hard glare on Kane. "And you? You don't tell me anything! You don't tell me where you got your scars from, you don't tell me about your past, but you want me to tell you everything. And any time it seems like we're getting somewhere, you bolt like a coward."

Kane crossed his arms and said nothing, though his lips pressed together tight.

Tiffany leveled one more look Kieran's way, to the stoic alpha who managed to still look detached despite the way his cock hadn't gone down, the way it still showed beneath his hastily pulled up jeans.

"And you—"

"What about me?"

She narrowed her eyes. "You want me to open up and to trust you, but you're giving me a timeline. You expect me to be happy with being one out of a long fucking line of omegas for you. Guess what? It's not enough!" She rose, anger pushing her as she didn't hide behind the lies they'd told her, the lies she'd told herself. "None of you are giving me enough, and I'm not going to be happy with getting something. I've done that, accepted things because I pretended they were enough, because I pretended I could still have what I wanted, but I'm done with it. I'm over making do with things that aren't what I want."

Marshall kept part of himself locked away and refused to talk about it. He wouldn't even tell her why.

Kieran had signed a contract for her for a year and had given her no reason to think he wanted more than that.

Kane had scars covering his chest that he would not speak of or let her ask about.

They kept taking her body, but none would give her more. None of them even gave her the feeling she might get more in the future.

She swallowed hard at the reality, at not being able to do a damn thing to fix it. Yelling made her feel better for a moment, but it wouldn't change anything. She couldn't fix people who didn't want to change, and the three stubborn assholes didn't want to change. She'd yet again chased after something recklessly, ignoring that it wasn't real, that she couldn't catch it.

After everything, this is where we are?

She pulled the necklace, the chain catching her neck, likely leaving a mark, until it broke. She hurled it against the wall, as if that could release the hurt inside her, the anger, like breaking it would solve anything. She'd worn it like some protection charm, like a testament to some nameless omega who had suffered, but suddenly the life of an omega seemed too painful.

No matter what she did, she wanted three men who wouldn't give themselves to her.

Their voices followed her as she left the room with hard, sure steps, but she ignored them when she shut the door with a click, shutting them out like they had done to her.

They could fuck themselves for all she cared, but she'd reached her limit of arrogant, selfish, emotionally-inept alphas.

She was done.

Chapter Seventeen

Marshall ground the heels of his palms against his eyes as he sat outside. The crisp mountain air did nothing to clear the haze in his head or the discontent in his chest.

He'd hurt her.

The fact had been written across her face as she'd withdrawn to her room, as she'd not only closed the door but locked it. Even as he hated himself for hurting her, he didn't regret his decision.

Something tapped his shoulder. He turned to find Kieran standing there, beer bottle held out.

"Thanks."

Kieran pulled over a chair and sat beside him. "Well, that could have gone better."

"You think?" Marshall twisted off the cap and took a sip of the cold beer.

"Could have gone better? That shit was a cluster-fuck." Kane always was the linguist. Instead of pulling over a chair, he sat on the railing of the patio. "The fuck is wrong with your dick?"

Marshall might have been angry at the blunt question if not for the absurdity. Instead, he chuckled and shook his head. "Nothing is wrong with it."

"Then what the hell was that?"

Marshall gave himself a moment by taking another drink, then set the beer on top of his thigh. "I've spent my entire adult life seeing what alphas were capable of. You can't tell me you don't feel that side of you, that it isn't there beneath all that civility you wear."

Kane and Kieran had the decency not to argue his point, at least not right away. They both cast their gazes down at their own drinks, the silence reigning as they all considered it.

Kieran answered first. "I've seen my share of damage alphas have done. It's not that they were alphas, though. Betas kill and rape, too, you know."

"Sure, anyone can, but that's a cop out and you know it. How many times do you smell an omega and want to mount her? How often does someone push your buttons, and that side of you, that animalistic part controlled by all that instinct want to tear their throat out?"

"Yeah, fuck, who doesn't want to do a little throat-tearing with assholes? Doesn't mean we do it."

"We don't do it because we control that side, but the fact we have to is what scares me. What if I lose one day? What if I'm not strong enough to leash it?" Marshall rubbed his palm over the top of his thigh to wipe off the sweat or condensation from the beer. "When I'm close to Tiffany, it's worse. The rest of my life I dealt with that side easily, but around her? It roars inside my head, and I'm terrified of what it could do if I lose control."

"You think if you knot her, you could hurt her?"

"Maybe. I know I'm not willing to risk it."

"Then you better be fucking willing to lose her, because that girl ain't gonna be satisfied with that." Kane held his own beer between his fingers, dangling down over his lap.

"And I'm supposed to take advice from you? Because neither of you has done a good job at this whole relationship thing."

Kieran huffed, leaning back. "Well, I knotted her at least. A step ahead from either of you."

That had Kane laughing, an odd reaction compared to the jealousy that usually sprang between them. "You're such an asshole."

"Fair enough." Kieran took another drink. "We have to make this right."

"And how the fuck do you suggest that? Because from where I'm sitting, we've all fucked that girl over."

"Yes, we have. So, let's fix it." Kieran took one deep breath before uttering words he didn't feel but had to say. "I'm willing to step back. I don't want to hurt her anymore, and this entire pulling her in three directions thing is only causing pain."

"Fuck that," Kane growled. "She's under contract with you for a year. Not like anyone would sign her over to me, so unless she finishes her year, she ain't getting her life back. I'll leave."

Marshall let out a laugh that lacked warmth as he shook his head, the answer obvious and frustrating when they failed to ever see it. "You two still don't get it, do you?"

"Get what?"

"Kane, what would have happened if Kieran hadn't been there to help Tiffany the night with Randy? Or with the judge afterward?" Marshall asked.

Kane drew his hands into fists. "She might not have made it since he helped take Randy out, and if she did, she'd have been thrown into the system like property."

Marshall shot a look at Kieran. "And what if Kane hadn't been there when she broke into that building? Or when she went to her apartment?"

Nothing showed on Kieran's face except for a tightening of his lips, the subtle, easy to miss shift that said the words affected him. "She might have been killed or abducted."

"And let's not forget the man who broke into my home looking for her. My point is that, thus far, it has taken all three of us to keep her safe. She isn't in there because she feels like she doesn't want one of us. She's in there because we've been too busy thinking about ourselves instead of her. We've been more worried about our hangups and our problems than her."

"You've been beating around this fucking bush for too long. Just fucking say it," Kane said.

"If we're serious about this, I think we need to consider making it official. Tiffany has proven to be more than any one of us can deal with on our own. She's outsmarted each of us repeatedly, and add in her recklessness? She needs a minimum of three to keep up with her. We've promised things that none of us can give on our own. I don't think any one of us could keep her happy alone, but I've got to say, I don't mind the taste we've gotten of the life all four of us could build."

Kane huffed a sound that was neither acceptance nor denial. "You think she's going to go for that? Because I ain't thinking having three alphas on her ass is something any omega wants."

"Shouldn't that be her choice? We've torn at her trying to get her to pick, and she hasn't picked. If anything, she's shown she wants each of us in a different way. And can either of you say you minded when she was in my lap while you watched? Do you think I couldn't feel how she pressed her chest out for the two of you? This is what she wants even if she doesn't realize it yet." Marshall tucked his hands into his pockets, hoping they'd see reason, that they'd listen to him for once.

The issue of him, of if he could ever let himself go, that he couldn't resolve. He had no idea if he'd ever trust himself enough, but he knew there was only one way this would ever have a chance of working.

"The only question is if you two are willing to try it," Marshall said.

Kieran exchanged a loaded look with Kane. So many years as, perhaps not enemies, but certainly not friends. Could they put it all behind them? Could they form something new with the omega they both were hopelessly in love with? Could they be happy with that future? All those things passed in the gaze between them.

Kane nodded. "Fuck it, I'll try."

"I will as well," Kieran said.

Marshall laughed, the chuckle softer than it had been before. "Well then, I hope Tiffany gets some good rest, because tomorrow she's going to have three mates to deal with."

Chapter Eighteen

The hot water had seared away the night before from Tiffany's skin. It didn't remove the memory of the fight, of the things she'd said, but at least it made her feel reborn, like the scolding water could help her start over. She'd stood beneath the water until it had turned cold, until her skin had wrinkled, and she'd been forced from the spray by a parched throat and a growling stomach.

The cold air rushed in when she opened the door, when she risked a peek into the hallway. She'd avoided the men all morning, having no wish to deal with the night before.

She would have taken back the words if she could have. They'd been true, but that made them worse. She'd rather have shouted something fake, something that didn't reveal so much of her. Instead, they heard exactly how much they'd hurt her, and how much she should have expected it.

Her bare feet pressed into the carpet as she braved the main living space, knowing that avoiding them any longer wasn't possible. She wasn't the type willing to starve.

In the living room, she found them. Kane sat on the kitchen island, a puzzle cube in his hands, his gaze locked on it. He wore no shirt, the colorful expanse of his chest tempting her even as she waited for him to notice her. *How could he think I wouldn't want him?*

At the other side of the room, Marshall and Kieran sat around the table, pointing at the computer screen, discussing something there.

Had she gone too far? Would they decide she was no longer worth the trouble? What would she do if they kicked her out? Could she handle being tossed aside by the men she loved?

The word stuck the moment it broke free in her mind. *Love? Do I love them?*

The answer was obvious, even if she hated to admit it.

Yes, you idiot, you love them.

She sighed, and the loud sound drew their attention. Being the focal point of three alphas made her gulp. Kane's feet thudded against the tile floor when he hopped off the island. He set the toy down, forgotten as if she were a far more interesting puzzle. "How you feeling, doll?"

She winced at the pet name.

The more she stood there, the surer she was that they were going to leave. No, not leave. Not them. They'd protect her because they had to, and they'd throw her away afterward. They'd made their limits clear. They'd each made no secret of how they felt, about what they were willing to give and what they weren't.

They'd keep her safe because they were men of honor, and the moment they knew she was safe, they'd get rid of her. Tiffany would have nothing, yet again.

Only this time, she'd know what she wanted, what she'd almost had. She'd gotten a taste of it and losing it would hurt her beyond what she was ready to deal with, more than she thought she could handle.

The best defense...

"I'm fine," she said with a haughty attitude. "Nothing to worry yourself about."

Kieran's eyebrow cocked up, but he said nothing.

Tiffany turned and slipped past Kane, trying for nonchalance, for that general attitude of 'I don't give a fuck,' that other people managed so well. "Look, there's been no movement on my apartment or the other houses, and we haven't figured out why anyone would be after me. I think maybe we made a big mistake."

"Excuse me?" Marshall asked, still seated at the table.

She pulled together her courage and turned to face all three of them. "We came up here because we thought I was in danger. I'm not. So, why don't we head back into town? You guys have lives to get back to, and you don't need me getting in the way of them. Besides, I have a life, too."

"You're too smart to say something that fucking stupid," Kane said. "You know damned well we ain't taking you back until we're sure you ain't in danger anymore."

The nobility bit at her. He hadn't said he wanted her to stay. No, they couldn't get rid of her until they were sure she was safe.

She set her hands on her hips and tried to press her chest out like they did, tried to look as big and imposing and impossible as they all managed. "Fine, then I'll disappear. Sure, starting over sounded nice, but I've been on the run for a year. I can do it again."

"You're not running again, and don't you try to tell me that's what you want."

"What I want is to not be trapped in this cabin anymore." Tiffany let her voice rise, covering her panic at being thrown away by the frustration at being trapped. It was easier to let them think she hated being there than it was to let them see the real problem. "I want my life back, and I'm sure you all will be thrilled to get yours back."

Kieran took a step closer, his body seeming even larger. "That's not happening."

Tiffany moved backward, but without her realizing it, Kane had shifted so he stood behind her. She backed right into him.

Still, she drew her hands into fists and tried to sound calm and collected. "We all know this was a bad idea. You guys aren't interested, and I'm clearly not what you want, so let's call it. There's no reason to keep pushing when it isn't working."

Another step and Kieran stood only a heartbeat away. He tilted his head down to look into her eyes. "What is this? Are you trying to push us away?"

Tiffany dropped her head back so she could stare up at him, into his dark eyes. It made her lean more against Kane. "You don't want me." Her voice dropped to a whisper. "Let's forget it all."

Kieran brought his hand up and brushed his pointer finger along the neckline of her top. A line of goosebumps lifted in the wake of the teasing touch. His hair, dark with the bits that had turned silver, was pushed back. His eyes, as solid as ever, trapped her. "I don't think I'm inclined to forget anything about you."

The touch intoxicated her. It slipped beneath the fear and ignited something else inside her, something that made her pussy clench and chased away the worry. The scent of alphas overpowered everything else and made her needy, made her want all the things she'd told herself she couldn't have.

"Don't do this." Even as she spoke, Tiffany pulled her shoulder blades together and pressed her chest forward. "I'm tired of fighting, of wanting things none of you want to give me. I'm not going to pick. I can't play this game anymore."

Kane's deep voice rumbled against her ear. "This ain't playing, doll, and in case you missed it, we ain't asking you to choose. In fact, there's only one question you get to answer right now."

Tiffany gulped at the way his voice crawled down her body. "What's the question?"

Marshall grasped her chin to turn her face toward him, his large body closing her in, surrounding her so she was trapped between the three alphas. His eyes, dark and serious and familiar peered at her from his honest face. "Are you ready to take the three of us, omega?"

As if the rush of wetness between her thighs wasn't enough of an answer so she nodded.

Yes, I need this.

Kane groaned at the scent that wafted off the omega. She trembled between them, and never had she seemed so small before. All that attitude and mischievous nature damned near purred at the proximity of the three of them.

He snuck his tongue out to trace the shell of her ear, her natural scent filling his nostrils, not overshadowed by the lemon and lavender from the shampoo. She must have not used them, and he was fucking glad. He'd take her scent and the arousal that poured out of her over that fake shit any day.

Marshall dragged his thumb across her pouty bottom lip. "You know, I don't believe we're quite over you telling us off like you did."

Tiffany parted her lips to answer, but Marshall took the opportunity to slide his thumb into her waiting mouth.

"I think anything you have to say will only get you into more trouble. Your best bet would be to remain silent while we work out our annoyances with you."

Ah, there went that scent again, thick and heady and enough to make him drool. He wished he was buried between her thighs.

Kane leaned down and offered a gentle kiss to her throat before nipping the area over her racing pulse, scraping his teeth across her soft skin. He pulled away long enough for Kieran to remove her shirt and reveal the tantalizing lines of her stunning body.

The curve of her lower back and the sharp points of her shoulder blades stood out on her pale skin. The end of her braid followed her spine, and each muscle sat rigid beneath the surface.

Nervous?

Good. She should be.

Kieran dropped to a crouch as he pulled her jeans down her curvy legs.

Kane chuckled. "Nothing underneath, huh? You might want to snarl and pull away, but if that ain't a sign of what you're wanting, I don't know what is."

Kieran slipped his fingers between her thighs, and the way her hips rocked forward said she enjoyed the attention. "She's drenched."

All the reasons Kane had to be against this vanished. They disintegrated into nothing between the lust-drunk look in Tiffany's eyes as her full lips wrapped around Marshall's thumb and the way her hips shifted forward against Kieran's seeking fingers.

Kane pinned her with his grasp on her arms, watching her chest rise and fall with uneven and needy breaths, and between them all, they'd stripped her bare.

Not of her clothing—well, of that, too—but of her defenses. The way she'd argued with them and tried to pull away had been her trying to build walls around her. They'd hurt her badly enough, she'd needed to lick her wounds. She'd wanted safety, and it shamed him that they hadn't been the safe place she'd sought.

Why did I fight this so hard? Kane groaned when Marshall drew his thumb back, then pressed it deeper into Tiffany's mouth. The motion was so filthy, as if he fucked her with his thumb, her saliva clinging to his skin. Kane's cock hardened at the sight, at the memory of how good Tiffany's soft and giving mouth felt wrapped tight around his dick.

Her eyes drifted closed as she let Marshall slide his thumb past her lips, the tension sliding from her body. She leaned back against Kane's grip as if she trusted him to make sure she didn't fall.

And he'd make sure of it. Fuck, he'd do anything to keep her there, to keep her safe. Kane had spent his life looking out for himself, since no one else had ever bothered to worry about him, but for the first time in a long time, he cared about someone else more.

The memory of the scars threatened to come back, but he shoved it away. Fuck before. Fuck his whole past. None of it deserved a moment of thought, and certainly not there.

Tiffany arched her back, pressing harder against him, a cry on her lips.

"How many fingers is that?" Kane asked as he slid his hands from her arms to her breasts, toying with the hard nubs between his rough fingers.

"Two." Kieran's biceps flexed, and even without being able to see, Kane could picture those fingers fucking into her.

"Only two?" Kane tsk'd, tone soft but mocking. "I know you can take more than that, doll."

"She took my knot, so she can stretch." Kieran's arm moved faster, and Tiffany's breathing matched the frantic pace.

The fact that Kieran had fucked her and he'd knotted her should have drawn up some jealousy.

Those feeling didn't show. Well, he had some envy. He wanted to fuck her, too. He wanted to feel the way her pussy would grip him, wanted to lock deep inside her and hear her whimper as he wrung every last orgasm she could handle out of her and a few extra for good measure. It wasn't anger, though, wasn't jealousy exactly.

Instead of dissecting that shit, because Kane hadn't ever been an introspective sort of man, he tightened his fingers around her nipples in a harsh pinch. "You know, these tits would look fucking pretty with some clips on them. You ever try that?"

She shook her head even as she arched into his touch, trying to lessen the pressure.

He hadn't asked the question because he thought she ever had. Girl was too innocent for that shit. He'd asked because he wanted her thinking about it, wanted her realizing how far he needed to push her, all the things he wanted to do to her curvy little body.

It had him groaning to think of her at their mercy, spread out and all theirs.

Theirs. Hell, he didn't even think of her as his alone anymore.

Instead of thinking about it, he released her nipples, then rubbed across them, knowing how sensitive they'd be as the blood rushed back into them. Sure enough, she gasped and pushed against him, trying to get away from the stimulation.

Deny it all she wanted, the girl got off on it. It was in the sounds she made, in the shiver of her body, but most of all?

That she came—hard. She unlatched from Marshall's finger, mouth open on a silent cry. She shoved her hips forward as if Kieran's fingers weren't nearly enough, not deep enough, not thick enough, and her body went rigid.

Kane kissed her shoulder while she shuddered, as Kieran's fingers pushed more waves to rush through her sweet little body.

Her scent clouded his head, made him desperate. His cock ached, his balls heavy, even his knot throbbing from the need to lock into her and fill her.

Kieran pulled his fingers from her, slipping them into his mouth, rapture across his features. He nodded toward her room. "There's not nearly enough room for what we're going to do to you, omega."

And the shudder that ran through her? The way she whined in something between fear and excitement? That girl was going to get fucked, and she'd love every second of it.

Chapter Nineteen

The move to Tiffany's bedroom went in a flash. Kieran had pulled his fingers from her, and while the taste still lingered on his tongue, he missed her heat and wetness.

Still, Marshall had taken her lips in a rough kiss, so Kieran used the short distance to remove his own shirt. A trail of clothing remained as they moved through the living room, down the hallway and into Tiffany's room.

By the time Marshall lowered her onto the bed, both Kane and Kieran had stripped down. It gave Kieran a moment of pause as he noted the tattoos and scars across Kane. He didn't know how he'd gotten them, but Kieran recalled the first time he'd seen them. After a job they'd been forced to work together on, Kane had ended up with a knife wound across his chest. He'd pulled his shirt off, showing the tattoos and the scars that the color was intended to hide.

What had happened? Given his age, it had to have happened when he was somewhat young. Hardly an adult, if one at all.

Marshall pulled Kieran's attention back when he moved off of Tiffany, breaking the kiss despite the omega's complaints. He shifted away from the bed as he worked off his own clothing.

Kane took Marshall's place and crawled onto the bed to grasped Tiffany's hips in his large hands. A pull, and he'd rolled the omega over so she straddled him, her cunt poised above his hard cock.

Kieran huffed a soft laugh at the younger alpha's impatience. Then again, Kieran had been the only one to knot her. He couldn't blame Kane for wanting to feel her snug pussy milking his knot.

Tiffany reached between them, her hands small as she grasped Kane's dick. She rose to her knees as she positioned the blunt head of his cock against her swollen and soaked entrance. She took his length in an easy slide, no hesitation, no worry. Her body swallowed Kane's cock until they pressed together, and the same lust-filled moan left both of them.

From his angle, Kieran grinned. Tiffany leaned forward, lips straining for Kane's, begging for a kiss, but that wasn't what Kieran enjoyed seeing. Instead, he got a perfect view of how stretched Tiffany's pussy lips were around Kane's cock and a good look at her ass. He pictured how tight she would be around him, how he'd feel Kane's dick thrusting into her, how they'd take up every inch of space when he fucked her ass.

They'd own her entirely. Hell, Marshall could press himself past her lips, and they'd fill her in every way possible.

Unable to resist the sight, Kieran moved forward. He positioned his knees on the outside and behind hers, close enough he could feel the heat of her body.

He reached between them, taking the chance to slide his fingers against where Kane was buried deep inside her, feeling the way her cunt pulled tight around his width. Kieran even played there for a moment, teasing, knowing she'd have to stretch even farther when Kane's knot grew.

A whine left her lips, and Kieran had mercy, moving his fingers from her pussy. He'd gathered her wetness and trailed his fingers away from her cunt until he found her asshole. She went still, and the sound that left her throat was something between a warning and a plea.

Kieran pulled backward and landed a hard slap to her ass. The way it turned pink so quickly was a thing of beauty. "Don't give me that, girl. You'll enjoy it."

Kane chuckled, breathing rough as Tiffany rode him. "She likes to complain, but the last time I shoved my finger into her ass, trust me, she liked it." Kane's words broke off for a moment, then a deep growl. "Fucking hell, doll, the way you tighten like that around my dick? You remembering how good it felt?"

Marshall appeared beside Kieran, a small bottle of lube in his hand. Well, wasn't the doctor always prepared? Kieran took it, then Marshall settled on the bed beside Tiffany and Kane. Marshall wrapped his hand around his dick, stroking himself in slow and teasing motions. It seemed he planned to last a while.

Kieran flipped open the top of the lube with a finger, then drizzled some onto her. Her ass clenched and she pulled forward, but she could go nowhere, not with Kane's cock so deep inside her, not with Kieran's heavy body behind her.

Kieran set a hand on her ass, using it to spread her cheeks. He'd bet the sensation of being so displayed was uncomfortable, of having something so private being examined. The way she squirmed said he was right, but each twist of her hips, each time her body tensed and she clenched down, he wanted to do it longer.

Each thing she did challenged him. He wanted to push her until she surrendered, until she gave him everything. Maybe that was why he loved anal, because it was something women only surrendered to someone they trusted. It was something beyond the boundaries of what they thought they wanted, and nothing was more of a turn-on than to be buried inside a woman's ass, like having some secret part of her.

The thought of having that with Tiffany had his cock leaking, likely onto Kane's legs. *Too bad for him. Sex is hardly a clean business.*

Kieran pressed the pad of his thumb directly against her hole. He didn't tease or coax her into it. He wouldn't go fast, wouldn't hurt her, but he wanted her to give in. He added pressure, the slickness of the lube warm between his thumb of her body.

She resisted him, trying to keep him out. *Foolish girl.*

Kane took that moment to snap his hips up, slamming deep. It made her clench tight, but as soon as she loosened, Kieran pushed his thick thumb into her.

Kieran's thumb felt huge inside Tiffany, and somehow all her attention remained on that one spot. He didn't wait, didn't let her get used to the strange feeling before he pulled it back and forced it deeper. It caused sparks through her, so intense she wasn't sure if they were good or not.

She rocked her hips, but she could go nowhere. Each movement only made her more aware of how full she was. Kane's long cock filled her pussy, stroking her walls with each shallow thrust, while Kieran's thumb fucked her ass in tortuously slow movements. That was who he was, though. He was methodical and steady and unmovable. He showed it as they took her, neither touching her clit.

It meant the sensations tightened inside her, her awareness enough to make her fingers curl against Kane's chest, her body primed but not satisfied. All she needed was a stroke against her clit and she'd —

A slap to her ass made her tighten, made both Kieran's thumb and Kane's dick feel impossibly larger inside her. Kieran's growling voice told her who'd done it. "You've been trouble, omega. I don't think you'll get to play with yourself. You'll have to deal with our playing."

What? I wasn't going to — She realized her hand was halfway down between their bodies as if it had a mind of its own.

Tiffany pulled in an unsteady breath, then returned the hand to Kane's chest.

Kane laughed, low and amused before he stretched, grasping her ass cheeks in each hand. It spread her even wider, and she flushed as she imagined the way she must look, displayed to Kieran, not an inch of her private or secret.

"Well, who knew you could be helpful?" Kieran's jab lacked they edge from before. Had they worked out their issues?

The question floated away when Kieran withdrew his thumb and something thicker pressed against her ass. She struggled at the pressure, as if struggling had done anything before.

"Relax. It's just two fingers."

"See what I mean? Dramatic." Kane lifted his head to nip at her throat, a playful bite. "Relax or don't relax. Doubt it'll stop him."

Tiffany dropped her head to Kane's shoulder once he lay flat again. It spread her out over his body and let her try to relax, try to get her body to give in.

"Good girl," Kieran rumbled from behind her before he added strength to his pressing. Nothing could deny him and that included her, because those two fingers sunk into her ass, filling her more than she'd ever had.

She twisted her head to rest her cheek against Kane's chest, a broken whine on her lips. To her side, Marshall sat, one leg hanging off the bed, his other knee angled toward them. It gave her a look at his cock, at the way he stroked himself, his palm gripped tight around his length.

"You're taking them so well," he praised her. "You look beautiful like that, all flushed and breathless and overwhelmed."

Marshall's words soaked into Tiffany, driving her need higher like another set of hands on her. His voice was soft, and his approval reached deeper than even Kane's cock.

"Fuck, I've got to knot her," Kane shoved out through gritted teeth.

Tiffany ground her hips down, trying to get more of him, trying to tell him yes.

He flexed his hands on her ass, pulling her closer as a growl left Kane's chest, low and dangerous. His cock twitched, he rolled his hips forward and the telltale pressure of his knot growing sent her over the edge.

Despite having only been knotted once, Tiffany remembered the sensation as if it was already a part of her. The barely-there thrusts of his hips to force the growing bulge inside her, to lock it behind her pelvic bone, teased the primal part of her that knew exactly what she needed.

His knot grew, thickening until he could no longer pull out. It pressed against the sensitive area inside her, against the places made for that. He was thick, thicker than even Kieran, and she whined as her body struggled to accommodate the mass.

Even as she writhed, as she tugged against the knot, against his hold on her, against Kieran's body, she came again, harder than the first time. She muffled her cry with Kane's chest, and before she could think about it, bit down on him. The way her teeth closed around the firm muscles of his chest had to hurt, but it was all she could do as he stretched her body and stole her thoughts. Her pussy pulsed around him, lost to the overwhelming pleasure.

Kane didn't complain. He didn't shove her away or try to get her to let go. Instead, he gripped the back of her head and pulled her closer, a deeper growl leaving him.

Tiffany released her bite, brushing her lips over the indents she'd left in his skin. She lavished affection on the mark with her tongue and lips.

Even trapped by Kane's knot, even as her body trembled from the way his cock twitched inside her, the tiny movements as his cum filled her, she tried to relax.

At least, she did until a pressure at her ass brought her back to reality. Kieran had removed his fingers from her, probably when she'd been too distracted by her mind-blowing orgasm, and what pressed against her now were not fingers.

That stole away the ease she'd had, the relaxation. She tensed, flattening her hands against Kane's chest to rise. "Wait."

Kieran did, though he didn't pull away. "You'll enjoy it."

"I'm not ready," she whispered. Even if she'd enjoyed what they'd done so far, that felt too far. She couldn't stop the swirling in her head that said it would hurt, that said she couldn't trust him. Would he even listen?

A heartbeat later, he pulled away from her, a chill covering her from the withdrawal. As quickly as it had happened, though, he returned. His weight pressed her down as he fit his hard cock against the crevice of her ass, his hands cupping her cheeks to tighten them around him.

Lube made the glide smooth as he rocked forward and back again. It teased her still sensitive ass and made Kane's knot tug against her body where it refused to budge.

He brought one hand forward to hold his weight as he leaned over her, caging her between the hardness of his and Kane's bodies. He caught her ear with his teeth, nipping hard enough to sting. "I'll give you a pass this time, but trust me, you'll be begging me to fuck your ass before you know it."

Tiffany moaned at the friction, at the way his words almost made her ready to try it, to risk it.

A thumb on her cheek had her turning her head. Marshall knelt closer, his hand around his dick, pre-cum beaded at the top and catching the light from the window. He held it toward her like an offer, and Tiffany knew her answer.

She leaned as far as she could, trapped as she was, and flicked her tongue against the slit at the head of Marshall's length.

Marshall pulled in a ragged breath at the soft stroke of Tiffany's tentative tongue against his cock.

Sweat lined her brow, her skin flushed and her breathing erratic. She was entirely undone and overwhelmed, pinned between Kane's and Kieran's massive bulks.

He'd enjoyed the sight as she'd submitted to the two, the way her lust rose until it crested, until it dragged her under. He was ravenous for her as he stroked himself, and the sensation of his own hand wrapped around his shaft didn't come close to what he wanted.

He knew how it felt to be buried deep inside her. Her cunt had tightened around him and the base of his cock had tingled as he'd grown desperate to knot her. The cries she'd let out still rang in his ears, needy and wanton.

It had been easier to keep himself under control before he'd experienced the sweetness of her body. Each thing she'd done, each stroke of her body against his only rattled the cage of his alpha side, desperate to have her.

I can do this, he vowed to himself as he leaned closer to let her full, pink lips wrap around the head of his dick. Her lips were soft, giving, and warm against his length. Her seeking tongue traced each detail of his cock, and a moan was her response when another spurt of pre-cum escaped him.

Marshall thrust forward, sliding a hand into her long blonde hair. He used it like a leash, holding her still for him. He didn't fuck deeply into her mouth because his desire was sated by the act of pinning her.

She was trapped. They hadn't needed ropes or cuffs or anything but their bodies. She was caged between Kane's swollen knot, Kieran's heavy body that still fucked against her ass, and Marshall's grip in her hair. She couldn't move, could do nothing but take all they had to give.

And yet none of that frightened her. No stink of fear sat on her, no fearful whines or struggling. Instead, her body responded by her scent increasing, filling the room until he could happily drown in it. He didn't need air. He only wanted to breathe her in until nothing else existed but her scent and the warmth of her body.

A deep sound left Kieran, his hips snapping forward, each thrust sending Tiffany forward on Marshall's cock. Marshall chose not to think about why he found that such a turn-on, why knowing the omega who sucked on his dick was knotted by one alpha and had another thrusting against her drove his own need higher, but it did.

He'd been serious when he'd claimed alphas were meant to claim omegas in groups, and his reaction only furthered that belief. Taking Tiffany like that, owning every inch of space, possessing her in every way possible, calmed the beast inside him in a way he'd never experienced before.

A sense of completeness swamped him, especially as Kane shifted his hips up and said, "You're still so fucking tight around my knot, doll. Fuck, I think you don't want to let it go, huh? Got a taste and you ain't giving it up?"

Marshall groaned and held off. Even with the tightening in his balls, the desire to come, to spill onto

Tiffany's tongue and down her young throat, he held off. She was too much, the moment too much. Instinct wanted him to wait, to give her another minute until Kane could pull out, until he could plunge into her soaked pussy so deeply she'd never be free, to knot her and make her his.

A vicious snarl left Marshall's lips, the sound surprising even him as he forced himself to throw the thought aside. Sure, he'd admitted he'd need to do it eventually. Tiffany wouldn't accept anything less, wouldn't be okay with him holding anything back, but that didn't mean it had to be then.

He was too keyed up, the scents of her and the three alphas too strong for him to grapple his control. So, he forced himself to come, to release into her waiting mouth, to fill it with his thick cum before he had to make a choice about knotting her.

Her eyes fluttered closed on a purr as if the taste was the best thing she'd ever had.

Even as his cock released stream after stream of hot cum, he watched Kieran's thrusts turn broken and frantic. He pulled back to come, large hands spreading her cheeks so his seed landed directly on her ass. Kieran didn't wait, though. As soon as the last bit landed, he scooped some with one of his impossibly thick fingers and pressed into her hole.

Tiffany's mouth opened, but Marshall pressed forward, filling her with more of him even as he had softened.

Kieran used the silence as he gathered more of the stickiness he'd left on her and buried it deep inside her ass. "Next time, girl, I'm going to come inside you. We're going to fill you up in every hole you have, take you until you're a crying, cum-filled mess. Until then? Well, I'll make do like this."

Even as tired as she was, exhaustion hanging to her features, Kieran's words had an immediate effect. Tiffany pulled in a breath through her nose, quick and harsh, before she came one last time. It wasn't the loud, violent thing it had been at first. Had she grown too tired for that? Instead, it ran through her like a weak trickle, her face twisted into lines of something that was too intense to be pleasure.

Marshall pulled his dick from her mouth, since getting bitten wasn't something he wanted to try. Kieran withdrew his fingers, rubbing his other hand against her ass to help her come down, to assure her they'd finished.

Marshall stroked his fingers through her hair with a gentle touch. "Good job, Tiffany."

Even though he'd said it for her, it reached more into him. As he stared at her, he couldn't deny it.

I love her.

Chapter Twenty

Trying to ignore a snarling alpha wasn't easy, but Tiffany gave it her best shot as she reached for her toes. The tightness in her hamstrings eased as she stretched and reminded her that she shouldn't neglect her yoga.

Given the mess of the last few weeks, she'd missed out on most of her exercise. Her only run had been less about running and more about sex, though it had certainly worn her out. She'd had no time for yoga.

The results had been tightness in her back and shoulders. It meant that when Kieran and Kane had announced after dinner that they'd go check the fence line, Tiffany thought it as good a time as any for her own routine.

Marshall had a book — some thick intellectual thing that looked dreadfully boring — and sat on the couch. Except, the first time she bent forward, that snarl had started up. It had sent a shiver up her back, made her feel displayed, exposed and hunted.

The other thing it did surprised her — it made her feel playful. She wanted to be hunted. She wanted to play the game, to push at Marshall until he stopped holding back.

The snarl went silent, cut off almost as soon as it started. Sizzling energy passed through the room, and even without seeing him, without turning around, she could feel his heavy gaze on her. The rustling of paper said he'd turned the page of his book.

So, he's playing this game too, huh?

Tiffany flattened her back, her palms going to her shins, the action sticking her ass out. She'd normally have worn leggings but seeing as the only pair she'd brought had been ripped apart by Kieran, she'd gone with a pair of thin sleeping shorts and a sports bra she'd gotten from Alison's things. The woman had a smaller chest, which meant the bra fit tight and created more cleavage than she'd normally work out in. Where it had been a simple outfit that allowed movement when she'd put it on, it now felt like more.

The brush of cool air on the backs of her thighs and the bottom curve of her ass tantalized her. The way her breasts pushed together in the tight-fitting bra made her feel like a vixen. Warmth pooled between her legs, and she suddenly wished she'd put on underwear beneath the thin cotton shorts that barely covered her ass.

A deep groan slid into the tension of the room as Tiffany dropped back down, her fingertips reaching the floor. "You can't do that."

Tiffany bent one knee, rocking her weight down, then switched. It made her hips sway and knew it moved her ass like a teasing lure. "Do what?"

The growl he let out was nothing like the snarl or the groan. Those had been quick, silences as fast as they came. This was long, dark and drawn out. He didn't stop it, instead speaking at the tail end. "Don't push me, Tiffany." Had his voice always been that rough? That gentleness she'd grown used to with him was gone, replaced by a dominating edge that made her cunt pulse and her nipples hardened.

Still, instead of giving in, Tiffany rose and stretched her arms over her head. She lengthened, her chest out, an arch in her back. "I'm just exercising." She made sure to keep her voice as taunting as possible.

"What are you playing at?" Marshall's voice came from behind her, breathed into her ear in a rumbled voice. He slid his fingers over her bare hips, dancing them up her side to the line of her sports bra. "If you want some attention, you can simply ask. There's no reason to tease."

She frowned at his complaint. *He doesn't want me to tease?* Tiffany ignored the way he traced the bottom edge of her bra, venturing beneath the band as he went, sliding into the slight dip between her ribs. It hit her then. *He wants distance. He doesn't want to risk losing control.*

Tiffany didn't want him controlled. She didn't want him careful and leashed and thought-out.

So, instead of listening to his warnings, Tiffany leaned forward again, reaching for her toes. Her ass pressed against his crotch, and against his hard cock. She leaned back to put more pressure on him, pushing against his length.

There went that growl again, along with his warm hand sliding up her back in a steady stroke. He ground his hips forward, his dick rutting against her ass. His growl lowered further, so deep she felt it stroke through her. That was what she wanted from him, what she needed. Not him be careful, not him trying to be who he thought he had to be.

"You don't want this," he snarled.

"Try me." Tiffany hardly got the dare out before she found herself shoved to her knees, Marshall's heavy body over her.

He wrapped a hand in her hair and yanked her head backward, the hard lines of his body forcing hers to submit. Every curve of her form molded to him, giving in to his strength and his demands.

Her scalp stung by the grip of his hand, her neck arched and her mouth parted as she gulped in harsh breaths. The jeans he wore scraped against the backs of her thighs and his shirt made her wish she could feel all that warm skin directly against her.

He leaned over her, his weight settling against her as he dragged his nose up the nape of her neck, exposed by how he grasped her hair. He stilled, though, opening his hands then re-grasping. He released a harsh sound from his throat, something feral and full of frustration before he yanked away.

Tiffany turned, staying on her knees but catching his hand before he could get far. "Wait."

Marshall stared down at where she held his hand. "I can't do this."

"Why? What are you so damned afraid of?"

He released a harsh breath. "Of myself, and you should be, too."

Afraid of him? She couldn't even fathom that. He'd done nothing to make her afraid, nothing that made her think she'd be anything but safe with him. "I'm not afraid of you."

"Because I've been careful around you. Under all these layers of control, I'm an alpha, like the one who attacked you."

"You're nothing like him. He was a monster—"

"And so am I. I might be better at hiding it than others, but deep down, that's what we all are."

She shook her head, still gripping his wrist, not willing to release him. "You're not. I'm not afraid of you—"

Marshall dropped to his knees and caught her chin with his free hand, forcing her gaze to his. "I grew up watching what my father did to my mother, what alphas do to omegas. For years, he beat her because he could, because it was his nature. I will not do the same to you. I won't endanger you by letting that part of me free."

The sorrow behind those words tore at Tiffany. She'd grown up with loving parents, and to think of Marshall as a child watching that? "What happened to her?"

"He killed her. He wrapped his hands around her throat and he strangled the life from her."

Tiffany's stomach dropped. "How old were you?"

"Twelve. I tried to stop him, but a twelve-year-old isn't much of a match." His grip on her chin loosened, and he used his thumb to stroke her jawline. "What my father was is inside me, Tiffany."

She risked moving forward, setting her hands on his chest. "It's not. He did what he did because he wanted to, not because he had to. You aren't like that."

"How can you be sure?"

She leaned closer, moving until she was nearly in his lap, until her thighs were spread around his leg. "Because I know you."

He shook his head. "If you're wrong, then you would pay too high a price. The only way this can work is if I keep myself under control, if I never risk you with that side of me."

"That's not enough for me. I don't just want part of you."

"And I can't risk that."

"So, let's try."

His lips tipped down. "Try what?"

Tiffany curled her fingers in and dug her nails into the firm lines of his chest. "Stop holding back. Kane and Kieran are nearby, so I'll be safe. You don't have to worry."

He tightened his grip again. "I can't."

"We'll never know any other way. I'm not going to keep doing this, having you try to always keep yourself in control. I won't have it. We do this the right way, or we end it. I won't do it any other way."

He leaned forward until he brushed her lips with his, until the masculine taste of him made her want to moan. "You're too brave for your own good."

"And stubborn, too. I'm not going to force you to do anything, but I can tell you I want all of you or none of you. Either I see the real you, and we do this right, or we go our own ways."

Marshall didn't speak at first, and the silence weighed on Tiffany. What if he said no? What if he stood up and walked away? She couldn't blame him.

What had she done but caused him problems? How could she blame him for not wanting to deal with her anymore?

As she was ready for him to tell her no, he set his hand on the back of her neck in a firm grasp. "You want all of me? You want me to fuck you like I've wanted to, to pin you down and force my cock into you? Because, Tiffany, I've thought of having you in ways you can't possibly imagine. This is your last chance. Tell me no. I'll back off, I'll let you go. Tell me no."

Tiffany pulled back enough to stare into his eyes. "I want you."

The sound he released went straight to her core, made her body shudder and her breath quicken. The lust and possession in his eyes was heady, thick, and almost frightening in the depth. Even worse, though? The way his words rumbled from his chest like the more terrifying promise she'd ever heard. "Then you'll have all of me you can handle, omega."

Tiffany's body made it so Marshall couldn't think. She'd come into the living room in nothing but those tight shorts, the bottom curve of her ass showing when she'd reached forward toward her toes. The doctor part of him was impressed with her range of motion, but that wasn't the part of him in control. No, it was the part of him that saw the way her breasts pushed together, her nipples pressing against the gray fabric of the sports bra that pulled all the strings.

And she wanted him to do that? *What is she thinking? I could do anything to her.*

Still, it was this or calling it quits, wasn't it? He saw no other option, no way to appease what she wanted while keeping the tight reins on himself he'd always used.

So, it came down to this. He supposed there was some good in the idea. She'd see that part of him when in the safety of the other two, where he knew he wouldn't be able to do much harm. She'd realize her mistake, and she'd never wish to see him again.

At least she'll be safe.

And that ugly instinct inside of him, the one he hated without reservation? It reveled in the idea of taking her. It wanted to spread her thighs, to feast between her legs until she was dripping for him, until she trembled and writhed and lifted her hips in useless begging. Then? Only after he'd pushed her beyond what she thought she could handle, when he took her to that edge and shoved her over, he'd fuck her.

And it wouldn't be gentle. No, he'd plunge into her as deep as he could, spurred on by every sound she made, until he finally knotted her.

Marshall let out a groan at the filthy thoughts, and the fact they were coming true. He'd know how it felt to have a cunt milking his knot, to have an omega's sweet pussy wrapped around him. Even if it was just that once, he'd know.

Tiffany wrapped her hands around him, her fingers clutching his side, but Marshall didn't want that. Neither did she, if she'd been honest. *She wants to see the real me? She wants to me to not hold back? Fine.*

Marshall used a hold on her shoulder and another on her hip to twist her, then shoved her forward onto the couch. Her knees went to the cushions, and she caught herself with her hands on the back. It left her leaning forward and at his mercy.

The sight made his balls ache. She was a stunning omega. Tough and willing to challenge him but sweet enough to melt against him.

She went to rise, but Marshall set a hand on the nape of her neck while using his hips against her ass to keep her pinned. He reached beneath her and pushed her sports bra up so her breasts hung beneath it. A stiff nipple pressed against his palm when he cupped one with a tight grip.

Tiffany gasped at the rough touch, the sound surprised.

And it went straight to his cock. It slipped loose more of his control, let more of his alpha side roam free, showed in the tightening of Marshall's fingers as Tiffany whimpered like trapped prey.

He ground his dick against her ass as he tormented her stiff nipple with his fingers. He could already smell her, knew she must be dripping, drenching those tiny shorts and running down her thighs.

She whimpered when he released her nipple, when he kept a grip on her back to hold her still and undid his jeans with his other hand. His cock was full and heavy, the pressure almost painful as he freed himself. One look down her tight body, however, had him sure he wouldn't allow the moment gone so soon.

His beast wanted to taste her, first.

So, Marshall released her back, then snapped, "Stay put," when she tried to rise. Only when she'd resumed her place, tiny tremors running through her, did he drop to his knees behind her. He could have removed her shorts, pulled them down her toned thighs, but no.

He wanted her disheveled. He wanted her right then, and the scraps she thought passed for clothing did little to hide her. Instead, he hooked a thumb into the crotch of her shorts and pulled it aside to bare her.

Sure enough, she was soaked. Wetness clung to her folds, and the center of her shorts were drenched in her slick. He let out a deep sound, something like a groan but far more feral before he leaned forward and swiped his stiffened tongue up her center.

Tiffany shifted her hips as if to escape but he wrapped his hands around her hips, thumbs pointed in to pull her up, and growled a warning against her flesh. She went still, but a new rush of wetness against his tongue said she hadn't minded the sound.

Her taste in his mouth and down his throat drove him mad. Whatever control he had left broke free and he used his thumbs to spread her cunt wider. He dove in, his tongue devouring her in greedy lapping.

She squirmed, shoving herself backward as if to get more, then away as though the sensation was too much. Not that it mattered to him. The voice in his head, the wants of his alpha side, they'd taken over. The only thing that chanted in his head was one word — *Mate*. It repeated over and over again, as certain as his need for breath.

She was his, and he'd have her the way he needed, the way they both needed.

His cock hung heavy, pre-cum dripping from it as he feasted. He wanted to wrap a hand around himself but that would require releasing Tiffany.

There's no way I'm letting her go.

Her pussy tightened down, pulsing beneath where his thumbs held her open and his tongue dove inside her. She was silent as she came, not even harsh breaths escaping her lips.

He let her go before she'd recovered, before she'd even drawn a breath, desperate to be inside her. She hung limp over the couch, her forehead pressed against the cushions on the backrest, her shorts having slid back over her like some sort of protection.

Marshall grasped his thick cock with one hand, then pulled her shorts out of the way again. Her cunt still squeezed down around nothing. *I'll give her something.*

He dragged the blunt head of his dick across her pulsing entrance, then fit himself against her.

His strong hands went to her hips to brace her, then he shoved into her with a snap of his hips, claiming every inch of her body. The grip of her pussy around him, the tightness was enough to draw a snarl from his throat. Sure, he'd had her before, but he'd been so cautious that time. He'd sat still, let her take.

This time he took, and he planned to have everything. He wanted every moan of hers, every whimper and sweet plea, every gasp and shudder. She'd give it all to him.

Her hips rotated, the sexy curve of her back shifting as she sought more from him. Very well, he'd give her more.

Marshall pulled back, savoring the drag of her tight walls against his shaft, then plunged back into her. He set a hard pace, fucking her with deep and sure motions. Her body seemed so small beneath him, but she took each thrust with a wanton whine. He leaned forward to press more of his weight over her, to use that bulk to fuck her harder, as though if he took her deep enough, thoroughly enough, it would fix something inside him, too.

"Yes," she moaned, voice quieted by the cushions.

Marshall scraped his teeth across her shoulder, nipping the bared flesh there, tasting the salt from her skin. "Is this what you wanted?" How had his voice turned so deep? It held an edge of madness that frightened him, but he was too far gone to pull it back.

Besides, Tiffany pushed her body back toward him in need. "Yes. Fuck, yes, this is what I wanted."

Her words drove him onward. He buried himself into the heat of her body, into the tightest grip on his cock he'd ever felt. His balls tightened and his knot burned, the need to take her, to lock inside her and fill her with every drop of cum he had overwhelming. He pushed on toward that end, instinct moving him more than thought. Her scent and her sounds demanded he satisfy her, and he'd damn well do that.

The first pulse of his knot, the first swelling of it inside her was a shock. The sensation was localized in the base of his cock, yes sparks traveled along his spine, the backs of his legs, the insides of his thighs. His entire body trembled as he got as deep as he could inside her, his knot growing, welcomed by her soft cunt.

The wiggle of her hips, the way she shifted due to the pressure of his growing cock inside her sparked that need to dominate her. Whereas the in-control Marshall would have pulled out before he locked into place, would have coaxed her and sweet-talked her, she'd made it clear she wanted the real him.

The real him wanted her still, wanted her to take his cum pinned beneath him. That part of him, the one he'd spent his life running from, bit down hard on the thick area behind her shoulder, using his teeth to hold her still.

His knot locked inside her, and the first spurt of cum made him lean more heavily against her, like his energy was sapped. It was even more powerful when her pussy clenched and she came again, squeezing down around his enlarged knot. Each time she tightened, it was like a stroke, drawing more cum from him until all he could do was snarl against her skin, against where he'd bitten her and held her still.

The rhythmic pulses of her cunt kept going, after she shuddered and gasped, her orgasm fading. Each time either shifted, she'd release a muffled cry and grip his cock with her body again.

As soon as he could force himself to move, he released his bite and shifted them over, tucking her against his chest. Her small body shook, her clothing soaked in sweat and cum and in disarray. Still, he'd seen no better sight, nothing lovelier. His beast slumbered, the part of him that had demanded he take her like that sated.

The bite he'd left darkened before his eyes and ran his fingers over it, his eyebrows drawn together. "Do you want me to leave?"

Tiffany shifted in his lap, the action causing a tug to his knot. "Unless this detaches, I don't think you can go anywhere yet." Exhaustion saturated the words, even with the joke.

Marshall shook his head. "I'm serious, Tiffany. I'll leave. Kane and Kieran can handle anything that happens, and while I will always do whatever I can for you, whatever you need, if that's my absence, I'll go."

She caught the fingers he traced the bite with. *Is she going to tell me to go, now?* She brought them around and pressed a gentle kiss to them, then wrapped the arm around her tighter, settling in his embrace. "If you leave, I'll find you and annoy you until you come back."

He frowned at her simple answer, at her certainty. He opened his mouth to argue, to remind her that he'd been too rough, that he'd held her down and fucked her as if he were no more than an animal.

"Stop trying to argue with me. You're ruining the afterglow."

His mouth snapped shut at that, and, despite himself, he grinned. While he wasn't sure about this, fearing what could happen, and the alpha side of him scared him more than anything else, he settled in to enjoy the warmth of her body against his.

If anyone could handle that side of him, it would be his feisty mate.

Chapter Twenty-One

Tiffany emptied the saucepan of chocolate into the pan, the oven already set.

"Smells good." Kieran leaned his hip against the counter, his presence both reassuring and unnerving.

He made her not want to screw up. Maybe it was because Kieran managed to look so perfect all the time, because he seemed to have everything so together. The idea of being her normal mess bothered Tiffany.

She tried to hide the nerves beneath a grin as she set the hot saucepan on a potholder. "Well, I can't cook, but I can bake. You guys have made all the meals, so I figured I'd bribe you with some brownies."

Kieran huffed a soft laugh. "What exactly are you trying to bribe us for?" His voice came out playful and soft, and carried with it a lot of temptation.

All the things she could ask for crossed her mind, all the things his strong hands could do, the many uses for his wicked tongue, the things she was too inexperienced to know she wanted.

Kieran wrapped his fingers in the front of her shirt and stepped forward, crowding her with his wide chest. "I like that everything you think runs across your face. It's fun watching you get all tangled up." He brushed his firm lips against hers, then traced her bottom lip with his tongue, a teasing kiss that melted her.

Heat stirred in her lower stomach, her nipples tightening at the skilled movements of his lips to hers. She reached for him, wanting to pull him closer, to convince him to take her right on the counter there.

Before she moved more than an inch, his strong hand caught her wrist as he broke the kiss. "Careful," he chided.

Tiffany turned her head, clouded by his hiss and his scent, to realize she'd nearly hit her hand against the still hot pan.

"You should be more careful, doll." Kane came in and hopped onto the counter beside her before sticking his finger in the brownie mix.

"It wasn't my fault."

"Cooking is dangerous. You should watch what you're doing." Marshall offered the same amused tone as Kane.

"Oh, so now you're all best friends, huh?" Tiffany pulled her wrist from Kieran's grasp, then took the pan before Kane could steal another taste.

"Isn't that what you wanted?" Marshall asked.

"No. Well, I mean, yes, but not like this." Tiffany slid the pan into the oven, then turned to face all three, crossing her arms over her chest.

Dealing with them on their own was hard enough, but when they were together? How was she supposed to keep her wits when they worked together?

Kieran laughed, then retreated to the living room, giving her space. "I called Joshua. No sign of anyone at your apartment or any of our homes, and Sam hasn't found anything new."

"Maybe that guy was alone?" Tiffany didn't hide the hope at that thought. "When can I go home?"

All three men froze at that, like she'd uttered some curse. *Right. Home. The place we won't be living together anymore.*

Was she hoping for Kieran to say something? For someone to say something about what would happen after they went back to the city?

"Another week, probably." Kieran turned his back toward her, his words flat and empty.

Of course, Kieran wouldn't give me any idea there might be anything else.

She twisted away to set the timer on the stove, taking the moment to school her features. It wasn't that she expected him to say he wanted forever. She'd wanted some idea that he wanted...something.

He gave her none of that.

Once she'd hit start on her timer, she faced the men in time to see Kane offering a vicious glare toward Kieran before he twisted back to Tiffany, wiping it clear as if she hadn't seen it. He gave her that mischievous smile he so loved to use, the one that made him seem a few years younger than his age. "I thought you and I might do some self-defense later."

"Last time you saw me do that, you said you didn't want to risk it."

"I saw you nail a man in the balls, and that ain't my idea of a good time. However, you like me more now, and you like that area a lot more, so I think they're safe. Besides, from what I've seen, exercise seems to get you riled up." He waggled an eyebrow playfully. "Figured I'd better test that theory."

His jokes and his smile made it difficult to let Kieran's distance bother her. It was hard to be sad or hurt when Kane looked at her like that, when his stupid, childish jokes made her laugh.

So, Tiffany let go the issue with Kieran. They hadn't figured it out yet, and she doubted they would in the next ten minutes. Why let it ruin her evening?

"How long can you stay?" she asked Marshall. "With your cases, I mean."

"As long as I need to. Don't worry about that."

Still, the idea of forcing him from his life, his obligations, it hung on her. "I don't want you missing out on things because you're —"

The subtle lift on his eyebrow had her swallowing the rest of her statement. It reminded her that while he might seem the sweetest, he'd also been unrelenting when he'd taken her on the couch. The curl of his lip and the set of his shoulders sent heat coursing through her as she recalled what he could do when she pushed him too far.

"Never mind," she muttered.

Kane's bark of laughter shot through the room. "Never mind? Never thought I'd see the day when someone tamed you, doll. Guess the good doctor ain't as sweet as he seems, huh?"

Tiffany went to argue, but a soft grunt from Kieran stopped her. He crouched down near the wall by the bookshelf. "What's this?"

Before Tiffany could ask what he was talking about, Kieran stood, a chain hanging from his palm.

My necklace. The one I threw. Tiffany sighed at the broken clasp. She should have never thrown it like that.

No matter how frustrated she'd felt, the piece had been a part of those women she hadn't been fast enough to help. "Sorry about that."

Kieran didn't acknowledge the apology, shifting the necklace and holding it up to the light. It was then that Tiffany realized it didn't look right. The rectangle that had been the charm was bent and split near the bottom.

He clasped his fingers around the charm and pulled, the end coming off to reveal a USB drive.

Kieran held the drive up, his gaze narrowed. "Well, what do we have here?"

* * * *

The night was hot, and, despite having stripped down and left the covers off, Kane couldn't seem to get past the heat.

They'd spent the rest of the evening trying to pin down the damn drive. That was, of course, Kieran's area. He'd muttered about encryptions, but fuck if Kane understood a word of it. The brownies had burned in their work, and dinner had ended up as some sandwiches when they'd realized how hungry they'd all grown.

Finally, around ten at night, Marshall had herded them off to bed except for Kieran, who had rejected the idea with a single snarl.

Fine, the asshole could stay up all night if he wanted to.

Kane sighed and shook his head. That wasn't fair. He was pissed that they finally had some idea of what those fuckers were after, and he was useless. Kane could knock people around, he could track, he could kill, but computers? *Fucking. Useless.*

So, when Tiffany could have used him, when he could have maybe done something, he had nothing to offer. Instead, he lay in his bed, awake as fuck, and she slept next door.

Always falling short, wasn't he?

His door creaked open, and he fought the desire to tell Kieran to fuck off. The bastard probably wanted to talk about their next plan, and while Kane didn't have the same animosity he'd had for Kieran at the start, he didn't want to have a heart to heart in the middle of the night, either. Kane kept his mouth shut, figuring there wasn't a need for his piss poor attitude. Wasn't Kieran's fault he felt like a failure.

The door shut, and when it did, it pushed a breeze of air his way. On that gust? The delicious scent of Tiffany, and look at that, turned out his cock wasn't tired, either.

Kane lifted his head to find her slim silhouette moving toward the bed, steps quiet. "Hey, doll."

She paused, then huffed. "I wanted to surprise you."

"You want me to pretend next time? Because if you try to wake me up with those pretty lips of yours around my cock, I promise I'll play along."

She snorted, no tinge of insult in the sound. Nah, Tiffany wasn't the sort of girl to get offended over something like that. Hell, the increase in her scent wasn't his imagination, either. She crawled into the bed, miles of warm skin against his as she settled in beside him.

"You ain't wearing much," he said.

"Neither are you." Her small hand settled on his chest, fingertips brushing one of the scars there. "Besides, you came to my room last time."

He swallowed down the discomfort of her touching the scar, playing off the panic. "So, this is just tit for tat? Because, I don't mind tit."

Tiffany sat up, then leaned over him. Was she going to straddle him? His dick might have wilted a bit, but damn if she couldn't get him back up to snuff fast.

A click, then light poured into the room from the bedside lamp. After a moment, his eyes adjusted enough to make out Tiffany leaning above him, her blue eyes staring down at him with a lot worse than lust. Lust, he could deal with. Lust, he liked.

That shit there? It was pity, and curiosity and fucking steel.

"Don't ask," he said, voice somewhere between a beg and a threat.

Her shoulders dropped and she sat back.

He caught her hand to keep her there, despite the fact that she didn't look at him. "Doll…"

She shook her head. "Don't. I'm not going to force you, Kane. You've been there for me, never made me tell you anything. I'm tired of being on the outside. I want to know you, to understand you, but there's this huge part of your past I don't know anything about, that you won't tell me anything about."

"Ain't anything worth knowing."

Her gaze dropped, and he knew she eyed the worst of the wounds, the thick white scar that had been left when a knife had nearly pierced his heart. Still, she didn't reach to touch it, nodding at the scar instead. "These almost took your life. You wouldn't even be here if they had, and you're telling me that isn't worth knowing?" A soft sigh blew from her lips, warm and long. "And I'm going to bet that whatever it was left scars that aren't on your chest. The ones that make you snap and keep people away. You do it to me, too. How do you expect this to work if I can't even understand you?"

And there it was. The girl was too fucking smart, saw too much. He should have known she wouldn't let that shit go, that she would eventually figure it out on her own.

Kane pulled her in closer by the grip on her wrist, hiding the flinch as he set her hand over the worst of the scars. Ugly white ruined skin ran over his pec, and even the intricate tattoo couldn't hide it.

Her eyebrows drew together. "How old were you?"

"Fifteen."

Her short gasp made him want to laugh to break the tension. Sure, fifteen sounded young, but it wasn't, not in his world. By fifteen he was already watching out for his sister, already out on his own.

"So, what happened?" Her soft fingertips stroked along the thick line of scaring.

The gentle touch pulled the story from him. "I was living on the streets, my little sister Kasey and me."

"Where were your parents?"

"No idea who our dad was, or if it was the same man. Mom was an addict, and after the first time I found one of her dealers trying to crawl into my sister's room at night, we were out of there." He gritted his teeth at the memory, at the way he'd sleep on the floor of his sister's room when their mom had any fucker she thought could get her a fix over. Fuck, those were bad days. He pushed forward. "I was thirteen when we took off and Kasey was eleven. Making money ain't easy when you're that young, and when I couldn't make cash doing anything legal, well, only left one option."

Her lip was pressed between her teeth as she listened, and he expected to see disgust on her face. Girl was fucking perfect, with her perfect family life and her perfect past and he was nothing but a mess. When nothing like that crossed her face, he figured she either didn't get it yet, or she was good at hiding shit.

"Started with easy shit. Did a lot of break-ins, stole shit they needed back, got information. Kid that young doesn't get noticed much, and it let me slip into places other people couldn't. Got good at it, developed a network of people who passed information. I wouldn't say Kasey and I lived in luxury, but she never had to worry about food. We crashed at friend's places and she got to keep going to school. Kept her out of it as much as I could."

"What happened to her?"

The question made his scars feel like they'd rip back open. "Guy I worked for gave me a bad job. Wanted me to break into this mansion up in the ritzy area of town, said the asshole owed him a ton of money. Wouldn't be the first time I'd done that, gotten in real close and scared the shit out of someone, but he wanted more. Guy had three kids and a pretty wife, and he wanted me to kill one of the kids — didn't even care which one it was. Figured that would send the message that we could get to him anytime, and if he wanted to keep the other two breathing, he'd pay up. I've done shitty things, but killing a kid? Fuck, I couldn't do it. Told him he was crazy, that I wasn't going to do it. I left and gathered all the cash I had stashed, figured I'd pick Kasey up and we'd leave. Guy was faster, though. By the time I got to the friend's place we crashed at, friend was dead, Kasey was a bloody mess on the floor, and the asshole left me for dead after he and his buddies carved me up, too. Spent a couple months in a hospital, few more in physical therapy, and realized that doing the right thing is shit." He offered a short shrug. "Never got to bury Kasey. Fuckers liked to dump bodies, figured it made it easier to hide shit. No idea where they left her."

Tiffany leaned in, moving slowly as if she knew how wound tight he was, and pressed her lips to the scar. It was a chaste kiss, like soothing the wound that had never healed, would never fully heal. "I'm sorry."

"Don't get shit twisted here. Kieran wasn't wrong about me. I am shit. I steal, I lie, I fuck people up for the money. Don't look at me like I'm some fucking hero when I ain't. Kasey got killed because I got in deep with the wrong people, because I fucked up and I couldn't keep her safe. I ain't a good man, doll, never have been and I don't see that changing. This?" He waved at himself. "The scars and fucking ink and the way I talk, this bullshit, is it what you were so desperate to know about? Because it ain't like I didn't already know you were too good for me, but I guess now we're both clear on it, ain't we?"

She said nothing, and the silence chipped away his bravado. He'd done the metaphorical bearing of his teeth to warn her off, tried to make it clear what he was, and now he waited for her to get it. *She'll realized she's better off without me. Good. Better now than years down the fucking line, huh?*

Even as he fed himself that line of bullshit, he held his breath. For the first time, he didn't want her to go. How many people had he frightened off the same way? At the first sign they might get a look at him, a real look, he'd give them a reason to write him off then take off the other way when he knew they wouldn't follow.

He didn't want to do that with her. Fuck, the idea of watching her go, of having her look at him like everything else did, like he was a piece of shit, killed him.

Still, he didn't take any of it back. He let the ugly truth sit between them and fester.

Tiffany broke the standoff, leaning forward to cup his cheeks and take his lips in a kiss that was far sweeter and gentler than he expected. Sex was always rough with him because that sweet shit? Too personal. Too dangerous.

When she slid her lips against his, coaxing as if he were some virgin in need of reassurance, it melted him. He returned the passionate exploration, deepening the kiss by slipping his tongue past her warm lips, dipping into her mouth to taste her. She ran her hands over his pecs, not following the scars but rather paying homage to his entire chest, as if the scars were no more or less important than any other part of him.

He broke the kiss with an uneven breath. "I tell you I'm a shitty person and you kiss me? You ain't got a lot of sense, you know that?"

The smile she gave him sealed the deal. The omega was tough enough to stand against his snarling and his asshole personality and still grin like that. Damn, she was perfect for him.

The point was only made clearer when she slid a leg over his hip, her heat covering him. "I've got enough sense to not worry about your snarling. You're not as scary as you think."

"Really?" He grasped her hips and rolled her, pinning her wrists above her head and using his weight to hold her down. "Let's see if you feel the same way after I have you knotted, doll."

Chapter Twenty-Two

Tiffany found Kieran seated on the front porch, his laptop perched on his thighs, his eyebrows pulled toward one another. His eyes were red and dark circles sat under his eyes.

"Why are you out here?" She sat on the bench beside him.

"I was typing too loudly, and it was easier to move out here than to listen to Kane complain."

"Were you up all night?"

He shrugged. "There was a lot to do. I wouldn't have been able to sleep even if I had gone to bed."

The idea of staying up all night made Tiffany want to nap. After her time with Kane, she'd dozed off in his bed. Later, when the sun had streamed in through the windows, she'd found herself alone. Kane must have moved to the living room to complain about the typing at some point, but it didn't shock her.

He'd admitted when they'd still spoken by text and on the phone that he never slept well.

Admonishing Kieran wouldn't do anything, so Tiffany didn't even try. "Find anything?"

The question finally stilled Kieran's quick fingers on the keyboard. He reached up to grasp the top of the laptop screen and close it, then faced her. "Some. A lot of the information I couldn't make sense of. I'm good at what I do, but to fully access these files, it's going to take more than just me. What I could find?" He sighed, setting the laptop aside. "It's not good."

Tiffany crossed her legs, trying to look at ease despite the fear. "What do you mean?"

"That drive didn't belong to an omega there. It has files from the people who abducted them."

"Why would it smell like an omega, then? Because an omega wore that, I can guarantee it. I could smell her on it."

"My best guess? They hid it on one. Maybe the mate of one of the alphas to protect it, to hide it. It doesn't change that what is on that drive is the reason people are after you, and they won't stop until they get that back."

She shouldn't have been surprised. She'd known whatever reason these people were chasing her wasn't good, but to think she'd had the answer all along and hadn't even noticed? Tiffany tried to push down the nerves, to think through it. "So, what do we do?"

Kieran leaned back, his face that hard and distant mask he wore that she couldn't read. "I've already put in some calls contacts I have in the FBI. This is a delicate matter, because criminals like this usually have more than a few people in their pockets. The men I contacted, I trust. We can turn the information over to them."

"And what about me?"

"Ideally, we'll have enough information on the drive to sweep up any threats. The agents I spoke with want to talk to you tomorrow to discuss specifics, but I suspect we'll turn the drive over and you'll finish out your year with me. After that, well, then you'll be able to start your life."

Tiffany stared at him, not sure how to respond. His eyes were flat, face giving nothing away.

After everything, he was saying she could walk away? Was she nothing but a contract to him? He'd said nothing differently, hadn't promised her more, so why did it hurt?

She tried to keep her voice steady. "So that's it?"

"What do you want from me, Tiffany?" He asked it as if he didn't know.

How can he not know what I want?

"Nothing at all," she whispered when she knew her voice would give her. She rose, ready to walk away, to swallow down the hurt at how quickly and easily it was for him to toss her aside.

He caught her wrist. "I understand that you have some feelings for me. That's not uncommon, especially because you don't have much experience."

She drew in a deep breath and pressed her lips together to keep from snapping at the arrogant bastard. Was he sitting there and explaining that she didn't even know how she felt?

If he noticed her reaction, he didn't let on. "The fact is, after that year, after you are able to go on your own, you will realize that this infatuation is based on a lack of options. You're young, Tiffany, and you don't know what you want yet."

"But you're so sure that it can't be you?"

His thumb stroked over the pulse on the underneath of her wrist like some consolation prize. "I've been through this before. I've had omegas who were swayed by the dynamic, not the alpha. It's why I stopped taking care of omegas, because once I helped them get on their feet, they realized I wasn't what they wanted. You, who haven't done enough or lived enough to know yourself, let alone what you want, are asking for trouble."

"So, you expect me to spread my thighs for you for a year while you offer me nothing? And I'm supposed to be okay with that?"

"Yes. It's for your own good as much as mine. You're young enough, desirable enough, you could have any future you want. You have Marshall and Kane, both interested in something long-term. The last thing you need is a jaded alpha like me." Self-hatred dripped from his voice, and beneath that? *Fear.*

Tiffany stared back into his eyes, willing some crack to show his feelings beneath that mask of indifference he wore. "Isn't that for me to decide? Let me figure out what I want, but I can't do that if you take away the chance."

His eyes softened the barest amount, but a shake of his head was final. "I can't. I can't plan a future knowing you'll change your mind. All I can give you is the year, Tiffany, the year to get you on a good path. Trust me, by the end of it, you'll realize it's best this way."

Tiffany pulled her hand away. She didn't yank, but tugged and he let her slip away. Wasn't that the theme, though? He was happy to let her go.

All his pretty words didn't change that he didn't want her, didn't think she was worth the risk. A year? A year wasn't enough, and she knew it. Each day of that year would only make losing him worse. She tried to picture that year, tried to imagine it passing with her living with him, sleeping with him, and knowing he didn't want anything more.

It tore into her.

She couldn't do it.

Trying to live with him knowing he'd cut her loose as soon as he legally could would kill her.

There was only one option, and none of the men would like it.

* * * *

This isn't good.

Kieran could read situations and people, and the hard look on Tiffany's face said he would not be pleased with whatever she was about to say. After having spoken to the FBI agents herself for a few hours, she'd called the men together like some family meeting.

What had happened? What was that troublesome omega planning?

Whatever it was, he had a feeling he'd be objecting to it.

She probably would explain how she wanted to continue to help with the investigation. Maybe she planned to ask about getting an apartment away from Kieran, a neutral place where she would have time for Kane and Marshall as well.

Truth be told, Kieran had already broached that topic with the other alphas. He had no intention to sell his home, but they'd discussed moving into Marshall's house as it was the largest and had more than enough rooms for each to have their own space. He would rent out his house during the year, and Kane could sublet his apartment.

Marshall also was a good choice because he was less territorial than the other two. His house felt more like neutral ground than either of the other.

The idea of moving into Marshall's felt strange, but not as negative as he'd have assumed. Moving never was a comfortable idea, and while it was only for a year, he had enjoyed the company. He enjoyed when he was up late and found Kane in the kitchen, searching for food. He liked that if he rose early, Marshall would be poring over some book. Yes, he liked the relationship with Tiffany, the sexual tension and passion, but the stranger comfort was that of the household unit.

However, with the way Tiffany bit softly at her nails, he had no doubt she planned to say something none would be happy about.

Kane, as usual, had sat himself on the kitchen table. He never did seem to know how to operate furniture properly. Marshall was seated in a chair he'd pulled out from the table, one ankle crossed over the other knee, the vision of calm. On the other side of that was Kieran, who leaned against the wall to hide the tension inside him.

"Out with it, doll." Kane swung his long legs.

Tiffany took a deep breath, her small hands drawing into fists. "I talked to the FBI. They're sending over an agent to get the drive tomorrow morning."

Kieran had figured they'd come soon. The information on that drive, once they decoded it, would be invaluable to the task force that handled omega crimes at that level. Of course, that couldn't have been all there was to the little talk.

He waited for the other shoe to drop.

"And I'm going with them, too."

Like hell. The thought came so fast, Kieran couldn't hide the growl that passed his lips at the thought of her going anywhere.

Kane was faster, though. "The fuck you are. You giving a statement? They can do that here. They need you at their office? We'll drive you there, make sure you're safe. You're still in danger until those fucks are caught."

Tiffany didn't wilt beneath the rough words or harsh looks. "They're taking me into witness protection. There isn't anywhere safer I could be than that. They'll get the information off the drive, do whatever they can with it, but I'll be somewhere safe."

"The contract —"

" — is transferable. The agent already assured me they have alphas in place in their witness protection network who are qualified to take over the contract."

Kieran didn't trust his temper, so he remained silent.

Marshall, always the even-tempered one, didn't even shift in his seat as he answered. "Why would you want that? I can't imagine a stranger would be a better choice than the three of us, who you already know."

She met Marshall's gaze, and wasn't it obvious she avoided Kieran's? "Because I need to move on. I can start over after this, and I won't be putting anyone in danger."

"Fuck danger. If it's dangerous, that's the exact reason we ain't going anywhere."

"I can't risk you guys. None of you asked for this, none of you wanted me to walk in and screw up your lives, and if I stay, that's all I'll do."

"You aren't screwing up our lives, Tiffany." Marshall finally leaned forward. "I can't speak for anyone else, but I'm not feeling particularly put out by having you in my life. Don't make a rash decision because you are hurt or angry or afraid."

Rash. That's exactly what she was. Despite him not being willing to promise any sort of future, did that mean she should rush off like this?

"I…" She sighed, her shoulders slumping, and that hurt him worse than anything else. "I can't stay. Please, stop asking me to. Don't make this any harder than it has to be." With that, she pulled in a trembling breath and turned glassy eyes toward the ceiling as if to stop tears from falling. Her soft steps followed her, then the click of her door as she shut it.

Kane turned the sort of glare on Kieran that would have normally worried him. "The fuck did you do?"

"Nothing."

"I saw the way she looked at you—or rather didn't look at you. Clearly you two had some disagreement, and enough for her to go into hiding over it. Make no mistake, she isn't choosing that because she is afraid of whoever is after her. She's doing it to get away from you," Marshall said.

Kieran didn't respond. What was he to say? They were right.

Kane jammed a finger toward Tiffany's bedroom. "Get in there and make it right! I ain't losing her because you're an idiot."

"I can't. What she wants isn't possible. It's better she realizes it now instead of later."

Kane's lips pressed together until the seam turned white, then he released a vicious growl and stormed off toward Tiffany's room.

Marshall rose, more controlled, as always.

"What, nothing to say?"

The other man shook his head. "What would be the point? You've made up your mind, and if you are determined to allow fear to control you, there isn't much anyone can do."

"I'm not afraid," Kieran argued, voice hard.

A sad chuckle left Marshall as he went to follow Kane toward Tiffany's room. "Of course you are. No one gives up what they want most except for fear."

The door opening didn't surprise Tiffany, and neither did the scents of the two men. Of course, Kane and Marshall would come to find her, to check on her.

Not Kieran. No, he'd be sat out there, stoic as ever, as if the entire thing didn't matter to him.

Maybe it didn't.

I am not going to cry. I'm not some damsel, damn it.

She dropped the clothing she'd taken from the drawer into the bag she had open on the floor, hoping the simple chore would distract her.

The thought of leaving broke her heart. Could she turn away? Could she walk out and never see the three of them again?

Maybe, in a year, when she was free…

Maybe what? Maybe Kieran will have changed? I doubt it. You can't teach an old dog new tricks and I doubt he listens well enough anyway.

Her eyes stung.

Strong arms wrapped around her from behind, twisting her to and pulling her closer to a wide, warm chest. *Kane.* She breathed him in, his hands grasped her close, and when another hand stroked through her hair, she knew it was Marshall.

Even still, she refused to cry. What would tears change?

"Shh, doll," Kane cooed to her, voice surprisingly soft. "Whatever's going on, we're here for you."

Tiffany pushed back enough to look up and into his familiar face. "I'm leaving in the morning. Nothing is going to stop it, but morning is still a lot of hours away." She slipped her fingers into the waist of his pants, a question on her face.

Kane answered the question with a deep groan and a kiss that made her breathless and wanting. Marshall ran his hands up her sides, slipping his fingers beneath the fabric of her top to stroke her skin directly.

They both gave so quickly, and Tiffany allowed herself to be swept up by the moment.

She tugged at Kane's pants until the button came loose, then pushed at the waist. Her lips never left his as they stumbled backward and he collapsed onto the bed, her over him.

Marshall pulled her up then stripped her of her shirt. He made short work of her bra, his agile fingers undoing the hook.

Kane's palms enveloped her freed breasts, and he sat, so he could bring his hungry lips to them. He snaked his tongue out to flick at the nipple, then raked his teeth over the nub.

Meanwhile, Marshall had moved to her pants. He didn't bother to take them off, not at first. Instead, he dipped his hand into the front of the loose sweatpants and against her pussy. Her body wasn't drenched, not yet, but at the first brush of his seeking fingers she knew it wouldn't take long.

She couldn't wait long. Morning was coming and she was leaving. It sat in the back of her mind like a clock that wouldn't stop ticking. No matter how much she struggled to ignore it, it kept going, kept taunting her.

She didn't want to take it slow, didn't want to waste a single second. It made her desperate, so she pulled at the men, at their clothing. When one slowed, she urged them on. When one hesitated, she begged.

Pride didn't matter, not when faced with the reality that it was their last night. They each knotted her, their kisses and sweet words and rough touches seeing her through it all.

At the end, once they'd come, once she'd come time and time again, she curled into a ball on the bed.

Kane's heavy hand rested on her hip as he sat at the edge of the bed, a helpless look on his face. "Stay, doll. You ain't gotta go anywhere. You got a place with us, always."

She shook her head and shut her eyes. "I can't."

Marshall pressed a kiss to her temple, his lips pressing against her skin for longer than needed, as if he didn't want to break the connection. "Do you want us to sleep in here?"

"No. I think some time alone would be good for me."

It wasn't the truth, but it wasn't a lie, either. *Getting used to being on my own is probably good.* The depressing thought made her want to take back what she'd said, but she let it stand.

Every second would only make the next day harder on them all.

Kane squeezed her hip but said nothing else as the men left, her body chilled and her mind in chaos. The warm cum they'd left inside her had leaked onto her thigh, and she couldn't find the energy to wipe it clean.

Instead, she tried to sleep.

Chapter Twenty-Three

The dark shape of someone in her room woke Tiffany. She bolted upright, a scream already in her throat, before the scent hit her.

She swallowed down the scream. "What do you want, Kieran?"

His body language gave nothing away, especially with the darkness. Neither did his voice when he answered. "Did you know you talk in your sleep?"

She shook her head and brushed her hair from her face. "You didn't come into my room in the middle of the night to watch me sleep."

"Are you sure? Because if you are so determined to leave, that may be all I get to see of you."

"If you're trying to make me feel bad, don't bother." Even as she said it, the guilt clawed at her. And why was that? *Why should I feel guilty when he is the one who doesn't want me? Just because I walk out, that doesn't change that he's holding the door open.*

Still, facts didn't matter against her wounded feelings and his still-distant voice.

A sigh left him, deep and unhappy, before he sat on the side of the bed. "I don't want you to feel bad. Whether you believe it or not, I've always wanted what is best for you."

"If you try to tell me that's why you won't even try us, that it's for my own good, I swear I'll scream."

"I suppose it doesn't matter now, does it?"

"I guess not." Tiffany inhaled and grew wet at the scent of his arousal. Then again, that didn't surprise her. Kieran might try to hide how he felt, he might not want her for anything serious, but he'd proven again and again that he wanted her body. "Strip," she ordered.

Even in the darkness, even without being able to see his features, she could swear she *felt* his eyebrow lift. "Excuse me?"

"You're not here for conversation. You didn't come in here to talk me out of leaving because you know you won't give me the only thing that would make me stay. You're here because you want me one last time."

"Won't this make it harder to leave tomorrow?"

"Probably, but what does it matter? I'm not leaving because it's easy, after all."

"I don't want to make it more difficult, though."

Tiffany couldn't help the dark and humorless laugh that left her at that, as if Kieran had nothing to do with her leaving, nothing to do with why she had to in the first place. She wished she could see him. She wanted to stare into his eyes, to see his strong jaw, his dark hair and solid frame. How pathetic was that?

Instead of arguing it — *What's the point?* — she ignored it. "You're in my room to fuck me, Kieran. Let's not pretend it's anything different than it is. It's what it's always been."

The silence between them was full of anger, of lust, of all the things they wanted but couldn't have. She dared him to deny it, but no matter how much of a bastard Kieran could be, he wasn't a liar.

Sure enough, he stood to remove his shirt, then shucked his pants and underwear in a quick motion. Even in the darkness, the width of his chest, the outline of his body sped Tiffany's heart. How he could make her want him, she didn't know.

She was worn out from Kane and Marshall, sore from taking each of their knots, their scent still clinging to her, yet all she wanted was to pull Kieran against her and have him, too.

Kieran's body covered hers as he pinned her with his bulk, his warm skin against her still nude form. His cock, hard and leaking pre-cum, pressed against her stomach like a tease. "This isn't just about fucking you."

Tiffany reached down, her hands curling around his hips, her nails digging into him as if she could punish him with them. "Don't talk. Don't explain."

"You seem to think you're in charge, but as I recall that isn't how this has ever gone."

She wrapped a leg up and around his thigh. "And you'll risk this for some proof that you're in charge? I doubt it."

He lifted his body enough that he could stare down into her eyes. It looked as if he'd say something, but Tiffany didn't want to hear it. She wrapped a hand around the back of his neck and pulled. When he wouldn't budge, she rose to take a kiss, to silence him with it.

She didn't want to talk. She didn't want to hear his excuses or his reasoning or anything else.

Those things weren't going to change his choice or hers. He wouldn't even try to promise her a thing, and she couldn't stay.

So, she turned the kiss aggressive to distract him. Let him have the rough sex he craved, and he'd stop trying to talk, stop trying to fix things, stop leaving her with words that would only repeat in her head for years. She pressed her demanding tongue to where his lips were together, and, on a groan, he opened for her. Traces of beer lingered on his tongue, and she stole them.

His cock slid along her stomach as he rocked his hips forward, rutting against her without finesse or though. Instead, he did it like he couldn't not do it, as if the need to have her ran so deep he couldn't stop the motion. Wetness was left on her skin from his cock, and she moaned at the waste. She wanted to taste it, didn't want to lose a drop.

Kieran broke the kiss, breathless and panting. His silhouette above her, chest heaving and lights catching the reflection of light from the window, made him look like a monster.

That was fine by her. She'd let him consume her. The less of her left, the less there was to hurt.

Her thighs spread for him as if she had no part in it, as if she didn't need to even consider it. He ran a thick finger roughly up her slit, then pressed it into her. She moaned and arched her back, sore after Kane and Marshall but unwilling to ask him to stop.

She wanted him with a strength that made discomfort a trivial concern she wouldn't listen to.

He hooked his finger up then withdrew it, stroking against the front of her pussy as he pulled free. "Marshall and Kane both knotted you." When he stroked again against her folds, she knew his fingers held not only her own wetness but also the cum from the other alphas

Tiffany nodded, despite it not being a question, and gasped when his slick fingers found her hardened clit.

"You're too sore." Even as he spoke, he traced her labia, sliding against her and teasing each part of her entrance without pressing inside her. "Taking three knots in a single night when you're not in heat would be too much for you. No matter what you think of me, I don't want to hurt you."

His words didn't register at first, not with how warm he was, with how deftly his fingers stirred that need inside her. *Wait? He's turning me down?*

She forced her sluggish brain to work, then took her lip between her teeth as an idea came to her. A shove to his chest had him pulling back enough for Tiffany to twist, rolling onto her stomach beneath him.

His growl from behind her made her cunt tighten down, a whine from the deep ache inside her.

His hands cupped her ass, large and impossibly strong. "You said no last time. I don't want you doing something you don't want to." Even as he spoke, he kneaded her ass, spreading her like he had when she'd been over his lap.

"If I didn't want to, I wouldn't have suggested it." Venom dripped from her words, laced with hurt.

His hands slowed, as though he heard it and didn't care for it. Still, he didn't mention the tone before pulling back.

Her breath stilled at his retreat. Would he leave, now? Would he walk out on the last chance they had? How could he steal away this last night?

He delivered a swift swat to her ass, the sting pulling a strangled yelp from her. "Stop overthinking, girl. If

I'm going to fuck your ass, I can't do it dry, now, can I? I'll be right back, and I expect you to be in this same position when I return."

His fingers, sure and confident, ran up her cunt in a slow and possessive stroke before sliding across her ass like a threat.

She shuddered at his dark chuckle before he rose from the bed.

What did I get myself into?

Kieran held the lube when he re-entered Tiffany's room to find her where he'd left her. Her legs were spread slightly, her feet hanging off the end of the bed, her cunt visible in the light from the bathroom across the hall.

Damn, she was beautiful. The thought of her walking out, of him never seeing her again, dug deep. He didn't want that. He didn't want to watch her drive away with an FBI agent, to sign the paperwork to relinquish any claim to her. It made him consider how it would feel for her to have a new alpha.

Not Kane or Marshall, he'd not only accepted that but had come to be pleased by the thought. Some other alpha, though? His sweet, feisty little omega with some faceless alpha instead of him?

He clenched his hand into a fist at the thought, at what he might do to any alpha who touched her.

No. She won't be mine, and that's where it was heading anyway.

If he kept thinking about that, he'd ruin the moment, and he refused to do that. Nothing would take the night from him, especially when he had no future to expect. That night had to last him for a long time.

He tossed the lube onto the bed beside her, then stripped down. He didn't want anything between them, not a scrap of clothing to keep him from each inch of her soft and giving skin.

Tiffany tensed as he crawled back onto the bed, the muscles in her thighs tightening. She didn't twist to look at him, not even when he set his knees on the outside of her thighs. Her arms were folded, her chin rested on them, her long blonde hair bound and tossed over her shoulder to reveal her bare back.

If he could have picked a mate, any mate, he doubted he'd have picked a single thing she didn't have. She was fun, wild, brave, and would never let him get an upper hand for long. He never had to worry about life getting boring, because she wouldn't allow it. Each trait he'd have wished for in an ideal mate Tiffany had in spades, and yet it came in a package too young for him to trust.

She'd grow into herself and realize she wanted to explore, wanted to see what else there was out there. Hadn't it happened before? Any alpha and omega living in such close quarters would give in to instinct and biology, but that didn't mean they were meant for anything more.

Her ass fit into his hands perfectly, the muscles flinching as he kneaded them with his strong fingers. It wasn't right, but a part of him thrilled at the idea he'd be her first. Not just with sex, but the first alpha to take her ass. Even when she'd moved on, when she'd ended up with anyone else, he'd always be her first.

He couldn't have her forever, but at least she wouldn't forget him. That was something, right?

He used the grip on her ass to spread her cheeks wide, enjoying that same subtle squirm she'd done before. He released one hand to pick up the lube, flipping the bottle open with a thumb before drizzling some onto her.

His cock hardened at the sight, at the way she clenched against the chill of the lube. He pressed his thumb to her ass, and, despite the tightness, the way she resisted, a steady push let him sink his thumb into her.

Her whine came out thin and needy, a sound that only made him want her more.

"Relax," he growled out, not trying to soften his voice. She knew who he was by this point, knew his personality. No reason to pretend he was a soft person when he wasn't. "You'll enjoy it."

"How can you be sure?"

He fucked her slowly with his thick thumb as he leaned in to press a kiss to her shoulder blade. "Because you've already enjoyed any time we've played with your ass."

"A finger is a lot different from your dick."

He laughed softly at her tone, at the sharp way she snapped out the words. Her attitude would never fail to amuse him. "You can take me, girl. Don't forget, this was your idea."

She huffed a disgruntled sound but didn't argue. Her sound came out less sure when he pulled his thumb from her, when he added additional lube and stroked some over his cock. The last thing he would ever want was to hurt her.

He wrapped his hand around his cock and used his other to spread her, placing himself against her ass. "Do you want this?" He held himself still, giving her the chance to think about it.

A shudder ran through her small body, and it highlighted how well she fit against him, beneath him. Would she turn him down? Would she say no?

No, Tiffany was never a girl to give in to anything. She shifted her hips back to push against him. "I want this," she said, voice strong.

Kieran groaned then rocked his weight forward. Her body fought him, tight and unyielding. Still, with the continual pressure, her body gave. He slid into the hot tightness of her ass, only a shallow inch at first before he stilled, allowing her the time to adjust to his width.

And that took more control than he'd known he had to hold still while her body clenched around him, while he knew he'd have her moaning before long. Even so, he didn't move. He held her hips, his body poised above hers, his aching cock buried too shallowly in her snug body.

She breathed in deep lungfuls of air, her back arched, her toes digging into the blankets of the bed as if it gave her some sense of control. She twisted beneath him, the almost frantic little motions enough for him to slide another hair deeper.

"Easy," he growled into her ear as he lowered himself closer to her back, remaining the same depth inside her. "Take a deep breath, Tiffany."

Her name seemed to sink into her, and she followed the direction. She pulled in a single deep breath that shuddered from her, along with some of the tension. Her ass loosened around him, a surrender she couldn't fake.

"There you are." He retreated, then pressed forward again. She didn't fight him, and her whines transformed into moans as he continued, as the pleasure outpaced the nerves. It had never been about pain, not for her. She'd only been afraid, unwilling to trust him to not hurt her.

Funny that now, after he'd hurt her in worse ways, she was giving in to this.

Perhaps that was it? She'd realized this wasn't so risky a thing when he'd already done far more damage.

Kieran ignored the thought, unwilling to let it ruin anything. His body pressed against hers when he'd filled her entirely, when his cock was buried so deeply within her that only her panting moans could be heard.

He nuzzled her throat, drawing her scent into him, wanting it to brand onto him. She might be leaving, but he'd never lose the memory. No one could change their mind or take that from him.

"You're so tight," he whispered to her, his lips brushing her ear as he spoke. "I won't last long, not with how you're squeezing down around me."

She lifted her hips off the bed, thrusting herself back toward him. Always the demanding omega, wasn't she?

He gave her what she wanted, pulling back, sliding into her fully. He took her with sure and deep strokes, fucking her in a way she wouldn't forget, in a way he sure as hell would never forget. Each time he withdrew, she pressed against him again.

"Stay," he said, voice low, the request one he hadn't thought about before asking.

"I can't."

A snarl broke through his lips as his balls tightened, as he neared his release from the snug grip of her tight ass around his dick. "Stay," he said again, more demand in his voice. "Don't leave tomorrow."

A hollow whimper left her, and it had nothing to do with how he stretched her, with the way she'd be sore come tomorrow. "What are you offering me?"

"This?" His hips came forward on a rough thrust. "You're happy with me, I know you are. I'd protect you, take care of you."

"For a year?"

He opened his mouth to deny it, but the words stuck. He couldn't lie to her, and no matter how much he did not want to see her walk away, he couldn't commit to anything more than the contract. It was too risky.

She turned her face from him, the pillows pressing against her face to muffle her voice. "That's what I thought." Had any words been filled with more pain than those?

Kieran brushed his lips against the nape of her neck as he gave himself over to the sensations. Physical pleasure, that he understood, that was easy. He let the tension that filled him, the tightness of his balls, the need to fill her take over. He wrapped an arm beneath her, above her breasts, his hand grasping her shoulder to hold her still.

If only he could keep her still…

His hips pistoned, fucking her hard and deep until he couldn't hold his release back. He came on a vicious snarl against her neck, teeth bared. He filled her, his cum like some claim she would never wipe clean, a part of him she'd always carry. She could leave him, but that at least would remain.

By the time he came down, when his energy waned and he wanted nothing more than to pull her against his chest and bask in her scent and warmth, he pulled his softening cock from her tight ass.

Her whine was broken, and he reached down to touch her, to stroke her clit until she came undone for him.

A shove of her hand stopped him. He frowned as she rolled to her side, her back to him, and curled up as she had been when he'd entered.

"Tiffany—"

"If you care about me at all, don't. Don't explain, don't apologize, don't say another word." Her voice cracked. "Just go, please?"

Kieran moved numbly to his feet, backing away from the bed, the omega he'd always seen as feisty and strong lying so broken there.

He'd done that? He'd been the one to tear her down?

The tears that left her, nearly silent as if she'd tried to hide them, took layers of his skin with them.

How could he have done that to her?

Chapter Twenty-Four

Marshall sipped his coffee, thick tension filling the cabin. The FBI agents would arrive shortly, and when they left, they'd take Tiffany with them.

His teeth itched to be bared at that thought of his omega being taken away from him. Even if she went willingly, it didn't sit right. She belonged with him, with Kane and Kieran. She belonged in their bed, under their protection, in their arms.

She did not belong in witness protection, handed over to some alpha like a piece of property, and yet she had made her choice.

When he'd watched Kieran enter her room the night before, he'd hoped they'd work out their issues. The ghosts on the alpha's face when he'd returned, however, said they hadn't resolved anything.

A knock on the door had them all freezing.

"Fuck off," Kane muttered without rising.

Ah, Kane's personality was as sure a thing as the sunrise.

Kieran came from down the hallway to open the door when neither Marshall nor Kane seemed willing to move.

Three men walked in, and Kieran shook hands with one. "Thank you for coming, Daniel."

"Any time. It sounds like the information your omega found is well worth the trouble." He cast his gaze behind Kieran, as if to look for Tiffany. "Besides, from the tone of her voice, she could use some help."

Kane's growl echoed in the room, drawing the tension tighter. "She ain't yours."

While alphas couldn't scent one another, they still tended to sense others. The stance of the two men screamed alphas, and it seemed Kane didn't like the idea of them taking Tiffany.

Daniel lifted an eyebrow but didn't respond with any aggression. His voice came out low, as if trying to be non-threatening. "I don't want an omega. In fact, Kyle and I won't even be taking her." He nodded at the third man. "This is Agent Jake Morter, our liaison with witness protection."

"Like fuck I'm letting him take her anywhere," Kane said.

"Pretty sure that's my choice." Tiffany's voice broke through the tension.

Marshall, Kieran and Kane turned their heads as if their eyes sought her out of instinct so deep they couldn't resist the draw. Still, none spoke.

Tiffany had her bag slung over her shoulder and her gaze down. Marshall felt cheated. He missed her gaze and her smile and her eyes.

"Tiffany?" One of the men inclined his head but come no closer. "I'm Agent Kyle Hopkins. You spoke to my partner, Daniel, on the phone. You have the drive?"

She lifted the necklace still wrapped around her neck and pulled the cap off that hid the drive.

"Good. You'll keep that until you sign the paperwork. Once you do, you'll hand it over and go into witness protection. I've brought everything for Kieran to sign to turn your contract over, so you'll be covered legally."

She turned her gaze to the liaison, brow furrowed. "He's not an alpha."

Daniel nodded. "You're right. Betas work best for jobs like this. It helps eliminate any issues with heats or bonding. You'll remain in the care of betas until we find a suitable alpha for you to stay with."

The liaison, Jake, took a step closer. "Hey, Tiffany. Trust me, you'll be as safe as could be with me. We use single-man teams for transport to reduce anyone paying too close attention."

She wrapped her fingers tightly around the shoulder strap of her backpack. "Can I have a minute?"

The three agents looked at each other, then nodded. They said they'd wait outside before exiting the cabin, leaving Tiffany and the three alphas alone inside.

Tiffany scraped her foot against the ground, and he wasn't sure he'd ever seen a less happy person.

Kane broke the silence, as uncaring of social norms as ever. "Don't fucking go. You don't have to go with those assholes—you can stay. We'll figure this shit out. Hell, I'll kick Kieran's ass until he stops acting like a moron if that's what you want."

The corners of Tiffany's mouth tipped up. She lifted to her toes and planted a soft kiss on Kane's unyielding lips. "Thanks, but I don't think that's going to help."

"I'll find you. You ain't walking out that door and outta my life, doll."

"Please, don't. It'll just make it harder."

His lips pressed together, but he nodded.

Next, she turned to Marshall, offering the same gentle kiss. A selfish man, Marshall returned the kiss, needing a taste of her no matter how brief. When she pulled back, too soon for his liking, she set her forehead on his chest before letting out a slow sigh. She offered another press of her lips to his chest and moved away.

Lastly, she hesitated beside Kieran. He stared down at her, but she wouldn't lift her head. How two people so clearly in love could behave as if looking at one another were hard, Marshall didn't understand.

"I'm—"

"Don't tell me you're sorry."

He nodded, face hard. "What do you want me to do?"

"Sign the paperwork. Make this easier on me, at least."

He lifted his palm to the back of her neck, then pulled her closer. Instead of a kiss on the lips, he pressed his lips to the top of her head, his eyes shut tight. His chest rose as he inhaled, and his hand trembled as he held her close.

He didn't have the look of a man who would let her go, and yet, he did. He released her and took a step backward. "I'll sign the paperwork. If you need anything else, ever, no matter what it is…"

She wrapped her arms around herself, eyes glassy. "We both know I'm not going to do that. Take care of yourselves."

With that, she walked out of the cabin, leaving the three alphas alone and lost.

* * * *

Kane couldn't settle. He paced the long porch, rolling his shoulders as if that would shake loose the tension.

Watching the SUV holding his omega drive away had tested his control. He'd wanted to follow it, to chase it down and pull her out of the car. Instead, he'd let her go. He'd drawn his hands into fists and forced himself to stay still until the car drove out of sight.

"You're bonded," Daniel said.

Kane twisted to level a snarl at the other man. "Fuck off."

Daniel leaned back and laughed, shaking his head. "You guys are screwed, aren't you? If you're bonded, there is no way she's going to stay away."

"You don't know her well, then. If anyone is stubborn enough to ignore a bond, it's her," Marshall said.

"So, you're willing to let her go?" Kyle asked.

Kieran answered, his gaze not on any of them but on the horizon. "We're willing to do whatever is best for her. If she wants to go, then I'll let her go."

Kane wanted to argue it, but Kieran was right. If Tiffany needed space, if she wanted to go, he'd let her go.

Well, he'd find her difficult ass and look out for her, but he wouldn't let her know. He wouldn't get in her way or fuck with her life. She deserved everything she wanted, and if he couldn't give it to her, well hell, he'd stay away.

And it would kill him to do it.

"Should I ask who owns this cabin? The paper trail is more than a little questionable." Daniel nodded toward the front door.

Kieran shook his head. "It is probably best to not ask."

Daniel huffed. "You and your secrets. Tell me it's nothing I need to worry about, at least. The last thing I need is to find out this place has bodies in the basement and coke under the porch. That might look bad on me."

"I think you'll be safe." Kieran tapped his fingers against the armrest of the chair he sat in.

Tiffany had been gone for twenty minutes, and in that time, they'd updated the remaining two agents with as much of the story as they knew, hearing what they could share.

From how it sounded, Tiffany was lucky. The group had killed people for much less, and the information on the drive could do a lot of damage. While Kieran still couldn't open most of it, what little he'd found said they'd have auction locations and potentially hunting grounds.

That was something, right? But, fuck, Kane couldn't find any real happiness in criminals getting caught when it still felt like it was costing him his mate.

A ring had Daniel pulling his phone out, then answering. "Hello?" He rose and moved off the porch to take his call in privacy.

It left Kane staring at Marshall and Kieran and wondering what was left for them. What were they? Friends, he supposed, in a way. They'd found a sense of belonging between the three of them with Tiffany, but with her gone?

The thought of trying to replace her had his shoulders tightening. She wasn't just anyone filling a spot. No other omega could slide into the dynamic and work out.

Even the idea of finding someone else on his own sounded as appetizing as eating garbage.

"What?" Daniel's voice rose as he walked back toward the porch. "That's not possible. He was just here."

Kyle was on his feet a moment later, the two exchanging heavy looks, as if they knew each other well enough to identify the exact meaning behind an expression.

"No. I have no idea. Fuck. I'll call you right back." He dropped the phone from his ear and turned a look on all three of them. "We have a problem. The real agent was found dead in his apartment. Whoever took Tiffany isn't him."

Kane didn't bother to halt his snarl that time.

Chapter Twenty-Five

Tiffany ignored the vibrating of her phone. She'd thought she'd have at least an hour before the men called her. She'd prepared herself for it, been ready to ignore the calls.

At least for a while. She doubted she could keep that up for long. Already she missed the men's rough voices. She missed the careful way Marshall spoke, his words sweet and quiet. She missed Kieran's exact language, proper and always this side of annoyed. She even missed the way Kane cursed, his lips always pulled into a smile as he did so to lessen the sting.

How the hell was she going to last without them when even after twenty minutes she felt lost?

Her phone went off again, so she twisted to look at it. Kane that time?

Finally, she gave in and answered. "I know you said you'd find me, but I thought I'd have at least a day before you tried.

"I need you to listen closely, doll. Don't react, don't let on. Tell me it's nice to hear from me."

Tiffany frowned, but the seriousness in Kane's voice had her following the direction. "It's nice to hear from you." She lifted her gaze to the rear-view mirror where the beta driving stared at her with such intensity, she fought a shudder.

"Good girl. The driver isn't the agent the FBI sent. I don't know who he is, but I can guess he wants that drive. Answer my questions but don't make it obvious what we're talking about. Are you on the same road or have you turned off?"

A lump in Tiffany's throat made answering difficult, but she did it anyway. "No, haven't seen him in a while."

"So, you've turned off. Do you know the street?"

She shook her head before remembering he couldn't see that. "No."

"Did you make it past the freeway onramp?"

They played the game, a back and forth with him asking and her giving him answers she hoped he could understand. All the while, she tried to plaster on her normal 'everything is fine' face.

"We're going to find you, doll," Kane promised. "You gotta stay calm, though. Play along until we get there. I know you, I know you're all fire a lot of the time, but you gotta think shit through. You can do that, can't you?"

She wasn't sure right then. She wanted to yank the handle of the door and jump out, consequences be damned. She wanted to kick the back of his seat or grab the wheel and pull it hard to the left. Something.

Waiting wasn't what she was good at, wasn't something she did well. She tended toward impulsiveness. She liked to come up with a plan, no matter how far-fetched, and act immediately.

Kane's rough voice came again when she didn't answer. "You can do that, Tiff, I know you can. Just gotta hold out a little while."

She nodded. "Yeah, I can do that."

"That's my girl," he growled back. "We've mapped out about where we think you are. Coming up is a mall. Get him to stop there. Play along, do whatever you have to."

Tiffany drew a deep breath, trying to draw on Kane's belief in her. "Okay. I'll see you then."

The line went dead, and Tiffany slipped the phone into her back pocket.

"Who was that?" Jake, or whoever he was, asked. Despite his face still having that same smile, his voice had taken on a sharp edge.

Tiffany used her best fake smile, the one she reserved for difficult customers who ordered difficult drinks to be pretentious assholes. "A friend. Well, sort of." She tried to keep her voice steady. "I'm sorry, it's weird to not have to keep secrets, you know? It's one of the omegas I've been helping."

His eyebrow raised, but his gaze lost some of its suspicion. "Do you know many of these omegas? Because we have departments whose entire job is trying to help them. I hate to think of them out there, alone in the world at in danger."

No, you just want to be able to find them to sell them. You won't get within a mile of any of them, I swear.

"Really? Well, that would be great. I've got at least ten or so who could use some help."

"Ten?" The sparkle in his eye made her want to throw up.

"Probably more in the end. We keep things sort of separate, so no one person knows everything. It's safer that way. It's why I sent a copy of the drive to one of them."

His hands tightened on the steering wheel. "You sent a copy to someone? You didn't mention that. The alphas didn't mention that."

"I don't trust alphas, so I didn't tell them."

He reached up and pinched the bridge of his nose. "Very well. That information is important and if anyone knows she has it, she could be in danger. Call her and have her meet us at..." He moved his fingers over the infotainment center. "There is small mall up ahead, on Arrow and Sixteenth. Tell her to meet you near the south-west entryway and to bring the drive."

Tiffany nodded and pulled her phone again.

Perfect.

It would at least thirty minutes for the alphas to arrive. While the trip had taken nearer to an hour for the beta and her, they'd traveled the speed limit. She had no doubt that Kane would do a hundred and make the trip in a fraction of the time.

They sat on a bench inside the south-west entrance, facing the door. He had taken her phone after the call, telling her it could be traced.

She'd wanted to tell him to shove it. She'd wanted to use the phone and slam it against his temple. It would have done no good.

The beta had been quiet, his body language careful but not overly concerned. Then again, why would he be? He expected to get everything he wanted. More omegas, his missing drive and her silence.

"Where is she?" The beta's question held frustration.

Her time was running out. He'd only wait so long before deciding the risk was no longer worth it.

Tiffany stood and squinted. "Is that her?"

He followed her lead, staring off toward the other side of the mall. "Where?"

She pointed, taking a few steps in that direction. "That way. Tall woman, blonde hair."

He leaned in that direction, gaze locked on the far side of the square-shaped mall.

Tiffany took the chance and darted in the other direction, pushing between the crowds, trying to put as much distance between her and the man as possible. She needed to buy a little more time.

My mates had better hurry up.

* * * *

Marshall tried to remain calm as they approached the mall. Tiffany had gotten the beta to do exactly as they needed, and while she couldn't tell them the entire plan, it seemed she'd tricked him into believe she'd given a copy of the drive to a friend.

Daniel and Kyle had come as well—useful backup. They'd found the SUV the beta had driven first, and in the glovebox had been the original man's identification. Daniel had pulled the battery to ensure he couldn't make a getaway in that.

Still, they had to find Tiffany inside, and without being noticed.

The beta had seen their faces, and even if he wasn't expecting trouble, he'd realize the game the moment he saw any of them.

This is all our fault. If we'd only listened, she wouldn't have felt like she needed to leave, would have never gotten into this position, would have —

Kane elbowed him hard. "Stop thinking. There's time for that later."

"We were supposed to protect her. It was our only job, and we couldn't manage it."

"Well, this shit takes time, huh? You always make your worst mistakes at the start."

"This had better be the worst mistake. I don't think I can handle more of this." Marshall rubbed his heel against his chest as they made their way through the door. "How can you be calm?"

"Calm? This ain't calm."

"Then what is it?"

Kane nodded down toward his hip. In his hand, he palmed a blade near his thigh. "Let's say I'm looking forward to being able to explain to that son-of-a-bitch what a mistake he made in fucking with our mate."

And for the first time, Marshall was quite okay with bloodshed.

Tiffany curled her fingers around the USB drive still hanging around her neck. Her back pressed against a corner of the mall in one of the connecting hallways that went through the middle space. She'd ducked through crowds, trying to keep a few steps ahead of the beta.

Worse? She couldn't ask anyone for help. He had the badge from the real agent, which meant all he had to do was flash that and no one would stop him from hauling her off.

She had to stay out of his grasp until Kane, Marshall and Kieran showed up. That was what she held on to, the fact that her alphas were coming.

And she knew they were coming. No matter how unsure things were, no matter how much hurt she still held for the things that had happened, she knew they'd come. It was something deep inside her, a truth. If she needed them, they'd be there. Nothing would stop them, and she'd do the same for each of them.

She softly banged the back of her head against the wall, her hands trembling. She wanted to run. She wanted to not move a muscle. More than anything, she wanted to see her mates.

She'd evaded the beta for what had to be ten or fifteen minutes. That meant Kieran and the others had to be there. Hiding in a hallway wouldn't help her at all.

Tiffany took a deep breath, then walked slowly from her hiding spot. She set one foot in front of the other, steps soft, weight on the balls of her feet. At the end of the hallway, where it intersected with the main walkways of the mall, Tiffany peered around the corner.

People walked, unaware of what was happening around them. It made her want to shake them, to wake them up.

Instead, she peered through the groupings of people, searching for a glimpse of her alphas.

Across the mall, down the walkway, she caught sight of a face that made her knees weak.

I never knew I'd be this happy to see that grumpy alpha.

Kieran's gaze searched the passing people, his face hard. Ah, that was the look she'd missed, the one when he was focused on a goal, when nothing else mattered.

Tiffany pulled the drive from her neck, holding it in her hand as she tried to make her way toward him. As soon as she reached him, she'd be safe. Together, she was sure nothing could touch her.

Kieran spotted her. His focus locked in so fast, Tiffany's breath caught. He took a step toward her, all but shoving someone in his path.

She went toward him, twisting to move through the crowds, so close she could see the flash of anger in his eyes, that temper she already missed.

As she neared, as she rejoiced in feeling like they might make it out alive, she was yanked to a stop by a hand around her arm and something sharp pressed to her side.

"Not so fast," snarled a voice into her ear.

The beta had found her.

Kieran stopped short, his lip pulled up to bare his teeth at the man who had Tiffany. The widening of her eyes and the way her body leaned away said he'd pressed something to her side. A gun? A knife?

No one touches my mate.

His mind roared, all the reasons he should let her go disappearing. There was no question about whether he'd keep her, whether he was good for her, whether she'd run off the moment she had second thoughts. In that moment, the only thing in his head was that she was his, and he didn't plan to lose her to some asshole.

He kept coming forward until only a few feet separated them, until Kieran could spot the knife pressed against her ribs. One hard thrust as he could drive it into her, possibly even pierce her heart.

"Stay there," the beta ordered.

Kieran held his position. "You have to know you can't escape this."

"All I want is the drive. Let me have that, and I'll walk out of here."

The lie was easy to spot. It was in the puffing of the man's chest and the tremble of his hand. He wouldn't let her go.

Tiffany pulled at where he held her, a soft jerk, as if testing. "You're not getting it, you asshole."

The beta responded by digging the knife in deeper to her side. "You know, I've dealt with a lot of omegas. You all think you're so special, but you know what I've realized? You aren't. You're no different than any other cunt."

"Why? Because none of us want anything to do with you?" She bared her teeth, the same temper Kieran had, the one he loved in himself and terrified him in her.

The beta twisted his wrist, dragging the blade against her side. It opened a wound, shallow but long, before he pressed the pointed tip against her again. "You think you'll be the first I've done away with for a smart mouth? I'd planned on handing you over, on seeing you get taken down a few pegs in the auctions. You wouldn't be so high and mighty once you were passed around like a party favor. Too bad, though, it looks like you'll bleed out here, and I'll take the drive."

He reached up to her throat, feeling for the string of the necklace, only he couldn't find it.

Tiffany met Kieran's gaze before she shifted, her arm coming forward. Across the short distance, she. tossed the drive, the beta too distracted to stop her before it came sailing at Kieran.

He lifted his hand to catch it, but right then, he didn't care about the drive. All he cared about was his mate and the asshole who still had a knife to her.

Red leaked from her side, the sight forcing energy to buzz through Kieran's body. His mind circled around his desire to tear the beta apart. He wanted to spill his blood and lay what was left at Tiffany's feet.

However, that would have to wait. For now, the drive was their bargaining chip. And her trusting him with it humbled him. She could have done anything, but she'd chosen to rely on him. He couldn't let her down.

The beta moved the blade to her throat. "Give me that!" He leveled a frantic look at Kieran. Frightened people made bad choices, which meant Kieran had to be even more cautious.

Kieran held the drive up, keeping the beta's gaze locked on it. If he charged forward, if he went for his gun, Tiffany was dead. One hard yank and the blade would slice into her throat. There'd be little chance to save her if that happened.

That can't happen.

What were his options? His mind searched for another way, for another path. If Tiffany moved or struggled, she risked the blade. If he did anything, they risked the same.

Indecision wasn't something he liked. What the fuck was he supposed to do?

Movement behind the beta caught his attention. Not the mindless running from people who noticed the altercation, who saw the knife and took off. Instead, it was his only chance.

Like before, he'd come to realize the real lesson he'd been forced to learn over the past few weeks. He took a deep breath before twitching his hand to keep the beta's attention as Kane and Marshall crept from behind him.

The sharp blade against Tiffany's throat made each swallow dangerous. It pressed tight enough that she'd likely have a mark even if he didn't kill her. *He won't. Kieran won't let it happen.*

The thought made her frown. She'd never trusted someone else like that, had never been willing to listen, to wait. Yet, she'd known the moment she'd seen him that doing things on her own had gotten her nowhere. All that struggling and fighting had only landed her in trouble and broken her heart. The only time in her life she'd ever been happy, ever felt complete, was when she'd given in and trusted.

Not just Kieran, but Kane and Marshall as well. So, she had to do that then. She had to remain still, to not fight it, to do the one thing she'd never done before. *Trust.*

"Throw it to me!" The beta slid his hand in to her hair and held her tight, pulling her head back to expose her throat more fully. "I have no problem killing her."

The drive dangled in Kieran's grip like a lure. "How do I know you'll let her go?"

"You don't have another choice."

Kieran leveled his gaze on Tiffany, that hard face so familiar, his eyes telling her something. The exact words she didn't know, but she got the point of it. He was telling her, in his own hard-headed way, that he was sorry.

She didn't have time to consider it before he moved. He tossed the drive toward her.

No, not to her, but to the beta, who was forced to release her to reach for the drive. He let go of her hair, the blade moving from her throat. The drive landed in his palm, and everything spun.

Tiffany was pulled against a hard chest, a furious growl rumbling through it. She shoved, wanting to get away, but a hand behind her head pulled her face against a body, and she recognized the scent. *Marshall.*

Her body went lax, the same relief she'd had when she'd spotted Kieran. She wasn't alone.

Even as she enjoyed the moment of reprieve, she pushed against him, needing to see what was happening. Kieran was there, the beta, and she had to know everyone was safe. Marshall let her twist her head enough to find Kane rising, the beta's body on the ground, blood dripping from a long blade in Kane's hand, the drive clutched in his other. He turned his gaze up to Tiffany's, that hardness there she'd glimpsed before, and not a speck of regret.

While Kane was gentle with her, this was her first glimpse of what other people saw. This was the Kane that other people feared.

Still, he only dropped the bloodied knife beside the beta's unmoving body as if it didn't matter and handed her the drive like offering her up flowers.

She shuddered as the adrenaline slipped from her, as she rested against Marshall's grasp. She'd survived. They'd all survived.

But where did that leave them all?

* * * *

Kieran sat in the conference room at the FBI headquarters. Marshall and Kane also sat around the large table, Daniel and Kyle present as well.

The fallout of the disaster at the mall had taken a few days to clear up. The security cameras had cleared Kane for the killing of the beta.

The drive was safely in the care of the FBI who had already started to decrypt it. It appeared to hold slave auction data, and while they didn't share everything with Kieran, they were hoping to find someone to infiltrate the next auction.

And now? Now they waited for Tiffany to show up. She'd spent the last few days with her friend, Claire. Kieran had accepted it only because he knew the woman's alphas were protective to a fault. She would be safe, and the distance would be good for her.

That time away ended today, however, and they all had to face one another.

The paperwork sitting in front of Kieran was all he had to offer. It hadn't been easy and had taken more of his favors than he liked to give, but it was worth it.

The door opened, and all three alphas lifted their gazes.

Damn, I missed her. Tiffany's hair was down, the blonde waves cascading over her shoulders. Her snug shirt was pulled tight across her chest, accentuating her cleavage, and her flared hips begged him to grasp them.

They'd only been apart for a week, but not a day had passed without Kieran thinking about her. He'd fallen asleep missing her scent, her warmth.

Hell, he even missed her smart mouth.

Even so, he'd not messaged her. Neither had Marshall or Kane, all agreeing to give her the space she'd wanted. They'd respond if she reached out, but she hadn't.

Seeing her walk in, he felt inclined to forgive her for it.

Her gaze sought Kieran's, those blue eyes of hers locking onto his.

"You look well," he said.

Tiffany wrung her hands together so tightly, Kieran fought the urge to tell her to stop. He had to rein in his protective instinct.

She sat beside Daniel and Kyle, across from her mates.

And they were mates. Even if she walked away, even if she fought their bond and never wished to see him again, it didn't change a thing. They were mates and losing her would hurt more than anything he'd experienced before.

Tiffany tucked her hair behind her ear. "Thanks."

Kane's soft growl said what the alpha didn't. It said he'd missed her as well.

Tiffany offered him a smile, one that tugged at Kieran's chest. If she left, it wouldn't only be him to lose a mate. Hell, they'd all lose the group they'd formed, the family.

Marshall leaned forward, his elbow on the table. "How's your side?"

"Good. The doctor you recommended is great." She shifted in the seat, a soft wince saying she wasn't fully healed.

"Are you not taking your medication?"

"I did the first day. They made me sick."

The shift into doctor mode by Marshall was so fast Kieran swore he saw a lab coat appear. "I can prescribe you something that won't make you sick, or anti-nausea medication—"

She stopped him mid-tirade. "I'm fine, really."

Marshall huffed out a soft laugh. "Sorry. It's a hard habit to break."

Everyone fell to silence, the unasked questions between them all.

Daniel broke it. "So, Tiffany, we've got quite a bit of paperwork here for you."

"Right. We're going to sign over my future."

"Not exactly." Daniel pushed paperwork over to her, the folder sliding across the table. "We've worked out a better deal."

She frowned as she opened the file and ran her fingers down the page. Finally, she lifted her gaze. "What does this mean?"

Kyle answered. "That's freedom, Tiffany. No more contract. A new identification, an account with enough money to get you started wherever you want. You can go anywhere and start over."

Her lips tipped down. "I thought no judge would sign off on this without the year under the care of an alpha."

"Well, seems like your lucky day. Your help with the drive meant this one went for it. With the new name, you won't need witness protection. Be smart, be careful and once we finish our investigation, you'll be able to contact your family again. In the meantime? Well, you can do whatever you want."

She stared at the paperwork, her fingers stilled on the page.

Kieran held his breath. He'd offered her everything she needed to leave. It was the right thing to do, but damn, it was hard. Staying still took everything he had, having to sit there and say nothing.

Not beg her to stay, not promise her the world, nothing.

She had to have choices. It had to be up to her.

She had to choose a future with him, with Kane and Marshall because she wanted it, not because it was all she had. For that, she needed to have options.

Between the three of them, they'd pulled all the strings they had to give her that option. She could go anywhere, start any life she wanted. It was, in the end, the only thing they had to give her.

Her freedom.

* * * *

Marshall tipped the beer back, taking a gulp of the cold liquid. He wasn't normally much of a drinker, but then again, he didn't get his heart broken often.

Kane laughed as he took a step backward. "Well, look at that. You thinking to keep up?"

A grimace passed over Marshall's features as he remembered why he didn't care to drink. "Well, if I don't learn, what else am I supposed to do when I visit with you and Kieran?"

"How fucking sad is that, huh? The three of us assholes left, what? Fucking moping around." Kane took a drink that made Marshall's look like a sip. "Fucking pathetic, that's what."

Marshall settled onto the couch, drink pressed between his thighs. "I miss her."

Kieran took a spot in the chair. "I wonder where she is?"

"Texas." At the look from the other two, Kane shrugged. "She always talked about going to Texas if she ever had to run far. Said the sun would do her good."

Marshall grinned at the image of her — jeans, tank top, cowboy hat. She'd fit in well there. That blonde hair of hers would catch the sunlight and light up. Damn, he would love to see that.

"Did we do the right thing?" Kieran asked.

Ah, the same question he'd asked himself for day since they'd come up with the idea. "We did what we had to. She needed to have a choice to make, and we gave her that."

"And she took the chance to run off and break our fucking hearts." Kane huffed. "Yep. Great plan."

The words hung there between them all, the truth. When they'd all given in, when they'd realized what they wanted, she'd been the one to break their hearts.

Kieran was the first to break the silence. His laughter started slow, deep. He leaned forward, holding the beer away so he didn't spill it. "I never thought I'd end up like this," he gasped out between bouts of laughter.

Kane joined in, his laughter deeper, rougher. "Who'd have figured a fucking omega would put us on our asses, huh? Figures, don't it? Some spit of a female does what no one else could."

While the moment wasn't all that funny, Marshall joined in. There was some sense of camaraderie with the other alphas, with all of them feeling the same pain. "We are a pretty pathetic group, aren't we?"

Then a voice that haunted Marshall broke into the laughter. "I don't appreciate people talking about my mates like that." *Tiffany.*

The sight of her three males had Tiffany's heart speeding. Walking into the house with the key she'd already had felt right. *I feel like I'm home.*

And the laser-like focus they had when they turned their gazes to her? She'd missed them. Every night away, she'd thought about them, woken up swearing she'd heard their voices in her sleep. Worse, the more she'd thought about it, the surer she was they'd been involved.

"What are you doing here?" Marshall asked.

Tiffany tossed the folder she'd received from the agents onto the coffee table. "I'm not as stupid as I look. I knew the only people who could have worked this out for me were you guys. Why'd you do it?"

No one answered at first, feet shuffling as if they were children caught doing wrong.

Finally, always the brave one, Kieran gave it a shot. "You deserved whatever future you wanted. We figured the best thing we could do for you was give you the chance to figure that out for yourself. If you wanted us, well, you needed to really want us."

"So, you set up everything for me so I could have a life that didn't include any of you?"

"We want the best for you, and if that isn't here." Marshall shrugged. "Then we'd do whatever we could to help you."

Tiffany's gaze fell to the paperwork, to the proof of what they'd wanted to give her, to do for her. Despite wanting her, despite risking their lives for her, they'd given her a choice. They'd offered her freedom, because what she needed mattered to them more than what they wanted.

It made it clear.

I love them.

Especially as they sat there like lovesick puppies with nowhere to go. Three alphas who could strike fear into anyone had been brought to their knees by the idea of not having her in their lives anymore.

It melted whatever resistance she'd had.

Still, it made her ask one last question. She turned to Kieran. "You told me you couldn't give me anything but a year." She nodded at the papers on the table. "Does this mean I don't even get the year?"

Kieran rose and crossed the room until he stood before Tiffany, so close she had to crane her neck to look into his dark eyes. He didn't touch her, though. Even standing so close a deep inhalation could cause them to brush, he didn't cross the final inches of space.

"I don't want a year. I said that because I thought losing you would be too painful to risk. After almost losing you to that beta, I've realized losing you would hurt no matter what, and pushing you away wasn't going to help. I've always done what I had to do, but with you, I see what life can be. I see the fun, the unexpected, the parts I've always thought weren't for me. The fact is, I don't want a year, girl — I want forever."

Kane's large body stood to the side of her, tattooed up and imposing and undeniably beautiful to her. "I ain't been the sort of man who could ever earn a girl like you, but I'm sick of letting that stop me. If you're willing to put up with my stupid ass, doll, I'll take that as a win for me. I don't want you to go, don't want you to be gone for a fucking second. Ain't saying any of us will be easy to live with, but hell, if anyone could put up with it, it'd be you."

Marshall, the last to speak, the one always to consider his words to carefully, offered his piece before she could interrupt. "I've always been afraid that if I let myself go, if I ever cared about an omega, that I'd turn into my father. I was terrified that I'd end up like him. The funny thing is that the exact thing I was doing to stop it caused the fear. My alpha side is vicious, but I know that it's only drive is to keep you safe. You taught me I don't have to be afraid of it, run from it. There is nothing in the world I want more than to be with you, than to wake up to your laughter and go to bed exhausted and covered in your scent."

Kieran's voice dropped low, unsure when she didn't respond to their declarations. "If that's what you want."

Tiffany took her lip between her teeth, considering the life she could have. It didn't take more than a moment for her to gaze around, to find Kieran's eyes, Marshall's, Kane's, and know she wanted exactly that.

She crossed the space Kieran had left and slid her lips against his firm ones. The kiss was quick, only a heartbeat before she pulled back, her hand pressed flat against his chest. "I haven't made a lot of good decisions in my life. In fact, my life has pretty much been a string of bad choices."

Marshall's hand came to rest on the small of her back, the comforting weight, that quiet strength he had reassuring her. She reached out, wrapping her fingers in the fabric of Kane's shirt, gripping it tightly.

"I think this might be the only good choice I've ever made."

Kane huffed a laugh before catching her behind the neck, twisting her to face him. "Nah, doll, I'd bet this is another shitty choice, but like I'll complain." He pulled her in for a kiss that was nothing like what she'd offering Kieran. No, Kane's was deep, his tongue taking as if to tell her how much he'd missed her and how badly he wanted her.

He broke the kiss only to have Marshall steal the next one. It wasn't gentle, but rather let out that dark edge he had hidden for so long, a low growl in his throat as he forced her head back to deepen the kiss, his fingers tightening on her lower back. He broke the kiss with a stinging bite to her bottom lip that only had her growing damp. "You won't regret it," he swore.

Kieran caught her hand and lifted it, offering a kiss too chaste for the things she was thinking. His lips twisted into a smirk, one that promised such filthy things, her cheeks warmed at them. "I say we take our mate to bed and show her how much we've missed her."

Kane and Marshall agreed with their bodies more than words as they all pulled her toward the bedroom.

And Tiffany followed, following her mates, the family she'd found and the home all of them had made. No matter how they'd fought it, they'd created something between them that they'd all needed, and Tiffany wouldn't let anything get in the way of that.

She'd never been as happy as she was being shared by her alphas.

Want to see more like this?
Here's a taster for you to enjoy!

Taming the Beast:
Mastering the Beast
Tina Donahue

Excerpt

Zoe stormed toward a treatment room, ready to rumble.

As the top enforcer at From Crud to Stud, *the* New Orleans' makeover service for supernatural beings, she didn't take lip or attitude from anyone. She'd made that fatal mistake in the past. First with hard-nosed villagers during the Salem witch trials, which had been way worse than the fluff shown on the History Channel. Then with Satan after he'd wooed her to Hell using his typical bait-and-switch scheme. What a creep he'd turned out to be.

Twice in her existence, she'd let guys determine her future. No more. She was her own woman now, uninterested in men. Her work here was all she needed, guided by her determination to do things the mortal way—suffer and endure, no supernatural powers allowed.

She pushed open the door and faced a sickly looking vamp who sported a pasty complexion and a man bun. Hardly a babe magnet. Only fierce dedication and hard work would turn him into Mr. Charm. "Yo. On the table. Now." Before the staffers helped him to suppress his inner beast, she had to strap him down. An easy-peasy job for a reformed demon with hardcore ways.

He licked his fangs flirtatiously. Some might say hungrily. "Hey. I'm —"

"I'm not going to ask again."

"Easy, cupcake. I'm just trying to make conversation. What's your name?"

"Kim Kardashian."

"Yeah?" He regarded her scrawny figure. "You changed. Like a lot."

"It's an illusion. Call it my work uniform. Once I'm on my own time, I blossom."

"Cool."

They circled each other, both ready to pounce.

Given his powers, he struck first and sank his teeth into her neck.

She tapped her foot but let him do his thing.

"Gah." He gagged and recoiled. "Damn, you taste like hell."

Surprise, surprise. "Time for you to learn some manners. Good thing you came to us."

He eyed a female staffer strolling by and gave her a toothy grin.

Zoe got in his face. "Park your butt over there now."

"When I'm good and ready, sweetheart." He craned his neck to watch the staffer. "Run along."

Zoe rammed her saddle shoe into his foot and her elbow into his gut, wrestled him to the table then strapped him in so he'd never get free. Not even if he morphed into a freaking bat. His frustrated hiss mingled with a reaper's wail, zombie grunts and were howls.

Lovely sounds, ordinarily. However, tonight something was off, the evening heavy with tension that breathed danger. Similar to when another demon slunk nearby.

Warily, she approached the last two treatment rooms. Both were empty. The walls bore claw marks from former inhabitants.

Maybe she was overreacting due to the calendar date. Halloween approached, the dumbest and most inaccurate holiday ever.

Heather, a healer and the good fairy receptionist there, had decorated her desk with plastic skulls. Fake cobwebs hung from the faux gas fixtures. Rubber spiders stuck to the coral walls and spelled out *Boo*! on the artificial brick floor.

Zoe resisted the urge to roll her eyes or say anything unkind, since Heather was her BFF.

Heather smiled adoringly at Daemon, a former satyr. He'd come to the service more than a year ago to ditch his horns, tail and hooves in order to look fully human so he could boogie with mortal babes. Not only did he work there now as an enforcer, he and Heather had shacked up, their love more enduring than Romeo and Juliet's. They laughed easily and gazed at each other with tenderness and respect whenever they weren't busy making out like sex-starved teens.

Loneliness tightened Zoe's chest. She ached from unexpected longing but shook it off.

Romance wasn't what she needed or could risk. She'd learned that brutal truth centuries ago when she'd had wanted one guy, just one, more than life itself. What a hot mess that had turned out to be, especially after she'd sold her soul to get his affection. Talk about false advertising. What she'd ended up with was a one-way ticket to Hell along with Satan's negligent shrug and pissy explanation about what had happened.

"It all boils down to free will." He'd grinned. "The guy doesn't want you. What can I do?"

Satan made first-class louses look like Prince Charming.

However, he had taught her an important lesson. No way would she ever fall for another man and give him her heart, if she'd had one. These past years, she'd sworn off dating, companionship and especially sex even though celibacy was killing her. Especially tonight.

The only thing she couldn't figure out was why.

"Zoe." Becca, another BFF and the half-mortal witch who owned this place, motioned her to the other hall. "Can we have a word in my office?"

That same edgy feeling returned and grew stronger. She expected a demon to pounce from behind the feathery ferns or potted plants that adorned the reception area.

No one was there.

"Now?" Becca led the way. Her harem pants rode low on her voluptuous hips and swished around her legs. Her tie-front crop top hugged her ample boobs. Both garments were iridescent blue that matched her eyes.

In her office, she gestured Zoe to the needlepoint sofa that faced the antique desk. Displayed on the cabinet behind it were numerous photos of Becca and Eric, a minor god she'd met and had fallen in love with when he'd come there for treatment.

Melancholy hit, followed by dread. Zoe worried another staffer had found her man and now that guy was going to work here like Daemon. A new enforcer would cut even deeper into her territory. The only thing she had left.

Rather than sitting, she squared her shoulders prepared to defend her turf.

Becca smiled cautiously. A sure sign she wasn't certain what to do, like when she practiced her witchcraft. Poor thing had been studying hard but managed more misses than hits when she concocted spells or potions. If not for her mom, Rowena, helping with those things, she would have been shit outta luck.

Zoe lifted her chin and got bolder than she felt. "Is this about Constance?"

Another BFF and the resident voodoo priestess here. Given that Constance liked men big time, it was a miracle she hadn't been the first on their team to hook up.

Becca frowned slightly. "What about her?"

"Shouldn't she be in here, too?" Seemed reasonable if she had a once-in-a-lifetime romance to gush about.

"No. She's with a client, removing some of his memories."

Zoe suspected those involved the dude's former girlfriend that Constance wanted him to forget. "So the client is the one she's in love with?"

"Love?" Becca pressed her hand to her chest. "Oh, my God, is she serious about someone? I didn't know she was even dating on a regular basis. What have you heard?"

Confused, Zoe shook her head. "Nothing. Is this about MJ?"

She was a genie who'd used to live in Daemon's ring before he set her free. Currently, she was his and Heather's houseguest and also worked there granting wishes to clients for a price. Like Constance, MJ enjoyed doing the nasty with guys. Little wonder she'd found her man. "She's hooked up with someone?"

"You mean permanently?" Becca's eyes widened. The heavy black makeup surrounding them made them appear larger against her fair skin. "I don't think so.

Daemon had to separate her and a were earlier. They were really going at it. Once she left him, she had her eye on a warlock. Have you heard or seen something different?"

"Uh-uh. I thought you knew something and wanted to tell me about it in here."

"Oh...no." She made a face and shook it off. "This is about business. We've been really swamped this year, so I've decided to expand. I've already talked to the building's owner about taking over the entire floor and renovating it for our use."

Zoe's tension drained away. "Cool. You want me to keep the workers in line in between my other stuff?" She slammed her fist against her palm. "I'll be happy to."

Becca stopped fingering her short red hair. "I don't want you to kill yourself by working so hard."

"How could I do that?" She frowned. "I'm already dead, not to mention immortal."

"That's not what I meant." Becca waved her hand dismissively. "I want you to enjoy your work."

That funny feeling returned and made Zoe queasy. "Who says I don't like what I do here? Oh, hey, is this about Daemon horning in on more of my stuff? Uh-uh. He's already keeping the clients in line for the other staff. I don't need him to do that for me. I'm capable. Hell, I'm a better enforcer than him. I do not want him anywhere near my customers."

"No problem. He won't be." Becca cleared her throat. "Stefin, Anatol and Taro will be here for that from now on."

Footfalls rang in the hall.

Three guys strode into Becca's office, their movements fluid and assured. Each looked thirty or so, in mortal years, and had dressed in black, their shirts silk, their boots and pants elegant, like bouncers wear at an elite club.

No one was dancing in here, especially Zoe.

A faint sulfur scent emanated from the unholy trio. Flames flared briefly in their eyes.

Demons. The trouble she'd sensed earlier.

She froze, too stunned to move or speak.

The guy in the middle was easily six-three and nicely muscular, his blond hair shoulder-length. His rough good looks, bronze complexion and stubble put the va-va-voom in virile. Sin filled his light gray eyes, his mood dangerous and predatory.

Her belly fluttered.

He winked.

Disquiet and lust rolled through Zoe. Her legs went watery.

The guy on the right proved equally tall and powerfully built. Beautiful, he had rich-chocolate skin, dark eyes and long hair worn in dreadlocks.

Those babies would feel awesome gliding across her naked boobs and thighs — until he screwed her over like every other male had done.

She steeled herself against his allure.

He smiled.

A freaking dimple dented his right cheek, his grin an unusual combination of boyish mischief and raw sensuality.

Her pussy creamed.

Hot didn't begin to describe the last guy's masculine features, deep-blue eyes and thick auburn hair. Those wavy locks trailed past his ears and curled on his neck. His stubble called to everything female within Zoe, as did his height, big body and the assured way he regarded her.

The guys' enticing sulfur odor enhanced their musky scents, making the mixture wanton and unashamed. Their impressive cocks pushed against their flies.

She bet each of their rods jutted from blond, black or auburn curls.

The room spun.

"Guys." Becca lifted her reddish eyebrows. "This is Zoe."

The introduction seemed to come from far away, Becca's voice muted by the ringing in Zoe's ears. She tried to respond but only managed an odd noise, part grunt, mostly a groan.

Becca edged closer. "Zoe, this is Anatol." She gestured to the black hunk with the dimple. "Stefin." The blond god in the middle winked again. "And Taro." The blue-eyed hottie regarded her intensely. "They're our new enforcers."

Each looked in charge already, their stances saying they wouldn't budge one damn inch for anyone, especially a female demon.

Becca offered a nervous smile. "You'll be working with them from now on."

Working with or for, as in taking orders, yearning helplessly then losing out as she had with the last man in her life?

Like hell.

TOTALLY BOUND

Home of Erotic Romance

Sign up for our newsletter and find out about all our romance book releases, eBook sales and promotions, sneak peeks and FREE romance books!

About the Author

Jayce Carter lives in Southern California with her husband and two spawns. She originally wanted to take over the world but realized that would require wearing pants. This led her to choosing writing, a completely pants-free occupation. She has a fear of heights yet rock climbs for fun and enjoys making up excuses for not going out and socializing.

Jayce loves to hear from readers. You can find her contact information, website details and author profile page at https://www.totallybound.com